Welcome to Mountain Meadow, Virginia, where love is worth waiting for ...

The town bad girl is back, and this time, Erin Richardson is in need of protection. Years ago, her youthful crush on handsome older man Sam Barnes nearly led to scandal. Now she's on the run from an entirely different kind of trouble: a criminal intent on eliminating his witnesses—including Erin. As the local sheriff, Sam's duty-bound to provide a safe haven. Though tongues will surely wag once Erin is sharing a house with the sexy lawman....

Erin is still too young, too vulnerable, and too irresistibly beautiful. But when Sam lays eyes on her again, all he wants to do is shelter her in his arms. It won't be easy keeping her out of harm's way. But it'll be even harder keeping the woman he never forgot out of his bed—and his heart...

I0677334

Books by Laura Browning

Winning Heart

Mountain Meadow Homecomings
Special Delivery
Lost & Found Love
Erin's Way

The Barlow-Barretts: An American Dynasty
Bittersweet
Balancing Act
Remember Me
Broken Heart

Published by Kensington Publishing Corporation

Erin's Way

A Mountain Meadow Homecomings Novel

Laura Browning

LYRICAL PRESS
Kensington Publishing Corp.
www.kensingtonbooks.com

Lyrical Press books are published by
Kensington Publishing Corp. 119 West 40th Street New York, NY 10018

All Kensington titles, imprints, and distributed lines are available at special quantity discounts for bulk purchases for sales promotion, premiums, fund-raising, and educational or institutional use.

To the extent that the image or images on the cover of this book depict a person or persons, such person or persons are merely models, and are not intended to portray any character or characters featured in the book.

Special book excerpts or customized printings can also be created to fit specific needs. For details, write or phone the office of the Kensington Special Sales Manager:
Kensington Publishing Corp.
119 West 40th Street
New York, NY 10018
Attn. Special Sales Department. Phone: 1-800-221-2647.

Kensington and the K logo Reg. U.S. Pat. & TM Off.
LYRICAL PRESS Reg. U.S. Pat. & TM Off.
Lyrical Press and the L logo are trademarks of Kensington Publishing Corp.

First Electronic Edition: August 2018
eISBN-13: 978-1-60183-573-4
eISBN-10: 1-60183-573-6

First Print Edition: August 2016
ISBN-13: 978-1-60183-575-8
ISBN-10: 1-60183-575-2

Printed in the United States of America

This book is dedicated to all the students it has been my pleasure to teach over the last decade. Many of you have struggled to improve reading skills that were holding you back. You inspire me with your determination and hard work, and I am grateful every time one of you succeeds that I could help. The hugs are nice too.

Author's Foreword

Author's Note

According to the International Dyslexia Association, 15-20% of the population has a language-based learning disability like dyslexia. Reading delays are among the most common issues for students receiving special education services. Dyslexia knows no sex, racial or socio-economic bounds. Causes of dyslexia are both neurological and genetic. There is no cure. It's not a disease, and early intervention is a key.

Children who are identified by kindergarten and first grade and receive help become much more successful at reading on grade level than students not identified until later. However, even older children and adults can still benefit from a multi-sensory approach to understanding language.

As a reading specialist and the parent of a child with learning disabilities, I urge parents not to wait if they or their child's teacher notice reading difficulties. Dyslexia, or any reading difficulty for that matter, does not mean stupid. Many dyslexics are of average or above average intelligence. Learning ways to cope with the difference in the way their brain functions opens the door to a successful future.

For more information about dyslexia, you can visit: www.interdys.org

Chapter 1

Erin Richardson handed over some of her precious stash of cash and signed by the X for her rental car. Leaving a paper trail made her nervous, but reaching her destination quickly took precedence. Home sweet home. The black sheep of the family was returning to the fold.

Hating the heavy jacket she'd donned to keep out the last blast of winter cold, she tossed it in the back seat of the little sedan. The car would warm up soon enough. The bulky coat was a further reminder that she'd been forced to leave behind the warmth and her friends for the cold and uncertainty of the Blue Ridge…also known as home. Right. The place where she was headed had rarely felt like home, at least not as she had wanted it to be.

An image of a frowning face with snapping, dark eyes flashed in front of her. Sam. He was older now, but so was she. Not that it would make a difference. He was one more face lined up in judgment of her.

She slid behind the wheel and checked her reflection in the rearview mirror. A little different look than last fall when she'd dropped in on the 'rents so unexpectedly. Erin had kept the extra body jewelry but ditched the Goth-looking makeup and dyed her hair back to its natural color. This time when she returned home she wasn't aiming to shock as she had been at Tabitha's art showing. Erin was trying hard to fit the image of the senator's daughter. That would be a first. But now totally necessary.

After what had happened right before she left the Virgin Islands, it was important to lay low and fit in. Maybe she should get rid of the ring in her eyebrow. No. She'd keep it for now. That was one too many changes for her to cope with at the moment. If she suddenly turned up in plaid and pearls, she'd make her family more suspicious than they would be simply by her turning up at all.

One thing hadn't changed. Erin carried a bag of some high-grade pot, a few hits of ecstasy, and even a couple of Quaaludes she'd traded for with a guy from South Africa. She laughed humorlessly as she pulled out of Dulles and headed southwest in the rental. There was only so much goodness she could stand, and she certainly wasn't ready to give up her escapes from reality. It might at least brighten the dullness of where she'd grown up. Mountain Meadow. She shivered. Her last memories of her hometown were some of the most humiliating of her life. She was far from happy to be back, but life had a way of throwing curve balls. She wished it wouldn't throw so many.

With a long drive still ahead of her, she stopped at a Starbucks and wired up on a triple shot of espresso. As the miles slid by, her nerves tightened. She would so much rather still be on board the *Sprite*, but Andre Delacroix had certainly screwed that. Staying there after what she'd overheard? No way. She might be stupid, but she wasn't suicidal.

Just thinking of Andre made her stomach tighten. She was afraid Rick, the *Sprite's* captain, and the rest of his crew were underestimating how dangerous Andre could be. Rick was forever writing Andre off as nothing more than a spoiled, rich kid, much as he'd originally thought her. While his opinion of her had certainly undergone a radical change, his opinion of Andre hadn't, and Erin was afraid they were all making a big mistake.

Her hands clenched on the steering wheel, her left leg adding a rapid tattoo. She still had part of a joint already rolled. Maybe a few tokes would calm her nerves, take her stress level down a notch. After all, if Stoner and Catherine were as uptight as ever, she'd need all the help she could get once she arrived in the middle of nowhere. A little brain fog might help blunt how underwhelmed her parents would be to see her. Maybe she could even pretend they would welcome her home. Erin laughed. Like that would happen.

Suddenly, surprising them didn't seem like such a great idea. In the back of her mind, fear niggled that her parents would have asked her not to come if they had known of her plans ahead of time. How mortifying was that? She snorted. No more humiliating than being carried out of a party last fall tucked under Sam Barnes's arm like a little kid in the midst of a temper tantrum. That had accomplished essentially the same thing that evening. Erin had taken the hint and cleared out before they could actually kick her out.

She had never been able to do anything right in her parents' eyes. So now she was going *back*? Really. She needed her head examined. What was the definition of insanity? Oh right. Doing the same thing over and over again and expecting a different result.

Erin yawned. God, she had forgotten how truly boring this area was. No people, almost no traffic and certainly no lights. Nothing, as a matter of fact, to help her stay awake. Even worse, she'd already hit several icy spots where she felt the car's traction turn loose for an instant. After years of rarely driving at all and only in warm, sunny climates, the ice had certainly jolted her back awake. Erin shook her head and blinked her gritty eyes several times.

Shit, she was so tired she'd started to see things. Was that a deer in the road? Was it a pot-induced hallucination? That most recent bag had been a doozy. At the last minute, she stared into a white face and wide, startled, brown eyes and yanked the wheel hard to the left. The car plunged off the shoulder of the road and through a dark board fence. The air bag exploded back at her, smacking her forehead and making it burn. Finally, the car landed at an odd angle, one wheel hanging over the bank of a creek. The only thing breaking the silence were the moos of panicked cows roaming in the darkness. *Wow, this was some fucking trip.* She slumped forward.

She wasn't sure how much time had passed when she groaned and touched her head. It was wet and sticky. She shivered. Her heavy coat was somewhere in the backseat. Why did it have to be so god-awful cold? She yearned for blue skies, even bluer water and hot, steamy nights. She could use a drink. Something alcoholic and on the rocks would be perfect. She hurt. Where the hell was she anyway?

It was dark, but this didn't look or feel like St. Thomas. She fumbled with her seatbelt, and it finally popped open. Her legs refused to obey as she opened the door, so she stumbled and half fell out onto the frozen ground. God, it was slippery out here and so freaking cold! She rubbed her arms, her coat forgotten. Her teeth chattered, and that only made her head hurt worse.

Erin turned around and looked at the car. *Holy shit!* She was in the middle of a cow pasture, and her rental car was a mess. God, how stupid. As she surveyed the damage to the vehicle, she decided it would be a whole lot easier to handle with a little buzz going. Life in general was a lot easier to face when she was a little bit high. She'd discovered that early in high school. She went back to the car, pulled out her purse, fumbled around until she found another joint, and lit it. Breathe deep, hold, exhale. It was a routine. A couple of tokes and she felt her calm return.

She turned to look at the fence behind her. *Wow!* It looked even worse than the car, though God knew it was hard enough to see anything out here. Had she taken that much of it out? Erin giggled as she imagined a cartoon vision of fence pieces flying through the air like matchsticks. The image was like one of those old Road Runner cartoons where Wile E. Coyote keeps screwing everything up. Yep! That was her all right. Wile E. Coyote, the original screw up. Maybe she should check to see if the car she'd leased came from Acme rentals.

It all struck her as so amazingly funny. She sat on a rock, puffed on her joint, and giggled. Welcome back, Erin! Nothing like arriving in style in Mountain Meadow. *Daddy, I'm home!* A few more feet, and she'd have made a splash right into the bottom of a shallow creek. Wouldn't everyone be so proud of her?

Some things never changed.

As she toked the joint in her hand, she looked around blearily. Where was she? She couldn't be far from home. But God, it had been so long since she'd been here. Last fall didn't count. She hadn't even spent the night. So, yeah, where was she? A couple of blinks and she momentarily cleared her vision enough to see the dark silhouette of a cabin. As she looked at the hills and trees surrounding her, memories came back. Her cheeks flushed with humiliation. She was on Sam's land. Why did every mortifying moment of her life involve Sam? He was the only man who had ever made her breath catch and her heart pound, and he was the only man who had never shown any sign of wanting her. Life was so unfair.

* * * *

With his long, sock-clad feet propped over the end of the couch, Sam had nearly dozed off when his phone rang. It had been a crazy day what with deputies on vacation or sick. Sighing impatiently, he snatched the cordless phone from its resting place on the table next to him. "Barnes."

"Sam? It's Stoner. Carter called me. There are cows out on the highway. He's not sure whose they are. He's already out there trying to round them up. I'd be happy to help, but that whole electronic tether thing…"

"Dang it, Stoner," Sam snarled. "I'll call the department and tell them to ignore the alarm and why. The neighbor kid who helps me is sick with pneumonia, but I'll be out there as soon as I get my boots on to see what's up." Sam slammed the phone down with a bang.

At that moment, he would gladly have strangled the judge who sentenced former Senator Stoner Richardson to two years house arrest for pleading guilty to conspiracy charges. It was nothing but a major pain in the butt, when it wasn't a downright joke. In the last six months, Stoner had probably spent as much time away from home as confined to it. Now he was going off the property again. If someone didn't suspend his sentence soon, Sam might go beg the judge himself, so he wouldn't have to play watchdog for the wandering senator. He would have to talk to Evan about it. The guy had served half his sentence already and had been a model prisoner.

Sam's already taciturn mood grew even more thunderous as he yanked on his coveralls, slipped his big white-stockinged feet back into thick-soled work boots, and pulled a cowboy hat on. Sweet Mary. He'd be glad when spring got here. Better yet, summer so he could work in either a T-shirt or shirtless.

Most of all, he wished he wasn't going out in the dark to round up cows in the freezing cold. Just in case, he threw a roll of barbwire, some temporary posts, and his wire cutters into the back of the truck before he bumped down the drive.

Please let them be Stoner's Angus and not his Hereford crosses. It would please him to no end to have something to hang over the senator, but as he reached the road, he saw broad white faces reflecting back at him in the moonlight. It was his baldies. Stoner would never let him hear the end of it.

Crap!

Even in the dark, the tall, angular form of the former senator leaning against his pickup was plain to see. He spoke as soon as Sam got within earshot. "Carter's herded most of them through the gate, but we haven't located the break in the fence yet. You know, Sam, if you'd hire another hand or two..."

Sam spun on his neighbor, fists clenched, but only glared at him. "Not all of us drip money, Senator."

Stoner's two-way radio crackled. "I've found the problem, Mr. Richardson. An accident. Fence is busted pretty good here in the corner by the creek. Car's hanging with one wheel over the bank."

Sam instantly converted from farmer to sheriff. "Any injuries you can see? Do I need to radio for an ambulance?"

"Don't think so. There's a woman here. She seems okay, I guess. She's laughing."

"Laughing?" Stoner's mouth twisted.

Sam growled with anger. Probably some teenager out joyriding. Just what he needed, something else to drag him back into town tonight when all he wanted to do was crash. "Hop in, Senator. I'll give you a ride. You and Carter mind helping me put up a temporary fence?"

"Not at all."

"I know we haven't exactly been on the best of terms...."

Stoner cut Sam off. "That was years ago, Sam. Besides, looking back, I don't think you were the one at fault. Erin was out of control."

Sam nodded, deciding it was better not to respond. Erin always seemed to be at the middle of any discord. He might not be at fault for his actions, but his thoughts about the senator's daughter had been anything but pure. It was twelve years ago, so maybe it was time to let things lie. After all, Erin was gone and it didn't look like she would be back. Last fall hardly counted. He rubbed the back of his neck and frowned at the thought.

As they drove down the road, Sam used the radio in his truck to call in the accident and said he would handle it until they could get someone out in the morning. As he and Stoner climbed out of the truck in the darkness, Sam saw how much of his fence was smashed.

"Holy freaking cow! Could the stupid idiot have done any more damage?"

"Damn," Stoner added. "It almost looks like the driver did it on purpose."

"Or fell asleep at the wheel," Sam grumbled. Fools. Nobody needed to be out on a night like this one, especially just joyriding. Icy patches from the last storm were still refreezing at night, making driving risky.

In the pasture, on the other side of the car, they heard Carter's deep rumbles and a higher pitched voice.

"I'm fine, man. Hey, jerk, get your hands off me. Ooh! Was that *cow shit* I stepped in? Oh, God. Oh *gross*. That is so freaking disgusting. Man, I hate this place! I *always* hated this place."

Stoner looked at Sam, who saw the same shock of recognition reflected in the senator's features before both of them slipped and slid down the embankment in a sudden hurry, running across the pasture to the car. Sam skidded to a stop, all of his thoughts jumbling together, but what lingered in his mind was, *not like this, Erin, not like this.*

Erin looked up as she heard them and grinned. The grin started Sam's heart pounding until he saw her bloodshot eyes in the glow of the flashlight. "Hi, Daddy! Hi, Sammy! I had a little accident." Then she leaned over and vomited right at a very surprised Carter's feet. Sam doubted it was the puke that floored Carter. Hearing Erin call Stoner Daddy probably accounted for the look on the foreman's face.

As Stoner slowed, so did Sam. They approached cautiously, as if they had encountered a wounded grizzly and weren't quite sure how it would react. But then confronting Erin had always been that way. He never knew exactly which Erin would show up. Would she snap his head off or twine herself around his heart? Sam had been struggling with that since he'd first met her when she was nine. No matter how much he'd tried to forget her over the years, it hadn't happened. His feelings had just changed.

"Erin?" Stoner ventured quietly. "What are you doing here?"

Sam sniffed the air, inhaling an all too familiar odor. Any nostalgia he might have been experiencing evaporated. "Darn it, Erin. Have you been smoking pot right here on my land?"

She straightened, her eyes wary as she looked between the two men. "Don't worry, Daddy...Sam. I'm fine, just a little head injury. So nice of you to ask, and nice to see things haven't changed. Oh wait, I guess they have, because the last time you two were this close together, Daddy, you were trying to choke Sam at the same time you were calling me... Let's see. What was it? Oh yes, a 'white trash tramp and no daughter of yours.' Fourteen was such a good year."

She glanced at Carter's gaping jaw and smiled coolly. "Another fond memory of childhood in the Richardson household." Erin tilted her head back and laughed. "Hi, Daddy. I'm home!"

"Damn it, Erin," Stoner muttered as anger and concern warred with each other in his expression, but when he reached for her, she stumbled backward, shivered, and glared at him. Her whole body trembled, and Sam wasn't sure if it was from cold, drugs, or just plain nerves.

Depression weighed on Sam. He rubbed the back of his neck where the muscles tightened with tension. Just once, he wished his encounters with Erin and Stoner could be different, but they all seemed to begin and end the same way with all three of them tense and on the defensive.

Erin scrubbed her hands up and down her arms as if she were trying to jumpstart the circulation there. "I can't find my coat. I thought it was on the backseat," she blurted angrily, "and I'm cold."

Sam saw she had on only a sweater. He pushed past her and searched the car, emerging in a moment with a polar fleece-lined ski jacket. He helped her on with it and zipped it. Then he saw the blood trickling down the side of her head. His breath hitched. Fear tightened his gut. He stepped in close enough to touch her head, nerves tightening when she looked up at him for just a moment with her guard down.

"Erin," he murmured, but the door had already closed. Her guard was up and her chin jutting. "You're hurt." Without waiting, he swung her into his arms and carried her back across the pasture. Somehow, he managed to get her up the bank without landing either of them in the mud. After ripping open the back door of the still running truck, he set her in the warm interior. Erin's face was pale and her eyes big and dark in the dim light.

"Stay here!" he ordered. His face felt tense, his brows drawn tightly together. "We have to fix the fence, then I'll run you and Stoner back to his truck."

Erin stared at him. As if the life had suddenly drained from her, she closed her eyes. She leaned her head back against the seat, grimacing in pain. "Okay," she muttered tonelessly.

"Erin!" Sam grasped her shoulder, thinking of last fall when she'd bolted as soon as he'd left her alone at Richardson Homestead after giving her a ride home. "You will stay, right?"

For a second he saw something hot and intense in her gaze, but she looked away and the moment was gone. "Yes. I have to. I don't have anywhere else to go."

He ignored that remark for now. In his experience, Erin appeared and disappeared wherever and whenever she felt like, as long as it was nowhere near him. He tamped down the ache in his chest that thought brought with it. The more drama she could create with her abrupt arrivals and departures, the better. Sam slammed the door and yanked the spool of wire and the temporary posts out of the pickup bed. He turned as Carter and Stoner reached the road.

"Let's get this fence up," he growled. "We'll run a couple of strands and use battens between the posts that are still up. That should hold until morning when it will have to come down anyway in order to get the car out." He looked at Stoner, "I guess you had no idea she was coming?"

Stoner grunted an affirmation. "When have we ever had any idea what Erin planned? Hell, she came out of the womb feet first just to be different."

Carter, who had only been with Richardson Homestead for the last four years asked, "That young woman is your daughter, sir? I thought you had only Evan and Tabby."

Stoner sighed, then explained, "Erin is Evan's younger sister. Tabby is their younger half sister. I'd better call Catherine and prepare her. No. On second thought, I don't want to break this to her over the phone."

Sam turned away with a frown and began anchoring the first strand of barbwire. In his mind, he saw again the brave little nine-year-old he'd met so long ago and the way she'd stood up to her father's chewing out even with the broken arm that had to have hurt like hell. Almost eighteen years later and nothing seemed to have changed. To Stoner, Erin was still a problem to be handled and hidden.

Sam's mouth tightened. He wanted to punch Stoner, or at the very least knock some sense into the man. Erin wasn't a problem. She was Stoner's daughter. Sam hammered the wire staple with enough force to anchor it in one swing. He was just as mad at himself as he was at Stoner. He had treated her the same way the last time she'd shown up. For a few minutes last fall, as he took her back to her parents' house, he'd gotten a glimpse through the attitude and seen the loneliness she so successfully hid. Something inside him had responded immediately, just as he'd always responded to her, but there'd been no chance to explore it before she had once again fled. Now she was back, and he had to wonder why.

Sam hammered the last fence staple in place, then hefted his wire and fence tools. "Thanks, gentlemen. That should hold everything until morning."

"No problem," Stoner's foreman replied. "'Night."

Carter climbed back into his truck, started the engine, and turned around, saluting Stoner and Sam as he drove back down the road to the caretaker's house where he and his young wife lived. Sam and Stoner walked side-by-side back to the truck without saying a word. Sam tossed the fence tools and the wire into the bed before opening the back door to check on Erin.

She was still there. Sam refused to examine why it mattered so much to him. His heart beat in a heavier rhythm as he took stock of her. She was curled into a ball on the back seat, her shapely little jean clad derriere pointed right at him. He pulled his glove off and checked her pulse. Steadier than his, that was for sure. He frowned when she didn't stir and looked across the seat to Stoner.

"She's always been a heavy sleeper," he said.

Stoner climbed in the passenger side in back and sat next to his daughter. It surprised Sam, but then Stoner was a changed man, so perhaps things would be different for Erin this time. Sam hoped so. The thought made his gut unknot a hitch.

"Erin, honey!" Stoner said. "Sit up. Let's see that head."

She struggled to open her eyes, blinking owlishly. Her brow furrowed as her glance went from side to side as though not sure where she was. When she finally focused on him, he saw no recognition in their depths. Sam wasn't sure if it was from the pot, the injury, or sheer exhaustion. She looked like hell.

"Think she needs to go to the hospital?" Sam asked.

Stoner shot him a meaningful look. "Your house is closer. Can we take her there for now? I still have to tell Catherine. It will be enough of a shock for her that Erin's here, but I hate to show up with her in this shape." Stoner's expression pleaded, and that made Sam very uncomfortable. Stoner Richardson didn't beg for anything.

Sam frowned as he looked at Erin. No hospital—because she didn't need it or because Stoner didn't want the embarrassment? Sam clenched his jaw, trying to leave his personal feelings out of it.

The cut wasn't bad. It looked more like a friction burn, probably from the airbag, so chances were she didn't have a concussion.

"She's your daughter, Stoner."

"You think I don't know that? You think this is something new? It's happened so often before, Sam, all through high school. We tried rehab… shit!" Stoner's jaw worked as he stared out the window, his fist clenching and unclenching.

Sam sighed. Stoner's struggle to handle Erin's abrupt and unexpected appearance was obvious, and it made Sam's heart ache. As much as he knew having anything to do with Erin would be like volunteering to step into a snake pit, he couldn't stop himself. He'd never been able to when it came to anything having to do with her.

"Yeah. Stay here," he finally told Stoner. "I'll see if she has a suitcase."

Sprinting back to the car, he found a small purse and a duffel bag in the trunk. Not many clothes if she planned to stay any length of time, but from what he understood, Erin rarely stayed anywhere long. From sporadic e-mails to her parents, they knew she'd bounced from job to job in the islands…even working as a hostess at a topless club for a while. Sam slammed the trunk with unnecessary force.

Better not to go there. Thinking about her without clothes would only lead to more trouble than he wanted.

When they reached the farmhouse, Sam carried her in and laid her on the couch in his den. The wood stove still sent out waves of heat. Stoner was right behind him with her purse and her bag. Seeing Erin in his house brought back memories Sam didn't want to think about…erotic memories he'd worked hard to put behind him with an astounding lack of success and a barn-full of guilt. She could stay for one night. That was it. Then she had to go. Erin in his house was more temptation than Sam could handle.

Stoner looked at him with steady, gray eyes. "I owe you, Sam. Catherine was so distraught over what happened last fall. I don't want to see her hurt again." His gaze slid to Erin, and Sam saw the shadows there, but whatever Stoner's true feelings were, he kept locked inside. Maybe that was part of the problem. Erin and Stoner had a lot in common. Everything that mattered, everything important, they locked deep inside, unable or unwilling to allow themselves to appear vulnerable.

Stoner looked at Erin's pale face. "You want me to stay? Help get her cleaned up?"

Sam shook his head wearily. "I'll do it. Take my truck and go back to Catherine. Call me in the morning."

Stoner put his hand on Sam's shoulder. "I owe you."

"Yeah. So you've said."

After the door shut behind Erin's father, Sam looked at his uninvited guest and sighed. He felt like he'd been picking up after this particular Richardson for years. He left her sprawled on the couch while he stalked off in search of his first aid kit. She was awake when he returned but, for once, not ready to start a fight. She leaned against him limply while he cleaned the scrape on her head. It wasn't big, but she did have a bump to go with it. She watched him from somber, blue-gray eyes. After a couple of minutes of her almost unblinking stare, he arched one brow at her.

"If you have a question, Erin, I wish you'd just ask it."

"Where am I?" she asked.

"My house. It was closer. Your dad thought it would be better for you to spend the night here."

A flush of anger quickly replaced the flash of hurt he'd seen in her face, but then she blinked, masking her expression. Long lashes dropped as she shifted her gaze away. Her eyes had always been the chink in her protective armor because they mirrored what she truly felt. Sam wanted to grab her, make her look at him, and for once tell him what she really felt.

"I see." Her mouth twisted with a cynicism he hated to witness. "Am I supposed to pay you for the fence while I spend the night? Is that the deal?"

Anger burned like acid inside him, but he wasn't sure exactly who he was angry with—her, himself, or her father. What he did know was he hated the hurt that lingered in those big eyes of hers, and he knew one surefire way of getting rid of it.

"I don't work that way. You might end up paying me for my fence, but it won't be on your back. The fence cost a lot more money than one night between your thighs is worth, baby."

The haunted look disappeared and fury replaced it. She twisted away from him. "You prick! You over-sized gorilla. Take your freaking hands off me."

He'd take her anger over her hurt. He was big enough to handle the fury, but he had no idea what to do with the wounded woman lurking behind it. Sam stood, set the first aid kit aside, and stared her down. "Let me have your purse."

She clutched it to her. "Why?"

"Unless you plan to spend the next little while in jail, hand me your purse, Erin. And tell me what you're on."

She tossed the purse at him. "Just a little weed."

"If it were anyone else, I'd say you need to be at the hospital, but you're a Richardson. Y'all have hard heads."

"I might have a concussion."

Sam arched a brow as he dumped the contents of her purse on the table and began going through them. He found the pot, the papers, her lighter, her stash of ecstasy, and the Quaaludes. How the devil had she gotten through customs with this stuff? It was a freaking pharmacy in here. Finally he held up an oblong package with pills. "What are these?"

"Birth control pills," Erin snapped defiantly.

Sam's hand tightened. What was he getting uptight about? She was nothing to him. He was nothing to her. She wasn't a kid. She was almost twenty-seven. Had he expected she would continue to hero worship him? *Save herself for him?* She'd had a teenage crush on him, but she'd obviously moved on. Maybe it was time for him to do the same. How much of a fool was he? "I don't see a prescription."

"It was on the box, not the compact."

He put the birth control pills in a different pile. When he was through, he picked up all the drugs, opened the door on the woodstove, and tossed them in.

Erin leaped off the couch. "What the hell are you doing? Do you have any idea how much all that shit cost?"

Sam glared at her over his shoulder. "I don't give a flying feline, and what I'm doing is saving your cute little butt from jail time, idiot. Darn it! I'm the County Sheriff. You can't have this stuff, especially not in my home."

She lurched toward the woodstove, staggered, and started to slip sideways. He caught her as she fell.

"Sammy?" her voice was thready and frightened. Big, blue-gray eyes stared at him, and again her defenses went down for an instant. That was all it took to turn him into a marshmallow.

"It's okay, baby. You're okay." His throat tightened. Maybe he did need to keep an eye out for a concussion. She was always so fiercely self-sufficient, wanting no one, needing no one, that it hurt his heart to see her weakened. He knew the lessons she'd learned years ago. He'd been an unfortunate part of more than one of them. He knew deep down she wouldn't want to lean on anyone. She would see it as a mistake because her experience had shown her that, in the end, everyone else would let her down—even family. Especially family.

"Lie down, Erin." Sam looked at her paper white face with real concern. Then he began to notice other things. The five earrings in her left ear and—*Jesus H. Christ*—was that an eyebrow piercing? "For heaven's sake," he ground out roughly. "Why the devil have you stuck all those holes in yourself?"

"It's a personal statement," she flashed, color starting to return to her fair skin.

"Of what?" he asked. "That you'd prefer life as Swiss cheese?"

"No… That uptight parents and nosy neighbors need to back the hell off. It's my life, my body." Her eyes narrowed spitefully. "I've got one in my navel too. Wanna see?"

Sam frowned with the memory, one that still aroused him. "I saw that one last fall." He saw the look on her face. She wanted to shock him, make him squirm, make him lose his temper. It had always been like this.

"Then how about my tattoos?"

He quirked a brow. He didn't remember seeing any tattoos when she'd shown up unexpectedly at Tabby's art showing, and she'd only had the barest essentials covered. Even though he knew better, he still baited her. "What would you do if I said yes?"

Erin smiled wickedly and teased the snap on her jeans. "I'll show you mine if you'll show me yours."

"For heaven's sake!" Sam spun away from her. He had to. The sight of her finger sliding along the waistband of jeans was making him hard, making him want things he shouldn't.

"Have some respect for yourself," he said.

Silence reigned behind him. Suddenly, Sam knew he'd gone too far, hit her where she was the most vulnerable. That had always been her problem. As tough as she might seem, Erin had no self-esteem, and he had never understood why. He turned to apologize. She had her back to him and had gone still and silent, but he could see from her stiff posture that he'd managed to hurt her.

"Erin…"

"Go to hell." It was barely an audible whisper, not her usual high volume bluster.

Sam raked his hand across his short hair in frustrated patience as he tried to explain. "The only room with a bed that's made is mine…."

"Thanks, but no thanks, Sheriff. As you've already made clear again and again, you don't want me there."

But he did want to be fairly certain she would still be in his house come morning. "You can have my room, and I'll sleep on the couch."

"Afraid I'll take off?" she asked, some of her bluster returning, but only for an instant. "No, I'll sleep on the couch. You're too big to be comfortable here," she mumbled. "I'm used to sleeping on a berth on board ship. This is fine for me. Leave me alone. I'll be all right, and I will be here in the morning. Like I said earlier. I don't have anywhere else to go."

It was the most she had said since he'd found her in the pasture, and it was without an attitude. She still had her back to him, still refused to look at him.

"Do you need anything?" he finally asked quietly.

"No."

"Well, good night then. I'm down the hall if you need me."

She snorted. "I won't."

* * * *

Stoner parked Sam's truck behind the house and stepped into the kitchen. Catherine had already gone upstairs. She sat propped in their king-size bed. Seeing her made him smile. That was something else that had changed in the last six months. She had moved back into his bed. It had been a long time, not since they'd taken Erin and gone to Washington. Dear God, that was more than a third of their married life. Their daughter's teenage years had been rocky not only for her, but for them too. In fact, their marriage hadn't been on a solid footing since Erin's birth.

When Catherine glanced up from what she was reading, he smiled, praying like hell Erin's sudden reappearance wouldn't erode what they had rebuilt. Guilt stabbed him for feeling that way. He wanted what was best for Erin, but in the past that had always translated into sacrificing the rest of the family.

"Did you find the problem?" His wife's gaze held only mild curiosity. Most of the time loose cattle were the result of a gate left open or a broken wire, common enough occurrences in a rural area.

"Yes." Stoner kept his tone casual. "There was an accident. A driver ran off the road and took out part of Sam's fence. It was his cattle that were loose."

"I hope no one was hurt."

He smiled. "Just a minor injury. She's okay. Carter and I helped Sam get the cattle back in and put a temporary fix on the fence."

"Well, that's good." She was too intent on what she was reading to pay much attention, and he was relieved. After stripping, Stoner showered, wrapped himself in a thick robe, and returned to the bedroom.

As casually as he could he asked, "Did you ever hear anything back from Erin after you e-mailed her with the pictures of Tabby's wedding?"

"No...not a word."

"Was she still in the—where was it? The Virgin Islands?"

"Yes. That job as a cook on the sailing ship must agree with her. She's been there longer than anyplace so far. Why do you ask?"

"No reason. Just curious." As soon as it came out of his mouth, he knew he'd said the wrong thing. Even his casual tone wouldn't fool her.

He had her attention now. Catherine was anything but stupid. "Stoner, you said 'she' when you mentioned someone taking out Sam's fence. Would that 'she' be Erin?"

He sighed as he sat next to her on the edge of the bed. They'd promised each other honesty when they'd healed their rift. "Yes."

"Where is she, Stoner? Is she hurt?" There was a pause. Disillusionment colored her voice when she spoke again. "Was she drunk…or stoned?"

"She's at Sam's sleeping it off. She was stoned, Catherine. She hit her head, but nothing serious."

There was a long silence before Catherine touched his arm. "Stoner… Something's wrong. She only came back last fall because of Tabby, then immediately took off again. Now she turns up out of the blue?" She shook her head. "Honey, do you think she's in some kind of trouble? It's not like her to come back home willingly."

The truth of that statement cut him to the core. Stoner knew how much it pained Catherine to acknowledge the depth of the rift between them and their daughter, but it was true. There had always been something about Erin that Catherine had never been able to touch, even when she was a little girl. Stoner might have been able to once, when Erin was small, but as the years passed his relationship with his daughter had gotten even worse than the one between mother and daughter.

Stoner laughed, but it wasn't with any true amusement. "When has Erin ever not been in trouble, Katie?" He raked a big hand through his gray hair. "God! She makes it so hard to love her. It's like from the moment she was born, she took one look at me, and thought 'what can I do to piss him off?' I don't want to feel that way about her, damn it. She's my daughter."

"I know, honey." Catherine took his hand and stroked the back of it. "Just a year ago, I would have chalked up your worry to concern about how Erin's behavior would reflect badly on our family, but in the last six months you've changed."

He took her hand. "How do I get through to her?"

She shook her head. "I wish I knew the answer. The two of you may be too much alike in some ways to ever have an easy relationship. You're both hot-tempered."

Stoner snorted. "Yes, but where I hang on to a mood for a long time, Erin is a flash fire."

Catherine nodded. "There's a lot to that. She could never understand how you could still be mad at her hours later when she had long since moved beyond whatever it was that triggered your argument."

"And I thought she was trying to deliberately provoke me with an attitude that seemed uncaring and unrepentant."

Catherine leaned her forehead against his shoulder. "God forgive me, Stoner. I don't want to turn her away if she needs our help, but I can't go back and relive what it was like all through her teenage years. It made our marriage nearly impossible to endure, and we weren't on a great footing to start. We've come such a long way recently."

She paused and took a deep breath. "There's a part of me that wishes she would stay away." When she didn't say anything more, he looked at her. Her expression pleaded for understanding, guilt and sorrow mixing in equal measure. "Whatever happens, for whatever reason she's come back, please don't let it come between us. I need you, honey. I need what we've found again. These last six months…"

"…have been the best we've ever had," he finished with a gentle smile as he leaned forward to kiss her lingeringly. "We could put her in the guesthouse."

"Stoner!" She drew back in horror.

"Think about it. She'd have her privacy. We would have ours. She's nearly twenty-seven, Katie. I'm sure there are areas of her life I don't want or need to know about. And quite frankly, I think we're due for a little privacy." He grinned at her. "Maybe a lot of privacy."

Chapter 2

Sam woke up and lay still for a moment, instantly alert, darkness thick around him. The time he'd spent in the military had left a lasting effect. He assessed his surroundings, listening for what had awakened him. He heard it again. Crying. Who? Erin.

She never cried. Even as a kid. It was one of the things he'd always remembered about her. With Stoner in her face, she'd been dry-eyed and defiant, as tough and hardheaded as any of the Richardsons.

Sam bolted out of bed, snatched a pair of sweat pants over his boxers, which were already a concession to having a female in the house, and padded silently along the hallway. She lay on the couch, curled on her side toward the woodstove. He started to say something to her, then realized she still slept. He approached her cautiously. God, when had he ever approached Erin with anything but caution? He squatted next to her.

"Don't hurt them," she mumbled. "Not Matty!"

"Erin," he coaxed. "Come on, baby, wake up. You're having a nightmare."

Suddenly he was pinned by her dark, blue-gray gaze. With awareness of where she was and who stared at her, her expression changed. She wiped away the emotion and her look became unreadable.

"You okay?" he asked, knowing any additional sympathy would put her on the attack.

"Yeah." She laughed cynically. "It was a stupid dream. Sorry if I woke you up. Was I yelling?"

Sam half smiled. "Yeah." No way would he tell her she had cried. He had never, ever seen Erin cry, not when she broke her arm, not when Stoner put her pony down because it jumped the fence and was hit by a car, and not even when he had dragged her out of Sam's bed. Erin never cried. To hear she did so in her sleep? It ripped his guts right out. Even if she believed him, he couldn't imagine how mortified she would be. "Uh. I was up anyway. You want a cup of tea?"

Erin snorted. "Only if you can lace it with some bourbon."

He looked over his shoulder at her. "Sorry, I got enough of alcohol when my father was alive." Sure he took a drink now and then, but he wasn't about to tell her he had booze in the house.

She rolled away from him. Once again, he stared at her stiff back. Obviously their conversation was over as far as she was concerned. Sam forced himself to walk away. He shouldn't think about her. He didn't want or need a complication like Erin. The problem was that every time he started dating other women, he compared them to her. Somehow, they ended up too boring, too stupid, or too weak-spirited. And boy would that be embarrassing if anyone knew, the bachelor lawman and the wild child of Richardson Homestead. Too much history stretched between them. He thought of the birth control pills again. She had moved on, and so should he.

Sam heated water in the microwave, dumped a teabag in, and waited for it to steep. He remembered when Erin had crashed the party at the country club last fall. She had been stoned out of her head, maybe drunk as well, but underneath, the feisty defiance that had always called to him was still there. It had been enough to make him step between her and Stoner when her father would have slapped her.

"Sam?"

He turned so abruptly he nearly spilled his tea. Erin stood there leaning against the doorjamb. She had changed into some kind of baggy cotton pants and a long sleeved, high-necked shirt that hung nearly to her knees. Such modest attire for sleeping made for a contrast that was hard to reconcile with what she wore in public.

"What is it?" he asked, rubbing the ache in the back of his neck. He didn't want to play any more games.

"I—tea would be okay." The defensiveness was gone from her voice. It actually sounded like she was making an effort to be friendly, even if she didn't quite meet his gaze. Sam wanted her to look at him with the same intensity; he was relieved she didn't. It didn't make sense, but then whatever it was between the two of them never had.

While he grabbed another mug, filled, and nuked it, she wandered restlessly around the room, her delicate fingers touching things here and there until finally she stood next to him. Next to, but not touching him. He'd encountered wild animals less wary than Erin.

She was still no bigger than a mosquito, he thought, smiling inwardly. The top of her head was no higher than his chest. He thought of Stoner... taller still than him, and Catherine...herself a tall, slender woman. Evan was also tall. Erin must have felt like a misfit from the very beginning in that family. Meeting Tabby wouldn't have changed her mind. Her half sister was somewhere around five-ten.

"Why did you come back?" Sam asked. He hadn't meant to. God only knew it was none of his business, and he didn't want it to be his business. He needed to be smart, remain aloof, but sometime what he knew logically, his heart wouldn't obey.

"Would you believe me if I said I discovered a desire for hearth and home?"

Sam chuckled. "No."

She grinned at him, but the shadows still lingered on her elfin face. "I came back because I have the hots for you. Would you believe that?"

His heart pounded, and other parts too, at just the thought of it.

"No." But he wanted to. Man, did he want to. "I hardly think we would be a perfect fit, Erin."

She flashed a smile. "The druggy and the lawman. Probably not." She prowled the room again, stopping and striking a dramatic pose and tone. "What if I said I ran away from a member of a notorious crime family, and I believe he might still try to find me and kill me?"

Sam stared at the way she had her hand clutched to her chest, and he laughed.

Erin tilted her head and grinned. "No one would believe *that*, would they? Silly of me. I'll simply have to think of something more plausible."

"Do you want something to eat?"

She shook her head. As she took the tea, he noticed the faint tremor in her hands and wondered if it was leftover from her nightmare, or a function of all the substance abuse. He pulled a chair out and sat, but Erin continued to prowl. If it wasn't so much a part of who she was, it would have made him uneasy, but she had been constantly on the move as a child too, always searching, always looking for the next diversion.

"I'm sorry about your fence." She paused, but almost immediately her gaze shifted restlessly around, looking anywhere but at him, as if she couldn't bear to look at him. Once upon a time, she'd worshiped him, now her avoidance was as painful as a slap. "I—I saw a deer, a cow, or something in the road and swerved. Let me know what I can do to fix it."

Sam studied her, sizing her up. He wanted her to stick around. Somewhere deep inside, he knew she was looking for an excuse as well. Gut feeling told him this might be the last chance they had to find out what, if anything, there was between them. As much as logic and reason told him to stay away, his heart had always carried another message. His heart won.

"I could use some help around the farm. My hired hand has pneumonia and calving season just started. I'd pay you, minus the cost of the fence of course." Before he'd even finished speaking, his subconscious was screaming at him. What was he thinking?

Erin stared at him. "Of course. What exactly did you want me to do? Cook? Clean?"

Sam blinked. Have her in the house? That would be too close for comfort. "I need help with the livestock. You'd have to check fences, water troughs. Ride out during the day when I have to be at work. Help feed and muck out."

Erin wrinkled her aristocratic, little nose. "You want me to shovel cow shit?" Her voice rose on a note of incredulity as she finished.

Sam grinned. "And horse manure too. How long do you plan to stay?"

Erin shrugged. "A few hours, a few weeks. I don't know, Sam. I guess until I've worn out my welcome. Last time that didn't take long. In fact, I think it was worn out before I even arrived."

"Are you on vacation from that job on the ship?" She never had given him a straight answer about why she'd returned.

"You could say that." She avoided his eyes, continued her prowling.

Sam clenched his teeth in frustration. She was as forthcoming with information as usual. "Isn't this your busy time?"

Erin set her cup in the sink with a distinct click of ceramic against porcelain. "I'm tired. If you want help, I'll help, but let's leave examining my life out of it, okay? It's not part of the deal."

"Right." Sam stood and came up behind her to put his cup in the sink next to hers. For a moment their bodies touched, and it was like the completion of an electrical circuit; sparks shot between them. Sam jerked away. "I'll show you what to do over the next couple days. Then I'm back to work on Monday."

She nodded warily, shifting away from him. So she felt it too, and it made her nervous.

* * * *

Erin caught the coveralls and baseball cap Sam tossed at her the next morning. "I'm going to ride out and check fences. While I'm doing that, you can muck out stalls."

Erin wrinkled her nose at the heavy, insulated coveralls. She preferred softer materials, but she knew this would keep her warm.

"Try some of the boots near the back door. You might find a pair that fits." Sam ducked out the door so fast Erin had to believe he was trying to get away from her. Her mouth twisted. Nothing new there.

After finding a pair of boots that would actually stay on her feet, Erin slogged across the barnyard. She paused inside the door and inhaled the familiar scents. She'd spent a lot of time in the barn at Richardson Homestead as a kid...until Daddy had put her pony down. Her gaze skittered around the storage area just inside the door. Erin grabbed a manure fork and the wheelbarrow and began shoveling the soiled bedding.

About mid-morning, she heard a vehicle pull into the farmyard. The nervous flutter in her stomach was beyond her control. The wheelbarrow was full, so Erin pulled the cap low over her eyes and pushed it outside, partly to empty it, partly to see who was there. With the cap on, chances were excellent no one would recognize her immediately. That might be the advantage she needed if... No, she wasn't going there. She was safe here.

"Hey, kid!" a voice she hadn't heard in years called. "You seen Sam? I brought his truck back. I need to pick my sister up and get him to drive us back to my parents' house."

Erin let the wheelbarrow drop to the ground and pushed her cap back. Evan's gray eyes, so like Daddy's, widened.

"Erin? What... What the hell are you doing?"

His tone, as much as his words, put her on the defensive. She stuck her chin out pugnaciously. "You're the freaking brain, Evan. What's it look like I'm doing? I'm shoveling horse shit."

"Why?" Evan's brows pulled together. "Did Sam *force* you to do this?"

She shrugged nonchalantly. "I wanted a job. Sam gave me one. It will pay him back for busting his fence."

Evan arched one thick brow. "Wouldn't it be easier to write a check?"

"He needed help. I'm helping." Not even a full day home, and both Evan and her father were questioning her every move.

Evan followed her into the barn where she picked out the next stall. As she worked, he watched her curiously, as if she were some kind of strange experiment. Hell, maybe she was. He didn't know her. Probably didn't know her as well as he knew the new darling of the family, their half sister, Tabby.

Since they had reached their teens, Erin's encounters with him and the rest of her family could only be described as brief and painful. Most of the time she had been in one scrape or another, or out of her head on booze or drugs.

"I'm supposed to bring you home. Mother and Daddy have opened the guesthouse for you."

She had her back to him. Good thing too. Erin pressed her lips together to contain the angry words that bubbled up inside her. The guesthouse. Not her childhood home, not the room she'd had growing up. She was relegated to the guesthouse. Erin had stopped in mid-scoop with a forkful of shavings and manure. She finished tossing them onto the wheelbarrow.

"How thoughtful of them to put their daughter in the guesthouse. Tell me, Evan, is that where the perfect Tabby stayed while she lived with them?"

"That was different, Erin. Tabby almost died. She was recovering from a serious accident."

Erin leaned the fork against the wall and turned to look at her brother. She tilted her cap back and simply stared at him. He looked imposing, successful. He looked like a younger version of their father. She wondered if his tongue was as sharp and suspected it could wound exactly like Stoner's.

Erin wasn't ready to face that.

"I'm not ready to go. I'm not done yet. Sam rode out to check the herd in the back pasture. I said I would finish this and I will."

But Sam rode back in at that point, his cheeks flushed from the cold. As Evan turned, Erin quietly returned to work. She heard Sam dismount and lead his mare into the barn. His dark gaze narrowed as it shifted from her to Evan.

"You've done enough today, Erin," Sam commented. "Grab your things and I'll run you and Evan over to the Homestead."

Erin wanted to tell him no. She wasn't ready for this, but she wouldn't beg.

Sam's gaze gentled as he continued quietly and evenly. "You have to see them, Erin, sooner or later."

Her chin rose. "You're not my therapist."

Sam ignored her. "I have to go to town anyway before the farm store closes, so I can get posts and boards to start making permanent repairs to my fence now that the tow truck's pulled your rental out." Sam stepped up and took the pitchfork from her. "I took the rest of your joint out of the ashtray. Get your stuff, Erin. Go home. I said you could work here… not live here."

She hated the way he saw right to her vulnerabilities. He'd always been able to do that.

"Who'd want to live with you anyway?" she snapped at Sam, "a middle-aged bachelor with the beginnings of a paunch." She pushed at him. "Get the hell out of my way, you goon."

She stomped past him and Evan and stopped just outside the barn to lean against the wall. Man, she didn't want to leave Sam's place. Just the thought of facing the rest of her family made her nearly sick.

From inside the barn, she could hear Evan and Sam. No doubt they thought she was long gone. Erin knew she shouldn't eavesdrop, but as she'd learned the hard way, sometimes a person could learn valuable information that way. Yeah, like Andre wanting to kill her.

"You know, Evan," Sam said from inside the barn, "I've never cared for your father much, but right now I almost feel sorry for him." Erin blinked at the stab of pain his words caused. After a pause, Sam asked, "Am I getting a paunch?"

"Hardly," Evan said, with a snicker, then continued, "Erin's always had great aim with her verbal arrows. Hitting at the heart of others' insecurities is a great diversionary tactic. I always assumed she did it to keep people from looking too closely at all of her less than desirable activities, but now I'm not so sure."

"What do you mean?"

"I don't know. It just seems like there's more to her coming home."

There sure as hell was, but Erin didn't want to share that. She should leave. She didn't like the direction this conversation was going, but she just couldn't seem to break away and go to the house.

"I am a bit concerned about her going back, Ev. The old Stoner would rip her to shreds. What's the new and improved one likely to do?"

"Hell if I know. She's been a thorn in everyone's side for years. You've seen that. I remember my parents missed my first varsity basketball game because Erin needed to go to the emergency room after she jumped from the hayloft onto the trampoline she'd pulled underneath the loft door and bounced off onto her head. Then at the party Stoner threw after I graduated law school, she turned up high as a kite. You wonder what the new Stoner will do? I have no clue, bro."

Erin crept toward the house. She shouldn't have stayed to listen. As she changed clothes and gathered her things, Evan's words kept echoing in her brain. If that was the way everyone thought about her, then she had made a mistake in coming home, a very bad mistake.

Sam and Evan were waiting for her. Without acknowledging either one of them, Erin climbed into Sam's truck. She sat silently in the back seat with her purse and her duffel bag clutched close to her side and glanced longingly out the window at Sam's receding barnyard. She'd had a decent time this morning feeding and brushing horses. Even mucking out stalls.

It had reminded her of spending time around the barn at home when she was little. It was the one place she'd felt at home. Animals didn't judge.

As much as it shamed her to admit it, she was scared to go back to Richardson Homestead. She was even more frightened to face her family. They had always intimidated her. Her brilliant, successful father and her mother, the perfect hostess, Evan with his brains and his athletic ability, and now there was Tabitha too. A new sister she'd barely even met who was a freaking artistic genius. Then there was her. Not much on her resume to brag about. Oh, wait, she did have a sadistic drug runner wanting to kill her.

"I'll need you at my place at six-thirty tomorrow morning." Sam caught her gaze in the rearview mirror as he spoke, and Erin quickly masked the insecurity and uncertainty she was sure must be showing on her face. "We'll be riding, so I can show you what you'll need to do during the week." He paused until she reluctantly met his gaze again. "Don't be late, Erin," he added quietly.

Her chin jerked up. "I'll be there." She wanted to beg him to let her stay, but his expression was closed, and his eyes focused on the road once more.

They turned up the drive to the big brick house on the hill, and Erin swallowed nervously. As soon as the truck stopped, she jumped out with her oversize purse and her duffel bag clattering behind her. With a nod to Evan, Sam turned the truck around and was off. She stared after him until Evan moved over to her.

"Here, let me take your bag into the guesthouse for you." He reached for it, but she jerked away.

"I've got it," she snapped, then bit her lip. "Just—just show me where to put it," she added more quietly.

Evan led the way into the guesthouse. Erin looked around with curiosity. It had been redecorated from what she remembered, but it was still essentially the same, a great room and kitchenette downstairs and two bedrooms upstairs. She set her duffel bag on the couch and took off her jacket.

"Do I bow before the king now or later?" she asked sarcastically.

Evan tilted his head. "There's no need to bow, but it might be nice if you came in to say hello to Mother and Dad. Jenny's here too with our son, Peter."

Erin took a shaky breath and looked around. It had seemed so simple when she was in the Virgin Islands. Come home. There would be shelter even if there was no comfort. But now she had to face her family. Maybe it would have been just as easy to take her chances in the islands. "Is there any booze in here? I could use a drink."

"It's eleven in the morning, Erin," Evan said softly. "How badly do you need a drink?"

Her chin lifted and her eyes narrowed. "I'm not a freaking alcoholic, Evan, if that's what you're implying."

"Alcohol, pot, drugs? It doesn't appear to matter much to you which one, does it?"

Erin's head jerked back at the distaste bleeding through his tone. Just because he was her brother, it didn't give him the right to look down on her. She glared at him. "You have no idea. You were always so perfect. Nothing I did could ever be as perfect as you." She brushed past him. "Let's get this over with. Maybe then I can figure out how long it will be before I get kicked out again."

Evan grabbed her arm. "They've never kicked you out."

She spun on him, effectively breaking his hold and putting herself out of his reach. Now Evan's eyes narrowed as he studied her defensive stance. Erin worked to control her breathing. That had been a mistake, a huge overreaction. She needed to be careful if she was going to keep her business to herself.

When he relaxed, so did she. She eyed him from his cashmere sweater to his neat khakis. "No, you're right, Evan. They never kicked me out. They froze me out. It got so freaking cold I had to go clear to the Caribbean to thaw out."

"Then why the hell did you come back?" he snapped.

"That's my business!"

She turned and left, digging her hands into the tight pockets of her hip hugger jeans and hunching her shoulders in an attempt to make her breasts appear smaller. All she wanted was to feel safe, to feel like someone cared. Sam's frowning face came to mind, but she forced it away. He'd made it plain years ago and again last night that he didn't want her.

* * * *

Stoner had ushered everyone to his study to wait for Erin and Evan to appear. Catherine and Jenny sat on the couch, keeping an eye on Peter, who played on a blanket on the floor, giggling as he rolled around. Stoner watched them with half a glance while keeping an eye on the doorway at the same time.

Evan appeared first. For a heartbeat, pain stabbed Stoner's heart, so sure was he that Evan would tell them Erin had bolted again. Then she stepped from behind her older brother, a petite woman who stood only chest high to him. Her hair was short and spiky, like it had been last fall, but Stoner was relieved to see it no longer had electric blue highlights on top, and now her face was almost completely devoid of makeup. In an odd way, it made her large, blue-gray eyes stand out even more against her porcelain pale skin than the dark, heavy eye makeup she'd worn when she'd shown up at Tabby's party.

For a fraction of a second, he was reminded of a doe in that instant she senses danger, but has yet to break and run. The minute Stoner stood, though, the impression disappeared. Erin's chin jutted belligerently, and her eyes narrowed.

"How are you this morning?" Stoner asked carefully as he crossed the room to her, uncertain of her reaction. "Did Sam take care of your head?"

"Yes."

She stiffened when he bent to kiss her, and Stoner straightened awkwardly. Inside he sighed. Why the hell had she come here when she so obviously didn't want to? He had never understood her, and it seemed he still didn't. Even a couple of years ago, he would have said that aloud, but circumstances had mellowed him.

"Come in," he invited instead. "Say hello to your mother and Jenny. You remember Jenny, don't you?"

Erin nodded and swallowed as her eyes met her mother's.

"Mama."

Catherine held her arms open to her daughter, and Erin moved as gracefully as a cat to her mother's side, briefly embraced her, then looked at Jenny warily.

Jenny smiled at her and laughed. "You have no idea how relieved I am to see someone in this family who does not tower over me."

Erin grinned, and even though it was tinged with anxiety, it was the most relaxed she had looked since she walked into the room. Stoner took a deep breath. Maybe everything would be all right.

"It can be overpowering." Erin's glance slid to the baby, and now she smiled genuinely for the first time. "He's cute. How old is he?"

"Five months," Jenny said, "and already has teeth."

At his mother's voice, Peter stopped what he was doing and looked at them both with a big smile, showing off two top teeth.

"Would you like to hold him?"

Erin shook her head, as she eyed everyone else awkwardly. "Could—could I just play with him?"

Stoner watched as his daughter and daughter-in-law sat next to Peter and teased him with toys to make him laugh and wave his arms and legs in delight. He had never seen such a soft expression on Erin's face. The baby calmed her down in some way, so that she didn't prowl like a nervous cat, something she had done for what felt like forever.

"Can I get you something to drink?" Catherine asked since everyone else had either coffee or tea. Erin's eyes darted to the brandy decanter and away.

"No." Her voice was tight. Suddenly, she was on her feet again. She moved restlessly around the room. "I—I'm sorry about last night, D— daddy. I swerved to avoid hitting a deer. I told Sam I'll work off what I owe him for the fence. He mentioned he needed help on the farm, so I'm working there."

"You're working as a farm hand?" Catherine asked softly. She tried to keep her tone noncommittal, but the implication slipped through that a Richardson did not do that. Stoner held his breath. Erin stopped in the middle of the room, and Stoner could almost see the tension vibrate through her. God! She was as taut as a bowstring. She smiled jerkily.

"I'll have to be up and about early in the mornings. If—if that's not convenient, I—I'm sure I can find a place to stay."

"For God's sake, Erin," Stoner finally exploded. "You're family, not some damn guest."

Her gaze was cool as it rested on him. "Am I?" The bitterness in those two words was there for everyone to hear. It slammed into Stoner with all the force of a slap. Did she really feel that way?

Catherine rose and approached her daughter, but all of them could see the way Erin stiffened at the contact. "Of course you're family, honey. And you're welcome to stay in the guesthouse for as long as you wish."

Silence stretched. Stoner pressed his lips together as Erin's expression subtly altered. It was as if she withdrew from them, though she hadn't moved at all. The shaft of pain that speared through him made him take a step back. He had never been able to reach her, and he didn't understand why.

Erin blinked a couple of times as though she was at a loss for words. Maybe putting her in the guesthouse had been a mistake. Her expression gave away nothing as she finally took a deep breath and looked around the room.

The instant she spotted Tabby's new portrait of him, she moved toward it. This time Stoner saw the flash of emotion in her eyes—amazement followed quickly by jealousy. He wondered at that. Certainly, the painting portrayed him in a way few people had seen him. Even Stoner had difficulty relating the image of the pleasantly relaxed man intent on the table on which he was working, his hands setting minute inlay into its surface, with the cold man he'd often felt himself to be.

"This must be the painting Tabby did." She pasted a smile on her face. "She's very talented."

Stoner stood behind her but didn't touch her. He wanted to. He wanted to wrap his arms around her, but the keep-off signals his daughter was throwing out were almost tangible.

"She and Joe will join us for dinner," he murmured. "We'd like you to be there too, Erin."

She continued to stare at the painting for the longest time, never turning around as she asked, "What time?"

"Six."

She nodded, edging away from him, as if she didn't know how to be around them or what they expected. Stoner stifled a sigh. Because she had been gone for so long, they were all but strangers to her. Before he could think of something to say to ease her mind, she spoke.

"If—if you don't mind, I'll go rest. I'm tired."

"I'll walk you over there." He started to take her elbow, but she edged farther away, so Stoner dropped his hand.

"No. No, Daddy... That's okay." Erin fled.

Stoner looked at Jenny after Erin left. "Well?" he inquired softly, hands jammed in his pockets to prevent anyone from seeing how tense he was. "What do you think?"

Jenny shook her head. "She doesn't appear to be on anything right now, Stoner. Of course, knowing for certain would require testing. She simply acted like..." Jenny paused, then rushed on, "Well, she acted like a stranger walking into an unfamiliar setting might."

"But she's our daughter," Catherine protested. "Why should she act like a stranger?"

Evan put his hand on Jenny's shoulder. "Mother, other than that disastrous visit last fall, I haven't seen Erin since she was eighteen. She is virtually a stranger. I'm not sure that we're dealing as much with a substance abuse issue as we are that she's running from something...or someone."

"What makes you say that?" Stoner questioned.

"While she got her things out of Sam's house this morning, he told me he dumped pot, ecstasy, and some Quaaludes out of her purse last night. She doesn't appear to have any one drug of choice, which is more like an addict; she seems to do whatever will get her high. It's an escape, not something she physically has to have."

Stoner's unease ramped up again. "Did Sam check her suitcase or just her purse?"

Evan grimaced. "He only mentioned her purse. You want me to call him to find out?"

Oh how Stoner wished he could say no, but it wasn't possible. He nodded reluctantly. Evan stepped out of the room to use his cell phone. Stoner moved to the window and stared out over the winter-brown fields, grateful that Catherine knew him well enough to leave him to his thoughts, uneasy though they might be.

Evan returned in a few minutes. "Sam didn't check her suitcase."

The instant Stoner met Evan's gaze, they hurried from the room toward the guesthouse. Stoner prayed this would not be a repeat of her teenage years.

Damn it," Evan said. "She's locked the door, Dad."

Stoner dug into his pocket. "Hang on. I've got a spare key here. Jesus! She hasn't even been here a day, and it's already started." He unlocked the door and opened it quietly. His eyes spotted the pills almost immediately. Evan examined them.

"Ecstasy."

"What the hell is that?" Stoner demanded.

"It acts like both an amphetamine and a hallucinogen."

"I don't even want to know how you know these things," Stoner grimaced.

Evan arched one thick brow, looking like a younger version of Stoner. "Prosecuting attorney, remember?"

Stoner raced up the stairs, heart pounding, opened first one bedroom door, then the second, smaller room. She was curled in one of the two twin beds in there, but when the hinge squeaked, she leaped from the bed and backed into the corner before her eyes cleared and she saw it was him.

"Daddy! What are you doing?" Her chest heaved, but a trace of panic lurked in her eyes.

Panic that she'd been caught? Stoner grabbed her and shook her. "What did you take, Erin? Damn it! How much?"

Her eyes were wide and shocked as she glanced from his face to Evan, who now stood behind Stoner.

"Nothing," she whispered. "I didn't take anything."

"You're lying," Stoner snapped. Concern made him sound harsh and cold, but he couldn't help it. She was scaring the shit out of him. "We saw the pills scattered on the table downstairs."

"But… I didn't take them," she protested again. "Please. Daddy, you have to believe me."

Stoner shut his eyes, feeling as though his heart was being ripped apart again as he admitted, "I can't believe you. You've never given me any reason to believe you." He turned to look at Evan. "I want Jenny to look at her."

"Dad…" Evan began uncertainly, his gaze shifting to the hurt evident on Erin's face.

"I want Jenny to look at her," Stoner insisted. He remembered a night when she was in high school, when he had given her the benefit of the doubt, and she had nearly died from an overdose. "I'll stay here. Get Jenny and flush that crap lying on the table."

Erin stood like a statue in the corner of the room, her eyes huge in her pale face. Stoner's heart ached. When he reached toward her again, she flinched, throwing her hands out to ward him off. "Don't touch me."

Her nostrils flared and her eyes glittered before she turned her face away from him, pressing her palms against the wall behind her. Stoner raked his trembling fingers through his hair. He had forgotten how many nights he had lain awake, worried sick about her. Now, she no sooner came back than it started all over again.

Jenny came into the room, took one look at Stoner and Erin's stiff postures, and ordered him out of the room. When he started to protest, she glared at him. "I am doing this only because you're her father, but she's an adult, Stoner. You will not stay in here while I examine her, not even while I talk to her."

* * * *

From the corner of her eye, Erin saw the door shut behind Stoner and Evan.

"Can I get you a glass of water?" Jenny asked.

Erin sucked a breath into a throat so tight it hurt. She shook her head and whispered, "I shouldn't have come back. I keep saying that. Maybe I'll eventually learn my lesson and leave once and for all." She cast her hand around the room. "The guesthouse is where they've put me. Not their home. I'm a guest, not one of them."

Erin blinked a couple of times as she absorbed the hurt and let it pass on through. All she had ever wanted from them was their love, their understanding, but how could they understand? Some of the fault lay squarely at her door. She could acknowledge that now, as an adult. She'd kept the real issues hidden, and done a damn fine job of it.

Jenny sighed, drawing her out of her introspection. Her sister-in-law sat on the edge of one of the twin beds. "It took me a long time to understand your father, Erin. A long time to forgive him. He is a man of very intense, deeply felt emotions."

Erin laughed bitterly. "As deep as a chest freezer."

Jenny shook her head. "I can't help you two with those issues, but I can deal with some of yours. Did you take any of the MDMA?"

"No. I thought about it, pretty seriously." Something about Jenny gave Erin complete confidence that Jenny would not doubt her. "My boss, Rick, never had a problem with us being a little loose, but I don't want to keep doing that."

"When's the last time you used anything?"

"I smoked part of a joint last night right after I landed in Sam's pasture with my rental car."

"Nothing since then? No alcohol, cold medicine, anything?"

"Nothing." Erin met her gaze without flinching. Jenny didn't need to know the mental battle Erin had fought to leave the pills untouched.

"May I examine you?"

Erin nodded and submitted to having her pulse, respiration, pupil response, and reflexes tested. When Jenny asked to see the contents of her purse, Erin dumped them out along with her duffel bag. Jenny flicked open the birth control pills and looked at Erin.

"This is fine for pregnancy prevention, but you should use condoms to protect against disease."

Erin snorted. "It's not an issue. I take them for severe cramps."

"But you make your partners use condoms?" Jenny's concern was evident.

Erin raised her brows and said again, more slowly, "It's not an issue. It's never been an issue. You're a doctor. Do I need to be clearer than that?"

"But…?" Jenny shook her head. "Are you telling me you're a virgin?"

Erin laughed bitterly. "What? I'm sure my family led you to believe I'd spread my legs for anyone and everyone, right? Just because…" Erin paused, grinding her teeth in frustration. "You know, never mind. It doesn't matter anymore. I'm almost twenty-seven. They won't change what they think, and I can't make them. Just…just tell my dad the truth, please. I'm not on anything. I'm exhausted. Last night was the first night in three days I've had any sleep… And I didn't sleep well."

"Why the MDMA downstairs then?" Jenny probed, her tawny eyes intent.

"I thought about it," Erin whispered. "But then I remembered Sam going through my stuff. I didn't want to disappoint him. What a joke, huh? I've always been a disappointment to all of them. I'm not an addict.

I need a break sometimes from my own head." She turned away. "Leave me alone, Jenny. Make Daddy leave me alone. I want to sleep right now."

"All right."

With a nod, Jenny stood and opened the door. When it had shut behind her, Erin slid down the wall and curled up on the floor in the corner of the room. Her lip trembled, but she refused to shed a tear. Why she had expected things to be different this time, she had no idea. It was another way of setting herself up for disappointment, and there were more than enough of those already.

She had come back because she feared for her life, and in some corner of her mind, she supposed she still associated home and safety with her parents. Or maybe she wished it were so. Erin rubbed her eyes. She was rubbing away the scratchiness from lack of sleep. Yeah.

Chapter 3

Sam couldn't shake the unhappy feeling hounding him as he pounded new fence posts into the soil and hammered up fresh boards. Evan's call to find out if Sam had searched Erin's duffel bag nagged at him. Had she taken something? He fought the urge to rush over there. She wasn't his concern. Stoner had made that plain more than a decade ago. Sam wanted to shake some sense into Erin at the same time he wanted to protect her from whatever hell Stoner was no doubt giving her. And the fact he couldn't get her off his mind bothered him. He swung the hammer even harder as he secured another board in place.

By the time his cell phone rang early in the afternoon, Sam had worked off most of his concerns. Then he saw it was the Richardson's number and his gut twisted as he answered.

"This is Sam."

"Oh, Sam. I'm so glad I caught you. It's Catherine." Relief surged through him. She sounded perfectly normal. Everything must be fine. "Tabby and Joseph will be here for dinner this evening along with Evan and Jenny. I thought I would invite you as a way to say thank you for giving Erin a job."

"I don't want to intrude on a family dinner." It was a convenient excuse, because somehow Sam had the feeling the reason behind the invitation was far from a simple thank you.

"Nonsense. We're all very fond of you."

Sam grinned. That was doubtful, especially when it came to Erin and Stoner. In fact, he had a hard time picturing either one of them looking at him with gratitude about anything. "You need me to even out the numbers, right?"

Sam knew there was more to it than that, but it would give Catherine a convenient reason without having to admit Sam would provide a buffer between Erin and her family.

"Well...partly."

He laughed, letting her off the hook. Besides, it would give him a chance to check on Erin. "I'll come. Your cook beats my cooking any time. I figure you'll tell me eventually why I'm really invited."

After sliding his phone back in its clip, he returned to the job of fixing his fence. It was hard sometimes not to envy the Stoner Richardsons of the world. He had plenty of money to hire a crew to fix something like this. But Sam's family had always been the poor neighbors.

Years ago, he'd resented that difference much more, but now, seeing everything that had happened with Stoner's family and his political career, Sam's envy had mellowed. Senator Richardson had certainly tumbled from the mountain top, opting out of a political career rather than facing exposure for some of his past misdeeds. Then there'd been the whole fiasco with Jenny and Evan's relationship. Stoner's interference there had split the two apart for more than a dozen years.

Sam shook his head. No. He no longer envied Stoner Richardson. Most of the time, except when he considered what having the kind of money the Richardsons had would allow him to provide for a family. He could update his farmhouse, maybe install an updated kitchen where someone who really enjoyed cooking would feel at home. Sam nearly smacked his thumb with the hammer. With a shake of his head, he returned to the backbreaking work of rebuilding his fence.

He knew some of his neighbors laughed at him for the wood fences when woven wire would have been a hell of a lot cheaper. When it came right down to it, though, he'd rather be hefting boards and pounding nails than trying to stretch wire in cold weather. He glanced along the road, eyes narrowing, at the neat line of fence that fronted not only Richardson Homestead, but his farm too. And there was the whole issue of appearances. Having Richardson Homestead as a neighbor wasn't easy, in more ways than one.

At six that evening, he knocked at the door, tired but dutifully on time as he'd promised. Peterson was there to let him in, looking every inch the British butler he was. Sam nodded to him, then looked past him to Stoner, who stood in the doorway to his study.

"Sam, come on in." Although his welcome was friendly enough, Stoner was tense. When Sam entered the study, he discovered why. Everyone was there except Erin. No doubt waiting to make an entrance. Creating dissension came as second nature to her.

Never one to ignore the obvious, Sam asked, "Where's Erin?"

"Just a little late, I'm sure." Catherine's smile was just a bit tremulous.

Sam studied all of them. Stoner, Catherine, and Evan looked ready to chew nails. Jenny, Tabby, and Joseph were calm, but then they didn't know her. Sam wouldn't put it past Erin to walk in wearing nothing but her diamond belly button stud. Never had he met anyone quite so able to throw things into complete chaos.

"I'll get her," he stated to Catherine and Stoner, totally unsurprised when they made no protest.

No lights shone in the guesthouse. When he knocked and got no answer, Sam's first thought was she had bolted again, and that was quickly followed by the thought she had found more drugs and was high as a kite. He tried the door and found it unlocked.

"Erin!" he called as he opened the door and stepped inside.

"Here." She stood near the rear window that overlooked the pool, her profile only dimly outlined from what remained of the waning light. Sam turned on the lamp next to the couch, half expecting her to be in a micro mini skirt and a halter top. She turned toward him, wearing a simple black jersey dress with high-heeled pumps that gave her some added height and did great things for her long bare legs.

"Everyone's waiting on you," Sam stated.

"I can't..." she began, swallowed, and started again, "No one wants..."

"To miss dinner," Sam interrupted. He stifled the urge to rub the tightness in his chest as he noticed the haunted look that had entered her eyes again. Wanting to erase it, he continued, "And as usual, you wait to make a big entrance."

Her chin lifted and she straightened to her full, if meager, height. "Shut up, Sam."

He held her coat for her and smiled behind her as he slipped it over her narrow shoulders. He would much rather have her angry than blue. As soon as they entered the house from the den, Sam took her coat and tossed it carelessly across the back of a chair. His hand rested lightly between her shoulder blades as he guided her into the study. She trembled, and for an instant he could see why. With the exception of Jenny, they were all tall and regal looking, but even Jenny had a presence that intimidated.

Neither Peter nor Melody, Joe and Tabby's adopted daughter, were there. Sam's mouth tightened. So, not a family night. Adults only probably meant a lot more serious discussion. Sam began to wonder if his presence was motivated by more than a desire to even out the numbers. He restrained the urge to wrap his arm tightly around Erin, an action that would make neither Erin nor Stoner happy. Joseph and Tabby were the first to smile and approach them. Was it his imagination, or did Erin shrink even closer toward him.

"Erin?" Tabby murmured gently, "I'm so happy to see you. This is Joseph, my husband."

She looked at both of them, Tabby with her black hair and golden eyes, and Joseph with his blond hair and warm blue eyes. Erin held out her hand to Joseph who smiled warmly and clasped it between his own.

"Tabby has so looked forward to this," he spoke in a melodic voice that made Erin's eyes widen. Her trembling all but disappeared.

"Sam," Joseph greeted him. "Good to see you again. I'm sorry we didn't say hello when you first came in."

Tabby and Erin stared at one another. Although Erin was older by three years, it was Tabby who appeared more polished and self-assured, an assessment that would surely amuse Tabby if she heard it. Sam knew enough of Tabby's background to know her upbringing had been anything but sophisticated. Logically, Erin, with her exposure to living in the nation's capital, should be the more socially aware. Tabby touched Erin's arm gently. "Please tell me about yourself. It feels so strange suddenly to have developed such a large family."

Erin looked around the room. Sam followed her gaze, trying to see it through her eyes, and realized that the dysfunctional family in which she had grown up had indeed changed. Her father had his arm draped around her mother's shoulders, Jenny was tucked firmly against Evan, and they all talked and smiled. When she looked back at Tabby again with wide eyes, Sam felt her shrink toward his side even more. "Wh-what have you done to them? What are you?" Erin whispered.

Sam's head jerked toward Erin in shock. What in the blue blazes? Before he could call her on being so rude, Tabby responded.

"I'm your sister." Her brow wrinkled with concern more than surprise at Erin's reaction. "And I'm hoping you'll accept me like Evan and Jenny have."

Erin was pressed so hard against Sam's side, he was certain the seam of her dress had left an imprint on him.

"Erin!" Sam growled, worrying that she was about ready to bolt.

"I don't want to pressure you," Tabby tried to reassure her. "I grew up as an only child. I used to dream of having brothers and sisters. I have Evan and Jenny, and now you, if you'll let me. I'd like that." Tabby held out her hand. "Please."

There was a tense moment in which Sam felt the entire room hold its breath. Sam held his breath too, for the instant it took Erin to set her hand, with its finely trembling fingers, into Tabby's. The infinitesimal pause in the conversation on the other side of the room disappeared, and Stoner laughed at something Jenny related about Peter. If there was an edge of relief in that laughter, no one commented on it.

Sam felt some of Erin's tension dissipate, but not all of it. Something was definitely worrying her, but it would take a lot to get her to admit that. He'd have to work on that. Whatever was on her mind had to be the reason she had returned.

Dinner went well. Erin watched Sam, Joseph, and Tabby all refuse wine with their meal; then she did too. She was so afraid of making any kind of a wrong move, it made Sam's heart ache.

After dinner, the conversation turned to colleges. Erin's expression closed right up. As everyone related their experiences, her discomfort was palpable, at least to Sam. Probably to Tabby too, as tuned in as she always seemed to be to everyone's feelings.

Joe, wanting to include Erin in the conversation, innocently asked, "What about you, Erin?"

"Erin dropped out," Stoner commented before Erin could say anything. Sam cringed. Stoner had done exactly the wrong thing.

"I may be the stupid one in this family, Daddy," Erin snapped, "but I can manage to explain that on my own."

"Erin…" Stoner began, but she jumped to her feet and stalked out of the room. She'd had enough. Stoner pursued her, with Jenny and Tabby not far behind. Sam raked his fingers over the top of his head. Yeah, call him chicken, but he was going to stay out of this one for now.

* * * *

Erin had nearly reached the door when her father's voice stopped her. "Was it really necessary to make such a scene?"

She spun on him, temper flaring. "Was it necessary to announce to everyone that I 'dropped out' in that offended paternal tone?"

Stoner glared at her. "It is offensive, Erin. You could have been anything! You're beautiful and smart, but you chose—you *chose* not to concentrate on your education."

"You're wrong, Daddy. You are so, so wrong. I was stupid then and I am now. Do you think I want jobs like I've had? A nanny, a cook, a lifeguard—a topless bar hostess, for God's sake! But it's always been much easier to blame that on laziness than face the reality that I just wasn't there when intelligence was doled out to the almighty Richardson bloodline."

Erin slammed the door behind her as she raced across the terrace to the guesthouse. She wanted a drink. She was tired of trying to play nice and fit in. Damn them all, and damn her for thinking she could come back, could make anyone change their opinion of her. There must be something to drink around the guesthouse.

She found the bar in the corner of the great room and quickly splashed two fingers of bourbon into a glass. She tossed it back in silent toast to Evan and Stoner who both enjoyed a shot of fine bourbon. She poured another one and had it halfway to her mouth when she heard the knock on the door.

"Leave me alone!" she snarled, her hand clenched around the glass, certain it had to be her father. Why couldn't he give it up?

"Open the door, Erin," Tabby said quietly. "It's Jenny and me."

It took Erin only a heartbeat to consider before she snatched the door open and spun back into the room, with the bourbon still in hand. She toasted them with it.

"Are we having a little girl to girl talk? I don't do too well at those. I always got along with guys much better. What do you want to know? How I graduated at the bottom of my high school class, but thanks to Daddy's influence managed to get accepted at a small college? How I dropped out of college before I could get kicked out because my grades sucked?"

Jenny gently removed the glass of bourbon from her hand, and led her to the couch. Erin shook with nerves. She didn't want to do this, didn't want to stay here. All she wanted was a chance to lie low for a while.

"Honey," Jenny prompted gently. "What is it? Every time I see you, you look ready to shatter into a million pieces. Don't lock it inside. Don't do what Stoner did. Don't wait until it's too late."

Everything inside Erin stilled. "Is something wrong with Daddy?" She choked the question out, her guard dropping as she had to ask, "Is he sick?"

Jenny looked at her strangely. "Erin, Stoner is serving two years house arrest on conspiracy charges. He pleaded guilty. You didn't know?"

Erin stiffened and flushed. How humiliating not to know something that had probably been all over the press, but then she had avoided reading anything about her family as much as she could. "No."

"Sometimes," Tabby said softly, "burdens are easier to carry when they're shared. Jenny and I both want to help. We wouldn't tell anyone else what we discuss here."

Erin glared at Tabby. "I'm supposed to open up to two people who are practically strangers?"

Tabby ignored Erin's rudeness, sitting on the edge of one of the overstuffed chairs. "Only if you want to. We both want to help, Erin. You're family."

Erin curled in a chair as far away from Tabby as possible. Her younger sister spooked her. She was as serene as a damn Buddha. "Couldn't we learn about each other in the regular way?"

Jenny flopped on the couch. "You mean we head to Roanoke for a shopping spree, gorge on fattening food, and ask each other questions over iced coffees? It might be a little late today for that. How about we take turns asking questions, and we have to answer?"

Erin snickered, as she eyed the two women who could have stepped from the pages of *Southern Living*. "You mean like Truth or Dare?"

Tabby laughed. "I played that in my dorm one time, but since I never wanted to answer any questions, I was always taking dares."

Erin grinned. It was hard to imagine that the perfect Tabby had things she didn't want to talk about. "Me too."

Jenny laughed. "I played with Evan in high school, but I always chose dare because all he wanted to do was kiss...and stuff."

"TMI. Certain things I just don't need to know about my brother," Erin said with a laugh. Amazingly, she found herself relaxing. She'd never had a lot of girlfriends. Matty and Stan were the closest things, but femme gay guys probably didn't count. Her thoughts clouded. She missed her crew mates. She hoped they were all right.

"You looked sad all of a sudden," Tabby observed. "Did you leave a boyfriend behind in the Virgin Islands?"

Erin tilted her head. "Boys and friends, but not boyfriends." She bit her lip. "I had a dream last night they were in trouble."

"Is there some reason to think they might be?" Jenny asked.

Erin smiled evasively. "That's not fair. I've already answered one question. Now I get a turn." She looked at Tabby. "Truth or dare?"

"Truth."

"How did you find out about Jenny?"

Tabby's smile was sad. "Mama was dying from cancer before she finally told me. Even if she'd told me earlier, though, I couldn't have left her." Tabby shook her head as if to clear it and looked at Jenny. "Truth or dare?"

"Truth. I only take dares if Evan's here."

"Is Evan going to run for another term as Commonwealth Attorney or is he going after a judgeship?"

Jenny wrinkled her nose. "He swore me to secrecy, so you can't say anything to him. He's running for another term."

Tabby smiled. "That's a relief. I was afraid if he pursued a judge's position you would move away."

Jenny grinned and looked at Tabby wickedly. "My turn. Were you and Joe virgins on your wedding night?"

Tabby blushed scarlet. "That's not fair, Jenny. You know Joe had to tell you that when you ordered my X-rays."

"Just answer the question unless you want a dare. We swore it won't leave this room."

"Almost."

Erin laughed. "What does that mean?"

Tabby giggled. "Well, we'd checked once before the accident to make sure everything worked, but then Stoner would hardly leave us alone together."

All three women burst out laughing. Erin felt herself blush and turned to look out the window, but not before she was sure Tabby had noticed.

Tabby sobered up first and looked at Erin intently. "My turn. I'm sorry, but I couldn't help overhearing you with Daddy. Why... Why do you think you're stupid, Erin?"

Erin's mouth twisted. "I was never any success in school. I was great at math, but nothing else. Mama and Daddy were always so busy, and I got bounced around from school to school more than Evan did, so that everyone seemed to think I was lazy, but I couldn't learn. I tried."

She looked at the two women and swallowed. "You can't tell them. You have to swear. You have no idea what it's like to be surrounded by people who are so brilliant. No one around here knows about this."

Erin closed her mouth. She hadn't wanted to share that. It had just happened. Why wouldn't Tabby and Jenny leave her alone the way everyone else did?

"Don't," Tabby whispered. "Don't shut down on us again, Erin. I'm so glad you're here, and we just want to help."

"They don't want me around," Erin spat. "You can see it in their faces. Daddy didn't even want me here last night. He practically begged Sam to let me stay there so he wouldn't have to bring me home."

She prowled the room again, feeling like an animal in a cage. Erin jumped at the knock on the door. She wrenched it open and stared at Sam's big frame filling the opening.

"I need to get home, bed animals down for the night," he rumbled. His gaze shifted from her to Tabby and Jenny before settling once more on Erin. "Just wanted to check to make sure you're okay."

She nodded and swallowed, drinking in his dark eyes and serious expression, wanting so desperately to stay with him, stay anywhere but Richardson Homestead. He had always been a refuge, someone who made her feel safe, and if not wanted, at least tolerated. "Please, Sam," she pleaded quietly. "I don't want to stay here. I won't be any bother. You wouldn't even know I was there...."

Sam shook his head. "No, Erin. It wouldn't work. I'll see you tomorrow morning, okay?"

She froze, feeling like she'd been slapped down yet again. "Yeah. I'll be there, Sheriff. Good night." She shut the door in his face. Tabby and Jenny were watching her. Her stomach knotted. "I think I've had as much family as I can handle for one night."

Tabby stood. "You need some time. Remember, Erin... We're here if you want to talk."

As Jenny and Tabby halted at the door, Erin knew she couldn't let them leave without saying something, but it was so hard to open up to anyone. She reached out awkwardly and hugged first Jenny, then Tabby. "Thanks. I know you're trying to help."

* * * *

When Sam entered the barn the next morning, the last thing he expected was that Erin would be there. He figured he would get one day out of her and that would be it. But as he looked around, the radio was playing in the background, and the horses were already munching hay while Erin leaned against a stall doorway with a hose in hand filling water buckets. He paused in mid-stride. She was here. He took his cap off and scratched his head.

"Good morning. I didn't see your vehicle anywhere. Did you get a ride?"

"I walked." She turned off the water, rolled the hose, and entered the feed room to carefully measure grain. He was impressed that she remembered exactly what each horse ate. "If you'll tell me which ones we'll ride this morning, I'll knock them off and tack them up."

He told her, and they worked together as the news played in the background. While he picked up eggs from the hens, she brushed the two mares. Sam listened to her talk nonsense to them. From a spot where he knew he would be unobserved, he studied her for a moment. She looked relaxed, the tension gone from her face and a bloom to her cheeks. Erin had always been gorgeous. Fourteen or twenty-six, it didn't matter. She still had a powerful, elemental impact on him, and it still made him uncomfortable. He didn't want to be attracted to her—but he was.

He'd already been an adult when she was just a kid. While he still had all his hair, he was getting a few gray strands around the temples. She needed someone closer to her age. Whoa, man. What was he thinking? As screwed up as she was, Erin didn't need a complication of any age in her life. And he had the feeling that as fragile as she seemed right now, a man—any man—would be more than she could handle.

When she stood practically on tip-toe trying to adequately tighten the cinch, Sam walked over and reached around her to easily pull it up another two holes. She stilled instantly, trapped as she was between his arms and the horse. She turned, bringing their bodies into almost perfect alignment.

Sam was only inches away from eyes that had suddenly gone dark and vulnerable. As he searched her face, her lips parted and her gloved hands trembled against the front of his coveralls. The desire to kiss her poured through every part of him. Her mouth looked soft and sweet. Instantly, his imagination thrust an image of her melting against him, her mouth opening beneath his. Sam leaned toward her. The mare shifted behind them and bumped Erin against him. He caught her, then instantly backed up to put distance between them. The moment was lost.

Her chin jutted. "Sorry. I'll go get her bridle." She ducked around him hastily. Sam watched her go, his gaze glued to her bottom, shapely even in the old coveralls he'd loaned her. He sighed. What the hell had he been thinking asking her to work for him? She was ten tons of trouble in a teeny tiny package. He'd been around plenty of women who would have been more than willing to jump if he'd just given them a nod, but Erin was different. When it came to her, he had no self-control.

A few minutes later, when he started to boost her into the saddle, she glared at him and vaulted onto her mare without help. Sam put his foot in the stirrup and swung up on his own horse. She wanted distance. Perfect. He'd play it casual.

"Let's go. You'll need to drive the truck out in the morning with feed and hay, but I like to ride the whole property as much as possible to check the areas not accessible by truck. The round bales will suit the cows closer in just fine."

He outlined how much food to put out as well as how many head were in each pasture. The cows ready to calve had been moved into a smaller pasture with easier access from the house.

"For the most part, they can take care of things themselves, Erin, but keep an eye out for a cow having trouble. If you spot one off by herself, check her posture. She might have her back arched or her tail raised. Once you see the water bag appear, give her about an hour, then check to see if she needs help. You know what a normal presentation looks like?"

Erin nodded. "Head first tucked between the front feet."

Sam smiled. "Yep. You see anything other than that, you call me. If you can't get me, call Carter or your daddy. I try to keep calls to Bill

Mitchell—the vet, you remember him—to a minimum. He's busy enough as it is. It's a lot to remember. You want me to write it down?"

Erin stiffened, instantly on the defensive. "No. I can remember it." And she proceeded to recite everything he'd told her back to him, including the feed amounts and livestock numbers.

He laughed. "That's pretty impressive."

"I have an excellent memory for numbers," she mumbled, not looking at him.

As far as he could tell, she seemed to have a good memory for almost everything. He turned his mare. "Let's get breakfast. We'll use the truck to feed after we eat. You wanna eat at the truck stop or go to Mercer's?"

"I could cook," she offered. "Don't you go to church?"

"Well yeah, but not every Sunday." Sam looked at her. He didn't know too many people who'd offer to cook over going out to eat. "If you really don't mind cooking, then let's feed first and we'll be done. I can get cleaned up while you cook. Uh... You could come with me...to church, I mean. I could run you by the guesthouse and wait for you to get ready."

Erin's eyes widened. For a second he thought he saw fear, but it vanished, replaced with a wary humor. "I don't think I'm ready for that, Sam. I'd kind of like to keep a low profile. Could... Could I stay here while you're gone?"

"Trying to avoid your parents?"

She nodded. Sam sighed. He was setting a dangerous precedent, but it was hard to refuse her anything. "Yeah, but don't make it a habit."

Erin working was one thing. Even taking her to church would be all right—public as that was, but Erin hanging around on a social footing was too much for him to handle. Every time he touched her, it was like holding his fingers to a flame. Sure he knew it was going to burn him, but it was so mesmerizing.

They rode out in the truck to spread more hay in the pastures that needed it. It was hard work, but Erin quickly found her rhythm, surprising Sam yet again with how hard she worked and how much she could do, given her small size. She didn't slack, and didn't complain. In fact, she didn't at all fit his preconceived ideas about her. She wasn't the screw up she always appeared to be, and he wondered if it was something she perpetuated, or just an image everyone had gained over the years. Where most of the help he'd hired had needed everything written and repeated for them, she remembered everything he told her is if she were a sponge.

Her cooking was another surprise. The eggs were fried to perfection, the bacon was crisped just the way he liked it, and she'd even made some of those hash browns with the peppers and onions. He studied her surreptitiously while they ate. She didn't eat much—an egg and some toast. He started to say something and stopped. He was afraid to spoil the tenuous peace between them.

Picking up their plates, he began to clear the table, but she protested. "I can do it. You don't need to help."

He stopped her with a touch to her wrist. "I know you can do it, Erin. I want to help."

Her eyes widened in surprise. "Oh. Okay."

After they finished cleaning up, Sam sat back in his chair to finish his coffee and studied her bent head. She pored over the Sunday comics with her brow furrowed, as serious as an archaeologist deciphering ancient hieroglyphics.

"Most people find them funny, Erin," he teased, "not something to frown at."

She jerked in surprise and blushed, and he realized she had forgotten his presence for a moment as she concentrated on the comics. His eyes flickered to the paper and back to her thoughtfully. Erin leaped to her feet, shoved the paper at him, and snatched her empty coffee cup.

"They're stupid anyway!" she burst out, as she ran water, quickly washed the cup, and set it in the dish drain to dry. "Aren't you going to be late? Does Joe give you detention?"

"You could always come and find out." He eyed the stiff set of her shoulders, wondering what had just happened.

"No, I'll just hang out here."

He nodded, picked up his suit coat, and was gone.

* * * *

Erin stared at the newspaper in frustration. She'd had to leave her laptop behind with all its software. All the blood left her head, leaving her dizzy for a moment. Her laptop—with her address book. Oh God! Her parents' address, Evan's... They were all there. She had password protected everything, but someone determined could get the information. Erin paced the floor. She would have to tell someone. She never meant to put anyone in danger. She'd tell Sam when he got back. He'd know what to do.

Erin finished the dishes, pushed the paper into a pile on the table, and stomped along the hall to Sam's bathroom. After stripping off her clothes, she stepped into the shower and let the water run over her and relax her. She dried off and looked at her clothes with a sigh. Sam wouldn't be back for a couple of hours. She could sneak in a nap. She still hadn't caught up on her sleep. And last night, she'd tossed and turned most of the night worried she would oversleep and be late.

She pulled a shirt from his closet, buttoned it, rolled back the sleeves that hung well past her hands and grinned at the shirttails that hit her just above the knee. Damn! He was huge. Why did it seem that every male she encountered was a giant? Her father and Evan were both almost six and a half feet. Joseph looked like he was about six-two, and Sam? He must be about six-four, but where Stoner and Evan were tall and lean, Sam was big. She knew he'd played football. She remembered Evan talking about it with awe when she was just a little girl. Of course, she also remembered there had been some injury that ended any hope of a professional career. He'd gone into the army or something.

Erin curled up in the king-sized bed in his room, feeling like a rowboat in the middle of the ocean, and snuggled under the comforter and flannel sheets. Mmm. It was just right. She was Goldilocks. It was so comfortable, and she'd still slept like crap during the night, jumping at every sound and suffering terrible nightmares. She inhaled Sam's warm, clean man smell and let her eyes drift shut. She was safe. Sam would keep her safe.

* * * *

Sam pulled into the farmyard and cut the engine on the truck. Everything looked quiet enough. He had thought a lot about Erin and the comics. She sure was touchy. He wondered if she wore contacts or glasses and was too vain or had simply forgotten them. He smiled as he entered the house. Somehow, he just couldn't picture her with owlish looking glasses perched on the end of that straight, little nose. When he didn't see her in the kitchen or the living room, he wondered if she had gone back out to the barn or home. He decided to change clothes and see if he could find her.

He was already down to his slacks, his chest bare, when he finally noticed the spiky, dark hair just visible over the top edge of his comforter. That lump in his bed was more than covers, he realized. Give her blond hair and he'd begin to feel like he'd stepped into "Goldilocks and the Three Bears." That would make him Papa Bear. The thought didn't amuse him. Was she sick?

"Erin?" He sat on the edge of the bed. "Hey, baby. You okay?"

She scrubbed at her eyes just like a kid, and made him feel every one of his thirty-eight years. Then her eyes popped open in alarm. "Oh!" She snatched the covers to her chin. "I'm sorry. I took a nap. I haven't been sleeping well, and…"

Her voice trailed off nervously, and the comforter dropped to her waist. Sam stared at her startled expression and her flushed cheeks. Eyes so big he sometimes wondered if he could fall right into them, and most of the time filled with the light of battle. Right now, though, they were soft, slightly befuddled, as if she'd momentarily opened the door to her emotions and wasn't sure what to do. The contrast drew him like a magnet. His body reacted. It knew what to do even if Sam fought it. Erin had been cute at fourteen, but at twenty-six she was all woman, and it looked an awful lot like all that womanliness was covered only by one of his dress shirts. What he wouldn't give to be his shirt. His eyes dropped to the open neck and the thrust of her breasts against the thin material.

"You're so beautiful, Erin," he murmured. Unable to stop, he trailed his hand gently down her cheek before cupping the back of her neck. He looked at the slumberous expression in her darkly lashed eyes and wanted her, just like he always had. Last fall or more than a decade ago, it didn't matter. Erin was stuck in his head and his heart.

He remembered the summer he had come home from Afghanistan. It was right after Evan and Jenny had broken up and gone their separate ways to college. To his shame, he'd been aware of Erin from then on in ways he knew he shouldn't. She had been a kid, even if she didn't look like one. To make matters worse, every time he turned around, he'd run into her. At fourteen, Erin had been desperate to escape her parents' house whenever possible.

His first sight of her after his return was indelibly burned into his memory. He had discovered her skinny-dipping in the pond in his back pasture, and also discovered that the little girl he remembered had grown up…too much for his comfort. She had ducked under the water to her neck when she spotted him, but then recognizing him, a wicked gleam had sparked in her eyes. Deliberately, she had turned her back to him and walked out of the pond, her bare, heart-shaped bottom swaying tauntingly.

Having just returned from two years in a Muslim nation where women were swaddled from nose to toes, Sam was shocked. He rode around the pond, his eyes averted. When he reached the other side, she pulled a T-shirt over her bare breasts, but since she was still wet from the pond, the shirt did little to hide a figure no fourteen-year-old had a right to.

He'd vaulted off the horse and approached her.

"Erin?" he'd asked in a choked voice, eyes glancing off dusky nipples. He'd last seen her as a gawky twelve-year-old. She wasn't that kid anymore. Not by a long shot. Christ. He'd looked quickly away.

"What the hell are you doing here?" He managed to choke out right before he swallowed his tongue.

"Hi, Sammy." She'd laughed with a mixture of shyness and tentative provocativeness that sent his starved senses into overdrive, his gaze once more unwillingly drawn to her. Sam was instantly hard, ready as any bull on his farm. No. Not happening. He'd shaken his head and backed away. She was a kid. Didn't matter if she didn't look like one.

Had Stoner not walked up on them at that moment looking for Erin, Sam wasn't sure what would have happened. As it was, he figured he had narrowly escaped jail. If Stoner hadn't already been furious with Erin for everything else she had been into that summer, he probably would have pressed charges, even though Sam hadn't even touched her, but publicity of that sort was the last thing a senator running for re-election needed.

That had been more than twelve years ago. They were both adults now. She was twenty-six, not fourteen. And him? He ground his teeth. Yeah. Still a lot older.

While he studied her, Erin returned the favor, reaching out to brush a lock of his dark hair from where it fell onto his forehead, the only place where it was long enough. Her lips parted as she looked at his chest. Sweat broke out on his forehead. He wanted her hands on a lot more than just his hair. Her breathing accelerated as she continued to stare. Sam knew the signs. He wasn't a complete idiot. She was as turned on as he was.

But he hesitated. She had worshiped him since the moment he put her on his horse when she was nine years old. She had offered herself to him when she was fourteen, and he had nearly taken what she'd not so innocently shown him. There should be nothing now to stand in their way. She was a woman, not a child.

Sam caught her wrist just as she was about to touch him, but he took advantage of her parted lips and brushed his mouth across hers. When he felt her response, he set her hand on his chest, shivering at the instant spark of heat racing through him. Unable to stop himself, Sam cupped her face in his broad hands and let his mouth cover hers. He had dreamed of this, even when he'd known it was wrong. He nibbled, tasted, and wanted even more. She was sweet, and her mouth was soft and willing beneath his. It was incredible. Erin all grown up.

She moaned and pressed her nearly naked body against him, then her hand slipped down to touch his flat stomach. Things heated up too much, too fast. Warning bells clanged in Sam's head. Sure she was an adult, but this wasn't right. He knew how vulnerable she was and didn't want to take advantage.

"No, Erin," he said quietly and firmly. "This is wrong."

"I'm not a kid anymore, Sam."

He hardened his heart and knew he needed her angry with him, not looking at him with those big, soft eyes. His gaze raked over her. "You think I don't know that? You think I can't see…feel?" He pushed her hand off him and spun away, putting ice in his voice. "I appreciate what you're offering…again. But no. I'm just a little too fastidious to want to follow where so many have already been."

Silence stretched tautly behind him, and there was just barely a whisper of sound before the bathroom door slammed shut, but he could still hear her through the door as she swore like a sailor. She ripped the door open in less than a minute, fully dressed, and jammed her feet into her boots.

"What time do you leave in the morning?" she asked stiffly. "I'll make sure I don't get here until you're gone."

"Erin." He frowned at her averted face. Guilt slapped him up side the head like it was his grandma. He'd meant to make her angry, not hurt her. "Wait. I'll run you home."

"No! I have to go. Now."

She raced out of the room, her feet pounding along the hall. The door slammed before he could get his boots and a jacket pulled on. He yanked the door open and looked down the driveway, but it was empty; then he saw her racing across the fields as if the devil himself was on her heels. Perhaps he was. Sam smacked the flat of his hand against the porch pillar. Maybe it was better this way, better to have her hating him than thinking he was some sort of safe haven.

But Sweet Mary, it eviscerated him.

Chapter 4

Stoner saw her trudge across the fields. Something in the way she moved, an aimlessness or listlessness, didn't seem at all like the Erin he knew. Already feeling her probable rebuff, he knew he still had to make the effort. Stoner pulled his coat on and stepped out the back door. Catherine hadn't returned yet from town. She usually stayed after church to visit with Jenny and Evan at the very least. Stoner met Erin as she rounded the house, obviously intent on reaching the guesthouse before anyone saw her.

"Erin? Are you okay?"

She looked at him with dry eyes glittering in a face that was deathly pale. "No."

Her admission startled him. Stoner swallowed, feeling more awkward than he would have imagined, more awkward than he'd ever felt talking with Tabby. "Do you want to talk about it?"

She jerked with surprise and eyed him suspiciously, but her wide gaze also searched his face for something, he wasn't sure what. At last she mumbled, "No. I don't think so."

She turned away, leaving him feeling as if his chance to reach her, to help this daughter who'd always been so defensive and prickly, was slipping away as quickly as water flowing down a stream. He was desperate to keep her there, to see if he might pry wider open the small chink she'd shown in her armor. He doubted seriously she'd open it herself.

"I was going to my wood shop to work for a while. Would you like to join me? There's a place where you can sit and watch if you want. You don't have to talk to me, but I wouldn't mind the company."

She shifted from foot to foot and glanced at his shop. "Yeah. I'd like that. I don't really want my own company right now. I'll change first."

He nodded and trudged to the shop, feeling defeat drag at him. He doubted she would turn up, but five minutes later, the door opened slowly and she stepped in. He glanced up, smiled as though it were the most natural thing in the world to see her there, and returned to his work. Stoner decided it would be best to ignore her, not make too much of her presence. For a man accustomed to demanding and getting answers, the task wracked his nerves.

She looked around warily, then found a spot in the corner, a bit like a cat, he thought. The next thing he knew, just like the cat he had already compared her to, she was curled up in an empty spot on top of his workbench, her head resting on her knees as she simply watched what he did. No pressure, he reminded himself and went back to work.

Stoner wasn't sure how long they stayed like that. He worked while she watched, quietly and completely still. It had made him a little nervous to begin with, but that quickly passed as his work absorbed his interest. After a while, he glanced up and smiled slightly. She had fallen asleep. Stoner finished what he was working on, put on his coat, then eased over to rouse her.

"Wake up, honey," he said softly, but she just mumbled in her sleep. He eyeballed her petite frame and simply picked her up as he had so many times when she was just a little girl and had played to the point of exhaustion. She was still tiny. Erin nestled against him, and his heart lurched. There were shadows under her eyes like bruises. He wondered again what had suddenly made her come home when it always seemed to him home was the last place she had ever wanted to be.

He took her into his study and laid her on the couch there. He tucked a soft, cotton afghan around her, a smile tugging the corner of his mouth as he remembered tucking her in as a little girl. Those moments had been rare, maybe too rare, he now realized. After covering her, he sat at his desk to work on the farm accounts.

About an hour later Erin finally stirred. She sat abruptly and looked around her in confusion. He thought he caught just a trace of fear on her face, and wondered why she would be frightened. Had Sam done something to her? Stoner's jaw clenched. There had always been some connection between Barnes and Erin that he hadn't quite understood. While Erin was a teenager, it had petrified him. Now, he was willing to admit Sam might be just what Erin needed.

"You fell asleep, honey, and wouldn't wake up so I brought you in here."

She ran a hand through her hair. "I'm sorry. Thanks, Daddy. I-I haven't slept well."

Stoner rose and came around to sit on the other end of the couch where he could study her more thoroughly. "Erin, if you think it would help, we can move you in here to the main house."

For a moment, it seemed like she wanted to accept the offer, but then she shook her head. "No. I'm fine where I am. I-I like my privacy, and I don't want to intrude on you and Mama."

That stung. He was hearing from her lips almost exactly what he and Catherine had discussed. Stoner touched her shoulder, encouraged when she didn't flinch from him. "Erin, what's wrong? Honey, please talk to me."

She stared at him, and as he watched, she began to shake. The need to protect her overwhelmed his fear of rejection. He pulled her onto his lap even though he feared she would rebuff him again. When she didn't, he cradled her against him as he had when she was just a little girl and frightened of a thunderstorm, sending a silent prayer for some divine guidance. This was like wading through a copperhead nest.

"Does it have anything to do with the job you had on that ship?"

"Yes." She closed her eyes and swallowed convulsively. When she opened them again, she stared steadily into his face. Stoner watched her inner battle, and almost wept when he felt her relax in his arms. He had to tilt his head to hear as she whispered, "I think the ship was being used to ferry drugs on some of our trips. I'm not talking about a bag or two of pot. I knew about that. I mean cargos of drugs. Lately, it seemed like all the time."

Jesus! What had she gotten herself into this time? He stroked her hair. "Did you ever see them?"

"No. But on our last trip, we had only one passenger, Andre Delacroix. His family is very wealthy, very influential there, kind of like an island mafia, I guess. Anyway, I jumped ship because he threatened Rick, he's the captain, and me. He didn't know I'd overheard him." She stopped, her hands balled into fists in her lap. "He threatened to kill me."

Stoner's heart went cold. "So you took off? But Erin, you're here now. You're safe."

She worried her lower lip. "Daddy, I literally jumped overboard with only my identification papers, my money, credit card, and cell phone. It was all I could fit into the waterproof fanny pack I had. I left my laptop on the *Sprite*. It has your address—and Evan's. If someone finds that…"

Like hell someone was going to hurt her! Stoner's arms tightened protectively around his daughter. "We'll keep you safe, honey, but I'll need to let Evan and Sam know what's going on."

She touched her father's face with her fingertips. "I'm so sorry, Daddy. I didn't come back to cause trouble, but I wasn't sure where else to go after I swam ashore. If you want me to leave, I-I'll understand."

His hand hovered just over the back of her head, and he closed his eyes as he brought it down to pull her close. "I don't want you to go." The tightness in his chest eased, and he realized that for perhaps the first time in his uneasy relationship with his daughter, he spoke the truth. "We need to get everyone together to talk about this. Sam, too, since you work for him."

Erin swallowed and twisted her hands nervously. "Not today. Please, Daddy. I—I don't want to see Sam again today."

Stoner frowned and held her slightly away as he gazed at her, his fatherly instincts flaring again into full alarm. Son of a bitch. Every warm thought he'd had about Sam flew right out the window. "Did he do something?"

She shook her head and said no, but the blush on her cheekbones told him she was lying. Stoner decided he would call Sam and Evan both that evening, and at least give them the bare bones of what she had told him, but Erin would have to provide everyone more details.

* * * *

Sam settled the animals for the evening and came back inside. He still couldn't forget the expression on Erin's face as she'd fled his house. He'd hurt her. Deliberately. Partly to stop her, partly to stop him. He could never provide her a life like she'd grown up in. There were other issues too. He was too old for her, too conservative. He was sorry if the truth was painful, but he was a fastidious man. While he was no virgin, he didn't hop into someone's bed at the drop of a hat. And after all, it wasn't like this was even the first time he'd found her in his bed.

It had happened that same summer after he'd seen her in the pond. She'd sneaked out on a hot night several evenings later. He'd still been drinking then—far more than the occasional social drink he now consumed. That night, Sam had swallowed enough bourbon to give him a buzz before he finally stumbled into his bedroom, stripped, and crawled between the sheets. When he awoke in the middle of the night, it was to feel a warm, naked female pressed against him.

He closed his eyes at the memory. He had nearly made love to a child. As soon as she'd whispered "Sammy" in that soft, shy voice, it had been like a bucket of ice water to his face and his groin. With a curse, he'd leaped out of bed, yanking on his boxers as he hopped toward the door of his room. Fear sweat, worse than anything he'd experienced in Afghanistan, trickled down his back.

He'd called Stoner. While a tearful Erin ranted and raged at him, Sam had pulled on his jeans and yelled over the phone at a furious Stoner to come get his daughter…to do something to control her.

Well, they had. Stoner had taken Catherine and Erin and moved to Washington, D.C.—making that their primary residence and leaving the farm in the care of a foreman. That had been the last time he'd seen Erin in person until last fall. Finding her in his bed today had brought it all back. She had been such a passionate little thing all those years ago, he wondered how many other men she'd pulled the same trick on. Then there were the birth control pills. She wouldn't need them if she wasn't having sex.

When his phone rang, he was somehow not surprised to find it was Stoner. A disappointing sense of déjà vu tightened his jaw. What did surprise him was that Erin hadn't had the gumption to call herself and quit. He was sure that's what this must be about. He was also sure he would get an earful from Stoner, but as he listened to the older man, his brow furrowed.

The tale Stoner was sharing was just short of unbelievable, and exactly what Erin had jokingly told him as to why she had returned. Someone was trying to kill her. She had told him the truth, but he hadn't believed her. Sam's gut hurt.

"I think she'll be safer at your place, safer than even here at the guesthouse."

"Whoa!" Sam snapped. "You want me to let her move in here? No! Stoner… That's a bad idea."

"Because of what happened today?"

"She told you?" Sam's heart pounded. He had hoped their exchange would be private, and he was somewhat disappointed Erin would be vindictive.

There was a pause on the other end of the line, and Sam swore silently. He'd just been taken in by a master.

"No. She denied anything happened, but you've now confirmed something occurred. I just saw her when she came back from your place. Erin wouldn't talk about it." Stoner's voice took on a harsh tone, "So help me, Sam, if you hurt her…"

Sam grabbed the back of his neck, "You think I hurt her, but you think it would be advisable for her to move in with me? What kind of crazy, screwed up logic is that?"

"Just think about it, okay? No one's likely to look for her on your farm. It will be easier for us to honestly say she's not here. I've already talked to everyone else locally who might have been on her laptop address book in case anyone calls looking for her... None of us knows where she is."

"Stoner..."

"Consider it. I'm letting her use my truck to get around, and she'll be over there tomorrow."

"She's coming back?"

"As far as I know. Think about it, Sam," Stoner said again. The line went dead.

Sam shook his head as he hung up the phone. He was amazed Erin would even set foot on his farm after what he'd said to her. But then if it was the simple truth, why should it bother her? He glowered as he sat in front of the TV. Sam had no idea what he watched. All he could see was Erin Richardson's luscious body wrapped in someone else's arms. And the idea made him growl in frustration.

* * * *

The last thing Erin wanted to see the following morning was Sam's cruiser still parked in the driveway. She realized as soon as she pulled up in her dad's truck that Sam had waited for her. Turning around and leaving was a real temptation, but a chicken wasn't what she was.

Sam strode down the steps dressed in his uniform and carrying his hat. Erin jumped from the truck and stood next to it, stomach churning. He looked even bigger and more intimidating in the tan and brown shirt and pants. Since the weather was still cold, he also wore a heavy brown wool uniform jacket that added more bulk to shoulders already impossibly broad. The duty belt around his waist included a side arm, an obvious reminder of the fact this wasn't Mayberry and he wasn't Andy Taylor. She'd be damned if she'd admit just how freaking intimidating he looked. And hot. Lick your chops hot.

As he approached the truck, Erin forced herself to stand her ground. "I thought you'd be gone already," she stated half accusingly, chin stuck out.

"That would have suited you, no doubt," he snapped. "Still smarting from having a man actually say no?"

"Go to hell." Her response was quick, but inside, the pain that spread through her was anything but quick. It seeped like a slow, insidious poison of uncertainty.

"Your father called me last night about your situation in the Virgin Islands. I left you copies of forms I need you to fill out so we can get information circulated about who we should watch for. You can get that done after you feed and ride fences. I'll be back to pick it up around lunchtime. Oh and there's a note in the barn about switching stalls around."

"But…" Before Erin could fabricate some excuse for why she couldn't fill out the paperwork and get him to tell her what the note in the barn said, he'd climbed into his cruiser and headed down the drive. As soon as he was out of sight, she ran inside the house to see what he'd left. Erin sagged against the table when she saw several pages of forms with instructions in small print. She could no more fill that out than she could fly to the moon.

As she moved through her chores of feeding, cleaning, and riding the farm, her mind worked frantically to come up with a way around the forms Sam had left. She thought about calling Tabby or Jenny for help, but was too embarrassed. Besides, there was no way she would have enough time to get them to read it to her. As for the note in the barn, she took one look at it and decided she could simply say she couldn't read his handwriting—which was partly true. It was hard enough to read typed print, but handwriting turned into one big confusing swirl.

If she had a laptop already set up, she could have just asked him to e-mail them. With her text-to-speech and voice-recognition programs in place, it would have been a simple matter to get it filled out, but paper forms were a major problem. *You could just tell Sam the truth.* She cringed from that idea as if it were a rattlesnake getting ready to strike. Right. Give them all one more reason to laugh at her.

Erin returned to the kitchen about eleven and sat. She had to try. Sam was trying to help. She spread the forms out in front of her and stared at them, but the harder she tried to read and understand what was in front of her, the more jumbled all the words looked. Erin's temper simmered along with her frustration. She had learned a long time ago not to cry. People made fun of you then and called you names, but they couldn't make fun of you if you just got mad or got even. Feeling like a complete idiot, but frustrated to the point of anger, she stood next to the table staring ambivalently at the papers with their empty, mocking white spaces. After setting her full coffee cup next to them, she deliberately knocked it over.

"What the *hell* are you doing?" Sam snapped from right behind her.

Erin spun around, stumbling back from the table in surprise, and hiding her guilt behind anger. "I'm not filling out your damn paperwork," she blustered. "Fill it out yourself, Sheriff!"

She started to brush past him, to escape, but he grabbed her arm. "You can darn well stay here and fill them out. I'll print new ones."

Erin panicked. This wasn't working out at all. She couldn't fill out what she couldn't read. Deciding hauteur was a better course, she responded coolly. "No, I can't stay here, Sheriff. I finished my work, and I have things to do. Bring them with you this evening. I believe my father has invited you for dinner."

"It would be a whole lot easier if you…"

Erin jerked her arm away from his grasp. "I have plans. You'll have to excuse me."

"Well la-ti-da…" He mimicked her haughty tone. "Excuse me, princess. Where did you pull that spoiled rich girl act from?"

She raised her brows. "It's no act. It's what you always thought I was anyway. I'm just trying to live down to your expectations."

Erin turned and fled. She had to get out of there. She knew she'd only put off the inevitable. There had to be some way she could avoid reading or filling out anything.

"Hey!" Sam shouted after her. "You need to go straight back to Richardson Homestead. You hear me, Erin?"

Erin flipped him a bird, hopped in her dad's truck, and drove to the computer store in Mountain Meadow. She'd been without her link to the rest of the world for long enough. The computer store, just off the main square, was a new addition, but otherwise, Mountain Meadow's business district looked the same as it had when she was a kid. She jammed the truck into park and leaped to the pavement.

Still clad in overalls and muddy boots, she glanced up to see a trio of older ladies eyeing her as though she'd just crawled out from under a rock. Busybody church ladies at ten o'clock. Lord, she remembered them from when she was a kid, still with those same pinched expressions. Times like these she wished she'd left all her earrings and the eyebrow ring in. That would give them something to talk about. Instead, she smiled and waved, nearly laughing when they turned their backs in unison. Good to know her reputation was intact.

When Erin entered the small store just off the square, she was relieved to find that they not only had the same kind of laptop she'd left behind, but also had the same reading and writing software she knew how to use. She looked at the kid behind the counter. He had computer geek written all over him.

She wanted more than just the same setup she'd had aboard the *Sprite*. Even though she'd had little luck in the past, she was determined to try again to get help to improve her reading. "I'm working with a little girl who's having trouble reading," she lied smoothly. "Do you have any suitable programs to help with that?"

"Oh yeah! There's a great one here. My little brother's dyslexic, and he does super with it."

"So he's made progress?" When the clerk nodded, Erin smiled charmingly, trying hard to keep the complete and utter relief from showing through. "That sounds just perfect."

"If you're working with someone having reading problems, you should talk to Ms. Hastings. She teaches at the high school and helps out with the reading program at the library. I bet she could help if you run into any problems."

Erin smiled. "Thanks. I'll keep that in mind."

Without enough cash to cover it, Erin pulled out her credit card, looked at it for an instant, and shrugged. She'd just have to take the risk. Surely Andre's reach didn't extend this far. She avoided using the card after her arrival at Dulles, so Florida would have been the last place he could trace her, but she just didn't have this much in cash.

Once she paid for everything, she drove straight to the guesthouse to set up the system and load the software. When she logged into her e-mail, she was surprised to find a message from Captain Rick. Erin frowned as she laboriously read what he had written, unwilling to wait until she'd loaded the text to speech software.

Sprite blown up. Stan and Roger missing.

Erin gasped and blinked in shock. This was worse than she feared.

Matty and I are looking for a place to lay low so we're headed your way. Call me on your cell.—Rick.

Rick was coming here. Erin grinned. He and Matty were her friends. They knew things about her she'd never told other people. It was unavoidable living so close together on board a boat. Maybe they could run interference between her and Sam. They'd certainly helped her out before when men had tried to get close. The other plus was they knew Andre. They could help keep an eye out for him.

While Erin installed her voice recognition software, she pulled her phone from her bag and punched the symbol she'd programmed for Rick.

It rang only once before a husky baritone drawled, "Erin, sweet girl!"

Erin giggled. "You sound like every girl's dream on the phone, Rick. How can you be so cruel as to like men?"

He laughed. "I've told you before, honey girl, any time you want to convince me I'm playing for the wrong team, I'm willing to listen."

Erin chose to ignore him. "What's this about the *Sprite*? Is it Andre?"

"I think. Matty and I would have been on board too, but we accepted a last minute invitation to play strip poker with some cute college guys taking a semester off. Girl, you should have seen the..."

"Rick!" Erin cut him off with a grin. "TMI. Where are you and Matty?"

"In a hotel in Miami. We may stay for a few more days before we head your way. Matty is doing a lot to restore my good humor over losing both my boat and my partner."

Erin closed her eyes. "I just don't want to know, Rick. You and Matty are going to have to play heterosexual around here."

"Do we get to be your beards again? You know how I love feeling you up."

"We can talk about it when you get here. There are only two bedrooms in the guesthouse…"

"That will be just perfect."

Erin sighed. "You don't understand. My parents are conventional, like Ward and June Cleaver conventional. In fact, I don't think they even share a room. I doubt they'll go for you staying with me, but we'll worry about that after you're already here."

After she hung up, Erin wondered what she was doing. She had tried to fit in, but it didn't seem to get her anywhere, certainly not with Sam, so what the hell? Maybe it was time the old Erin returned. Rick and Matty knew her and loved her, warts and all. She could be herself with them when she couldn't with anyone else. Sometimes she thought she was half in love with Rick, but then she'd shake herself out of it and realize it was just gratitude. He'd taken a big chance on her.

She finished installing her software and decided to try the reading program. After working on it for an hour, she quit with a tired sigh, rubbing her head. It just never seemed to get any better. Maybe it wasn't dyslexia. Maybe this was as good as it got.

She scanned the Internet with her text-to-speech application and found an article in the St. Thomas paper about the explosion. Two bodies were recovered and two more were missing and presumed dead. Rick, Erin was sure, would prefer things stayed that way for the time being. Pouring herself a stiff bourbon, she decided it was time to get plastered. After all, she'd been drug and alcohol free for nearly three days. That had to be a freaking record.

She raced upstairs, showered, and put on her baggy pants, but this time she added a tight cropped T-shirt, then returned to her laptop. She surfed the net again, returning to her favorite news…financial and stock analyses. With a few clicks, she was able to check on her own investments and saw that a company she had decided to invest in finally was showing the profit she had projected. Erin shoved the bourbon aside and asked the computer for additional information.

She was so lost in monitoring her finances she forgot the time until she heard a knock on the door. She jumped up, bumped the half-consumed glass of bourbon, which splashed onto her hand, and swore as she wiped it off. With the computer voice still speaking behind her, Erin rose and answered the door, rubbing the tiredness from her eyes.

Sam got one whiff of her and shoved his way in. "Darn it, Erin. You're drunk. Don't you realize what time it is? Everyone's been waiting on you for a quarter of an hour and you're over here three sheets to the wind and half-dressed." With scarcely a glance at the talking computer, Sam dragged her upstairs and pushed her into the room in front of him.

"I'm not...turn me loose!" she spluttered. "Get the hell off me."

Sam swung around. His angry gaze raked hotly up and down her, lingering on her breasts beneath the tight T-shirt. She'd opted for comfort and ditched her bra. Now she wondered about that choice. When his stare dropped to the waistband of her pants, his hand touched the drawstring as well as the bare skin of her midriff and he muttered, "You obviously have nothing on under the shirt... Just what do you have on under these?"

Erin curled her lip. His touch made her skin tingle and that just made her more angry. "Curious? I thought maybe you were old enough you couldn't..."

His eyes flared with fury, and he jerked her against his lean hips. "Does that feel like I *can't* Erin? There's a big difference between can't and won't."

She felt his erection press against her belly and saw the absolute disdain in his eyes. Unaccustomed and unwanted tears blurred her vision and she twisted away. Nobody made her tear up, dammit. He already had such a low opinion of her. Erin suddenly wanted to shock him even more. She turned her back on him, untied the drawstring on her pants, and let them fall around her ankles.

Over her shoulder she spat, "Kiss my ass, Sheriff!" She had the satisfaction of seeing his eyes widen at the small rose tattoo on one rounded cheek. "Oh, if you like that, Sammy, you'll really like this." And with one quick movement she whipped off her T-shirt and turned around to face him. His gaze darted straight to the small broken heart on the curve of her left breast.

"Sweet Heaven, Erin!" He swore and turned away. "Cover yourself."

Past caring now, she walked toward him and saw his eyes widen even more. She laughed and walked right past to her closet. She pulled on a skin tight knit dress that hugged every curve of her body and ended around mid-thigh.

"How's that?" she challenged. "That about fits your image of me, doesn't it?"

"You can't mean to wear that to dinner with your parents."

She stared at him hostilely. "Why not? It's what you all expected anyway. But Sam, what I don't have on underneath can just be *our* little secret." She stepped into high-heeled pumps. "And you can think about it all through dinner Mr. Can-But-Won't."

* * * *

Stoner ground his teeth when Erin waltzed into the room with a glowering Sam behind her. He absolutely would not rise to the bait Erin was throwing out. Evan looked at his sister sardonically.

"Ah," her brother drawled. "Now I see why you were late. It must have taken extra time to squeeze everything inside such a small amount of material. Nice dress."

Erin slanted him nothing more than a scathing glance. Her eyes glittered. Stoner knew that look. She was spoiling for a fight.

Catherine frowned and looked to him for help. He caught the way Sam glared at Erin and decided he would simply watch the two of them. Seldom had he ever seen the taciturn Sam Barnes so bent out of shape, and never over a woman. One look at Erin's expression made it clear she was deliberately trying to rile the big sheriff. Someday, Stoner thought, when things settled down some, he would show her the pictures of her great grandmother, a woman who had been on the wild side, even for the roaring twenties, and looked almost exactly like Erin.

But Erin was predictable for no one on this night. While Sam took notes, she obligingly gave them everything she knew about Andre Delacroix, his family, and the trade that transpired on aboard the *Sprite*.

"There's one problem," she said as she prowled the study after dinner, her hands fluttering over things, then moving on to something else. "The *Sprite* got blown up last night."

"How do you know this?" Evan asked sharply.

She paused. "Rick sent me e-mail. He was her captain, but he and another crew member had gone to a nearby boat to play poker. It was a last minute arrangement. Otherwise he and Matty would have been there too. Stan and Roger were. Their bodies have already been found, and Rick and Matty are listed as missing and presumed dead."

"Obviously, they're not," Stoner said dryly, his keen eyes taking in the agitation she struggled so hard to hide. There was just a slight tightness around her eyes to give her away.

She laughed, but it was brittle. "Oh no. They're in Miami sampling the nightlife. They decided it would be in their best interests to disappear for a while."

"And you know this from their e-mail?" Evan continued.

Erin stopped to look at him over her shoulder. "Do I get to cross-examine once you're done with your questioning? If you must know, I called Rick once I saw the e-mail to make sure he and Matty were both okay. *They* are my friends." Her glare raked Sam, clearly letting him know he wasn't among that group, and then moved on along with her graceful, nervous movements around the room.

Stoner looked at Evan and Sam. The latter rolled his eyes and reluctantly nodded his head. Stoner cleared his throat, drawing Erin's attention. "Honey, we think it might be safer for you if you moved in with Sam for the time being. No one looking for you would think to look at his farm. The guesthouse is…"

"Too close for you to feel safe from me, Daddy?" Erin whispered tightly.

"No. Honey…" But he could see he had lost her again. Her face wore that remote, frozen look he'd seen so often through her teenage years.

Erin turned to look at her mother. "Mama?"

"We're just trying to do what's best for you." Catherine kept her tone carefully neutral.

Erin's head snapped back. She turned a hostile gaze on Evan and Jenny. "So are you all here to help push me out the door in case I don't want to leave peacefully?"

"Erin," Jenny began.

She spun on Sam. "What do you get out of this? No, never mind. I don't want to know." She glared at all of them. "I'll go pack. There's no point in prolonging this, is there?"

"Erin…" Stoner began, but she cut him off.

"I dared to trust you, Daddy," she hissed. "For once in my life, I thought you meant it—that you would keep me safe, but some things never change. You and Mother should have quit with Evan, because you sure as hell never had time for me. You were always off at some fundraisers, or campaigning here and there while I got shuttled from babysitters to nannies and from one school to another. Let me guess, Daddy. That first night when you discovered I'd come back and you shunted me off on Sam, did you and Mama discuss how you could keep me from being a disruption in your life?"

Stoner was a master at hiding what he was thinking. Catherine too, but not that good. Erin's bitter laughter let him know in no uncertain terms that she'd caught the glance he'd exchanged with Catherine. With one more hostile glance at all of them, Erin stalked from the room.

"Well," Evan said, his mouth thin. "That ended about as badly as it could have."

Jenny glared at them. "You have no idea what or who she is, and I can't tell you a damned thing because what she told me was done in confidence. If you ever get her to open up before she self-destructs, all of you will be so ashamed."

Jenny rushed from the room after Erin, leaving everyone else to stare at each other open-mouthed.

A quarter of an hour later, Jenny returned and addressed Sam. "She's waiting for you in your truck. I couldn't get her to come back in."

Stoner's hands clenched in his pockets. One afternoon. Was that all he would get of the Erin he remembered from when she had been just a little girl? Now he wouldn't even be able to see her. "I want to see her before you leave," he said abruptly. He stalked out to Sam's truck where Erin sat in the passenger seat and stared stiffly ahead of her. She rolled down the window, but her eyes looked beyond him rather than at him. "Erin," Stoner pleaded quietly. "Please, honey, don't go like this. I just want you to be safe."

She looked at him with eyes that were empty. "Bullshit. Good-bye, Daddy." She rolled the window back up. Sam's eyes met Stoner's over the roof of the truck.

"I'll keep her safe, Senator," Sam vowed. Stoner nodded and walked back inside the big brick home, his heart heavy, though he still felt he was making the right decision in sending her to Sam.

* * * *

Sam climbed into the driver's seat and glanced at Erin. She kept her face slightly averted and her hands clenched on her knees. When they reached his house, he got out, grabbed her duffel bag, and her laptop case. Erin followed him without a word as he took her things up the stairs to the room that had once been the master suite. It was large and had a bath attached, similar to Sam's room on the first floor.

Erin looked around. "If you'll tell me where to find the bedding, I'll make the bed up."

"I'll get it," Sam said.

When he returned, she took it from him. "Thank you. If you don't mind, I'll do this myself and go to bed. I guess I'll see you in the morning."

"Erin, we're not done. We have some things we have to talk about."

"Like what?"

"Like why you deliberately ruined the papers I left you."

"I told you I wasn't filling that shit out. It's done now anyway, so what's the big deal?"

"The big deal is I have to be able to trust you."

"So I won't do it again. Problem solved."

She started to turn away, but he grabbed her arm. He felt her freeze, almost as if she feared he was going to hurt her. Sam forced himself to gentle his touch and his voice as he said, "Not quite. I left explicit instructions for what was to be done with my livestock this morning and you paid absolutely no attention."

For just a second he saw something like shame flash across her expression; then hostility replaced it. "How the hell was I supposed to read that chicken scratch of yours? If you have instructions, just tell me."

Sam ground his molars. She was the most stubborn, infuriating woman. "I'll do one better. Be out at the barn by six. I'll show you exactly what I want done. I can't afford mistakes with my Herefords, Erin."

"Fine." She turned her back to him. "I'm tired, Sam. Good night."

And that was the most he heard from her over the next two days. He'd shown her what he wanted done, and that was that. She did her work. She cooked him breakfast and left dinner for him, but in the evenings, by the time he got home, she had already disappeared upstairs. He knew she spent a lot of time on the Internet. When she'd failed to answer his knock the first night, Sam had opened the door a crack and seen her working on the computer, earphones over her ears and a calculator in her hand. He wondered what absorbed her so completely, but she was so remote he couldn't find an opportunity to ask where it wouldn't seem like he was spying on her.

Thursday, he pulled in the driveway to see his truck sitting there, but the house was dark. Seeing a light on in the barn, he opened the door to find that two of his Hereford heifers now had their first calves suckling at their sides. From the tackroom, he heard some public radio talk show. Erin was curled up on a couple of bales of hay sound asleep with a horse blanket thrown over her. She looked pale and exhausted with shadows beneath her eyes. On the ground next to her he saw pulling chains. He looked at the two healthy calves and wondered if she'd pulled one or both, then marveled that she had done it by herself.

He let her sleep while he checked the rest of the animals, then came back to the calves. Both cows and calves appeared to be just fine and everything had been cleaned with fresh bedding added. Sam looked again at Erin and rubbed his chest. For all she wanted everyone to believe she was selfish and irresponsible, he had seen how she worked her butt off on his farm, and how conscientious she was. He shook his head. It was like watching two different women, and he wondered if he would ever see the real Erin.

He thought about what Jenny said to all of them. Just what secrets did this tiny temperamental tornado, harbor?

When he took the horse blanket off, he noticed that her coveralls were stained with blood and fluids from the births. Sam ignored it as he bent and lifted her into his arms.

"I can walk," she protested in a groggy voice.

"I know you *can*," he said softly, "you just don't need to prove it to me right now."

He set her on a chair in the mudroom and took off her boots, then unzipped the coverall. He swallowed thickly when he saw the bra that was little more than a scrap of lace and a pair of panties that were barely big enough to sneeze at.

"Wh-what are you doing?" she mumbled.

"Getting your filthy barn clothes off. Do you want me to put you in the bathroom or the bed?" She struggled to focus. Even as he watched, she started to drift off to sleep once more. He smiled. "Bed, I think."

Sam set her on the edge of her bed and found the oversized shirt he knew she wore and slipped it over her head. She gazed at him now with that haunted, hungry look in her eyes that made his heart pound and left him feeling out of breath and unsettled. She'd always tugged at his heart strings, from the first time he'd seen her.

"Are they both okay?"

He knew what she asked. "A little bull calf and a little heifer. You did good, Erin."

She smiled as she snuggled into the pillow. "Not stupid. I figured it out. Saw the pictures."

"Go to sleep, baby," he whispered and stroked her short hair.

As he started to leave the room, he saw her laptop was still on and hooked to her cellphone. He decided to power everything down for her. When he moved the mouse, pictures of pulling a calf appeared. He smiled at her resourcefulness in finding out what she needed to know. As he moved the mouse over the text, he heard noise coming through the earphones. Sam picked them up and glanced over his shoulder to make sure she still slept before putting them over his ears. He clicked the back button. In every program he opened, whatever he highlighted with his cursor gave him an audio prompt. That was interesting, almost as if the computer was set up for someone who was blind.

Sam frowned. He'd wondered before if she had vision problems, but he'd never noticed Erin having any difficulty with any outside tasks, in fact, with anything other than reading.

His hand hovered over the mouse as images came back to him of a little girl who was constantly on the move and constantly in trouble at home and at school. He remembered her frowning concentration over the Sunday comics, then how she ignored his note to move the livestock, and finally the way she intentionally spilled coffee on the forms he wanted her to complete—then tried to give him that haughty attitude of how she wasn't filling out any forms.

Not because she wouldn't, he decided, but because she couldn't. Because she couldn't read. There could be no other logical conclusion. The idea floored him...and shamed him.

Sam closed the Internet and looked at the programs on the laptop. He really shouldn't be snooping, but he needed to know. If he was going to keep her safe, he needed to know what she was hiding.

Her computer contained all the usual programs he'd expect, plus a couple he found interesting. One was the reading and voice recognition writing program that was incorporated into everything on the computer, and the other was a remedial reading program. When he opened it, he saw she'd been working in it.

Sam closed the programs and left the room. He felt a twist of guilt. She would be beyond furious if she knew what he'd discovered. Merciful heaven! It boggled his mind to think of how she had gotten through school. Just functioning day-to-day had to be a challenge to whatever coping skills she'd developed. He slipped down to his room, changed into jeans and a sweatshirt, and wandered into the kitchen to fix something to eat. He missed the meal she would have had waiting for him.

How did she learn recipes? As he thought of all the things her obviously severe reading disability affected, he was more and more amazed at what she had accomplished. The most amazing thing of all was how she'd kept it a secret. He wondered if that was what Jenny had meant.

Erin thought she was stupid. She said it often enough. Had said it just this evening. Only this time that she was *not* stupid. He shook his head. She had figured out how to pull the calf from the pictures.

He wanted to wake her and ask her how she'd done it. Then he realized something else. As closely as she guarded this secret, she would be humiliated if she realized he knew. Between her and Stoner, he had never seen two more stiff-necked, proud people.

He checked on her before he called it a night, and she still slept soundly. As he studied her face, serene and relaxed in sleep, he wondered just what other secrets she had.

Sometime in the middle of the night, he thought he heard talking, but he'd already discovered that Erin was a restless sleeper who often talked in her sleep, so he ignored it. He awoke the next morning with a vague feeling that it was later than usual. When he came out of the bedroom, he found homemade cinnamon buns still warm in the oven. He wolfed them down along with a mug of coffee, pulled on his coveralls and boots, and headed for the barn.

She wasn't there. The animals had all obviously been taken care of, but there was no sign of Erin anywhere. He stomped back out into the cold rain and saw faint tire tracks. Beginning to feel alarmed, Sam strode into the house and bolted upstairs. Her computer was up and he accessed her e-mail, relieved to find she'd left herself logged in.

Hi, Sweet Cheeks! Did what you suggested. We're at the motel next to the truck plaza. Sorry you got the parental boot. Pick you up Saturday AM, and we'll have a lost weekend together just like old times. Nothin' like a girl pillow! Matty sends his love.—Rick

A lost weekend? Had she taken off to be with her lovers? Sam's fists clenched at his sides and he ground his teeth wordlessly. His first inclination was to run after her, but what right did he have? She had done her work. She wasn't his prisoner. She was an adult, and he had absolutely no claim on her.

The problem was that at the moment, the need to yank her back home, put his own brand on her, and never let her leave again overwhelmed him. Instead she was with two men. In a hotel room. Sam knew that just as soon as he could get some support, he would go after her, claim or no claim.

Chapter 5

Rick and Matty showed up just after dawn. Erin hugged them both and happily hopped into the back seat. This was just the break she'd needed. After breakfast at the truck stop, they drove back to Rick and Matty's room. While Erin sat cross-legged on the bed, Rick lay with his head in her lap, and Matty stretched out beside her.

"So are you seriously playing farmer Bob's wife?" Rick asked in amusement as he passed the joint he'd lit up over to Matty. He took a deep toke and handed it to Erin. She had no desire for it, but it was there, and she took a big hit before passing it off again. She finally exhaled the smoke, already feeling a faint buzz.

"You know me, Rick," she said with a giggle. "No sex, but I look after the farm and cook the meals."

Matty shuddered. "That is just too domesticated sounding for the original wild child." He rolled over onto his stomach and propped his face in his hands. He was such a girl. "Come with us, baby. We'll have a great time, and you don't have to worry about some man hands on you. They can have me instead." He laughed.

Erin blinked at him. Was that eye shadow on his lids or just her imagination? Matty always had been a bit more out there than the rest of them. While most of the crew could pass as just regular guys, Matty was a real queen. Still, he was sweet and wide-eyed enough that he was usually the darling of any older women on board. They surely knew he was gay, and maybe that was part of the reason they loved him. They could simply be themselves with no pressure.

Rick shook his head. "Seriously, girlfriend, you are wasted here on the farm. Do you know, once I got you hooked up with that software to read to you, your investment advice turned me into a millionaire in six months? Let's set ourselves up someplace sunny and warm and you can make us all a pot load of money."

Erin grinned and took another hit. If she left with Rick and Matty, she could be herself. No pretense. They knew exactly who and what she was. She didn't have to live up to some blueblood, by-the-book life that required the right education followed by the right marriage. Best of all, they demanded nothing from her. God! It was so tempting.

Except she wouldn't see Sam. Erin pushed that thought away. Sam didn't want her. He'd told her over and over. Was she so weak and pitiful she would stick around to have him kick her like she was some unwanted stray?

At some point, Matty broke out a bottle of rum. They played strip poker and did shots between hands of cards.

"My two pair beats yours because I have jacks high and you only have tens!" Erin told Matty. She slammed her shot glass down and waved her hand imperiously. "Off with your shirt!"

Matty stood up and made a production of unbuttoning his shirt and letting it slide slowly from his shoulders as he shimmied back and forth. While he looked at Erin, the show was really for Rick's benefit. Erin laughed, stuck her fingers into her mouth, and let out a loud wolf whistle. She smacked him on the ass and winked at Rick.

"Hands off the merchandise," the captain drawled, a twinkle in his eyes.

They were all completely smashed and down to their underwear when the pounding started on the door. Rick picked up Erin. As she giggled and squirmed, he dropped her on the bed beside Matty, who had already passed out.

"I'll get it." With one last look at Erin, who was laughing at him, he weaved to the door. Even though he was over forty, Rick's body was lean, muscled, and tanned. His sun-streaked hair fell around his shoulders, and he had tiny gold hoop earrings in each ear. Erin grinned. All the women loved Captain Rick.

He opened the door just a crack. Over his shoulder, Erin saw two dark-haired giants looming outside the door, one lean and sardonic looking and the other about the size of an angry grizzly with an expression equally welcoming.

"We're looking for Erin Richardson," her brother said.

Rick swayed a bit. "And whom shall I say is calling?"

"Her brother," Evan growled.

This was not going to be good. She should probably get up, but it was more fun to snuggle in the bed and watch what was happening.

Rick, with years of experience bluffing his way out of tight places, looked to Sam, who was doing his best grizzly bear imitation. "And who might you be?"

"Castle County Sheriff," Sam said in a voice as fierce as his expression.

Ohhh. Sammy sounded mad. He seemed to react that way around her a lot. Maybe it was just her who made him angry all the time, but Erin shoved that thought away. She wanted only happy thoughts.

"She's indisposed at the moment. Perhaps you could come back later?"

Erin couldn't suppress a giggle, thereby ruining the excuse. Over her shoulder, she watched Matty, who had come back to life, pick up her poker hand. She swatted at him ineffectually.

"No cheating!" she scolded.

"You are such a wicked girl," Matty purred. "Of course your jacks and aces will beat his hand and he'll lose his boxers. Maybe you can get the two hunks at the door to play too."

"I doubt it." Erin laughed as she heard Evan say, "Now Sam…"

She turned back to the tableau at the door just in time to see Sam's fist smash into Rick's nose, followed by the door slamming backward against the wall. Sam stomped into the room, his eyes going even blacker when he saw Erin next to Matty in just her underwear. Something tugged at her consciousness. What, Erin wasn't quite sure, but she scrambled from the bed and bent over to search for her shirt under the bed.

"Get up!" Sam bellowed. He hauled her to her feet where she swayed before she covered her mouth with one hand and delicately hiccupped. She smiled at Grizzly Sam. "Sammy! I love you." She looked back at Matty. "This is my friend Sammy," she slurred. "Do you know he didn't want to see my tattoos?"

She tried to look over her shoulder at the one on her butt and stumbled slightly. "Matty, the one on my butt looks okay, doesn't it? Sam doesn't like my ass, but you do, don't you?"

Matty grinned as he looked at her butt. "Sure, honey girl! I've seen a lot of asses and yours is perfect!"

She turned back to Sam's outraged expression. "See, Sam. Matty thinks I have a nice butt." She giggled and fell forward into his arms. She'd caught him off guard. A series of quickly disguised emotions came and went on Sam's face as fast as storm squalls before he glared at Matty.

"Get me a blanket and get her clothes together."

Evan handed Rick a towel for the blood. "Pinch your nose, asshole," he mumbled, then spoke in a voice dripping with ice and loud enough it could probably be heard through the whole motel. "She's tried so hard to get off the booze and the drugs, and the first thing her *friends* do is get her stoned and drunk. Well, listen, you two! He's the sheriff and I'm the fucking county prosecutor. There's enough pot smoke hanging in here that I'm sure just a quick search would find us enough to land both of you in jail for quite a while, but I'd like to spare my sister, so when we get Erin out of here, you get dressed, check out, and stay out of this county. This ain't your vacation paradise, and we take a dim view of strangers coming in and messing with family."

"Is that a threat?" Rick asked.

Evan paused and stared at him out of narrowed gray eyes. "No. It's a promise. Leave my sister the hell alone. She has enough problems."

Matty stood with Erin's clothes and her purse, and looked Evan over contemptuously. "It's always looked like to us that most of her problems came from her family. You didn't even know…"

"Matty!" Rick snapped.

Matty shut his mouth and thrust Erin's things at Evan. "Here."

Sam had her wrapped in a blanket from head to toe and cradled her against his chest. "Let's get out of here." He stared hard at Rick. "Sorry about the nose."

* * * *

When they reached Evan's SUV, Sam set Erin carefully on the rear seat, then climbed in after her. Evan slid in behind the wheel as Sam pulled Erin onto his lap and held her. She stirred and snuggled in closer to him with a contented little sigh. Sam found her smiling at him. "Did you meet Rick and Matty? They're my friends. That's Captain Rick. I love him too… and Matty. He helped me get away from Andre."

She leaned her head against Sam's chest. "They love me. Not like you."

Sam's arms tightened around her, and he stared morosely out the side window. Not love her? She infuriated him. She had knocked him off balance since the first time he had picked her up at nine years old. She fascinated him, amazed him, enthralled him, and made him want to slay dragons for her. Not love her? He'd wanted to kill those two men with her! He still did.

"Hush, baby," he rumbled. "Whatever you say and do now will likely come back to haunt you later. We'll get you sobered up. Then you can tell me how much you hate me."

When Sam noticed they were not headed back to his farm, he looked at Evan's reflection in the rearview mirror. "Where are we going?"

"I'm taking her to Jenny. She can get her showered and examine her. If either one of those assholes took advantage of her, I'll press rape charges." Evan snarled. "The whole situation just hits too close to home, Sam, reminds me too much of the way Jenny's father set her up so he could break us up years ago. Jesus, what if they…"

He didn't finish as he turned the SUV into his drive and pulled to the back of the house. Sam carried Erin inside. Jenny was in the kitchen starting dinner. When she saw Sam with a blanket-wrapped Erin, her eyes widened with concern.

"What happened to her?"

Sam frowned but was saved from explanations when Evan said, "She was in a hotel room with two men who'd gotten her drunk and stoned. I want you to examine her, Jen. I'll press sexual assault charges if I have to."

Jenny's mouth tightened. "Follow me to the guest room, Sam. Let me have her clothes, Evan. I'll take care of her if you'll go ahead and cook dinner. You'll join us of course, Sam."

He laid Erin on the bed, and started to straighten when Erin murmured, "Don't go, Sammy."

"It's okay, baby. Jenny's going to help you." He touched her short hair gently. "I'll be right downstairs. I won't leave you."

Sam returned to the kitchen to find Evan chopping vegetables. Sam leaned against the counter.

"That is so domestic, Evan."

"Fuck you."

The knife chopped rhythmically, but with enough force, Sam realized Evan was still venting pent up anger. Sam could relate to that. He rubbed his reddened knuckles. Punching that guy in the nose had felt extremely satisfying. Before he could contemplate how much better he would feel if he could do it again, Jenny returned to the kitchen and punched him in the gut.

Sam let out a big oomph. "What the heck? What was that for?"

Jenny glared at him. "For being an insufferable prick." She turned to Evan. "There is no reason to file any charges against her friends."

"They didn't do anything? You're sure?" Evan's voice was still filled with suspicion.

Jenny smiled. "As sure as I am that Joe is a preacher."

She left the room once more, and Sam looked at Evan in frustration. "That's all the information we get?"

Evan nodded and went back to chopping.

Finally Sam asked, "Doesn't it bother you that she knows a lot more than she tells?"

Evan sighed. "All the time, but I respect her for it, even if I don't like it. She wouldn't be much of a doctor if she didn't keep some things to herself. I'd say Erin obviously told her something about you that pissed her off. Care to share what you've been doing to my sister?"

"Not a darn thing," Sam said indignantly, "not that it hasn't..."

He clamped his lips tightly before he could say anything else and stared at his big feet.

"Not that it hasn't what, Sam?" Evan asked softly.

"I told her I wasn't interested," Sam said stiffly.

"And are you?" Evan inquired.

"Yes. No! It would never work."

"Never say never, Sam." Evan laughed, a dark, evil sound that made Sam nervous.

* * * *

The euphoria of Erin's pot and alcohol high had quickly evaporated, leaving her dragged down and depressed. As she stood beneath the spray of the shower, she thought back over what she'd shared with Jenny. Her brother certainly hadn't pulled any punches in how seriously he was treating her hooking up with Rick and Matty.

Right off the bat, Jenny had said, "Evan wants to know if you've been raped. Did those men touch you?"

It had struck Erin as funny. She'd stared at Jenny for a beat, then giggled. "I'm the last person Rick or Matty would touch. Evan and Sam were in more danger than me!"

Jenny's brows shot up; then she started laughing as well. "Oh God! They're *gay*? Well then why are you only in a bra and your thong?"

"We were playing strip poker. I was winning too, damn it. I had a full house, aces over jacks, when they knocked." She'd giggled. "I'd have had Rick's boxers next. Um, Jenny, don't say anything, you know, about Rick and Matty being gay. They don't advertise it. Well, Matty kinda does. He's pretty effeminate."

Jenny smiled. "So I can assume you are still...?"

Erin hiccupped. "As virginal as ever since Sam doesn't want me."

Jenny had plopped next to her on the bed. "Do you want him?"

Erin cringed now as she thought back on what she'd revealed. And then she'd just made it worse.

"Yes. No! He's mean and he hates me. He said he didn't want what so many other men had already had. I'd be crazy to want him." Erin sniffed. "Where's the bathroom? I'm going to be sick."

Jenny had helped her to the commode, then into the shower. Erin was mortified. As the water continued to run over her, she knew she would have to face Sam and her brother when she got out. Could someone stay in a shower forever?

Erin was quiet as she dressed again in her own clothes. It amazed her how quickly a person could go from falling down drunk to stone cold sober. With sobriety came humiliation. Her face burned. Sam and Evan had seen her nearly naked and falling down drunk. Had she really told Sam she loved him? Oh God. Then asked Matty about her ass? How on earth could she possibly face Sam or Evan again?

"Come on, Erin," Jenny said quietly from the doorway. "You can't hide here."

"I'm so embarrassed."

"We've all done stupid things at some point."

Erin looked up then, an expression of self-loathing on her face. "Some of us keep doing them. Oh, Jenny," she whispered, "I told Sam I love him."

Jenny put an arm around Erin's shoulders. "Don't worry. Nobody believes what you say when you're drunk. You need some food and some fluids."

When they entered the kitchen, Erin raised her chin stubbornly even as she averted her gaze. "I'm sorry if I embarrassed any of you in any way."

Evan came over and held her by the shoulders. "Are you sure you're okay, honey?"

She closed her eyes. Protecting Rick and Matty's secrets would make her appear even worse, but she owed them, especially Rick. "They're friends, Evan. Anything that happened was by mutual consent."

"Erin…" Jenny began.

She lifted her chin a little higher. "They've seen me in less than that before," she lied.

Evan and Sam's mouths dropped open.

"Erin," Evan began. "This area isn't like the Virgin Islands. People aren't as relaxed about some things."

It sounded remarkably similar to what she had tried to tell Rick and Matty, but she wasn't about to admit that. Erin stared at him. "Worried about your reputation, Mr. Prosecutor, or mine? 'Cause if you're worried about mine"—and now she looked directly at Sam—"people already think I'm a drug-addicted slut. I can hardly go any lower in their estimation."

"Erin," Sam began, his voice low and gravelly sounding, but she spun on him.

"Do you both have to gang up on me all the time? Do you think I haven't already had a lifetime of people pointing out everything I do wrong? You didn't have to go live in D.C., Evan. I did. It was like living in a fishbowl all the time. Daddy's name was always tied to the phrase 'potential presidential candidate,' so we were under constant scrutiny. If I said the wrong thing, wore the wrong thing, combed my hair the wrong way, it was in all the gossip columns… And everyone in school delighted in throwing it in my face."

When Evan tried to touch her, she stepped back and wrapped her arms across her waist.

"It didn't take long for me to become a prime target for all of them. Senator Stoner Richardson's troubled teenage daughter. And all I ever saw in Mama and Daddy's eyes was how tired they were of me. I was a liability. Even sitting on the bench for UVA you were more of an asset than I was. When they were finally able to ship me off to college, they looked relieved. Do you have any idea how that feels, Evan?"

Jenny started to reach out to her, but Erin backed away from the contact. "Do you have any idea how hard it is to grow up as the only idiot in a family of freaking geniuses? Even now… You're married to a doctor. I discover a bastard half sister who turns out to be another Georgia O'Keeffe and so squeaky clean she's married to a minister who sings like an angel." She began prowling, scarcely aware of how her fingers danced across surfaces as she walked.

"Then there's me, Evan," she whispered. She stared at him, feeling the humiliation of not living up to standards that had always seemed to be a little higher than other families. "The idiot who can only land jobs as a cook or a lifeguard. Oh, and now I can add shit shoveler. How does that stack up against your resume, bro?"

She continued to prowl the room, restless and agitated, before she stopped and stared at Sam accusingly. "The only person who ever really bothered to look at me as a person, you punched in the nose. And you and Evan both told him to leave. Rick knows me, knows my faults, and still likes me. That's almost unheard of for me."

"Sit down," Jenny said softly, but firmly. "You need to eat something, Erin, and get some fluids in you. I don't think now is the time to discuss all this."

Erin looked at her sister-in-law, and some of her belligerence faded. "You're right, Jenny. I don't want to talk about this. I spend most of my time trying not to think about it at all, but since coming back here, it seems like all I ever do."

By the time Erin and Sam returned to his farm, he was frustrated and irritable. She could tell by the way he stalked to the mudroom door. As he held it for her, he growled, "I'm sorry I punched your friend."

Erin stopped, staring at him incredulously. "That's it? That's your apology?"

Sam pulled at his already short hair. "It made me crazy. You'd disappeared.Then there you were, almost naked with those two guys. I lost it. Okay?"

"I'm safe with them."

"Are you?" Sam asked. "How the heck am I supposed to protect you if you invite people here to pick you up?"

"Am I a prisoner here?"

That stopped him. With one hand on the back of his neck he stilled, his dark eyes intense, his brows drawn together. "No. That's not what I want, but I need to be with you or know you're some place safe."

"Oh, so it's like being grounded. How quaint." Erin shook her head. "I'm going to bed."

She felt his gaze on her. As she crossed the living room, she heard the unmistakable sound of a liquor bottle rattling against the edge of a glass. Great. Now she was driving even Sam to drink. Erin was desperate for the oblivion sleep would provide. This day had been far too long already.

Erin was dreaming. She knew it was a dream because she had imagined it ever since she was old enough to imagine being with a man. She had comforted herself with stories and fantasies in which Sam Barnes was always the hero. Whether he knew it or not, Sam had been there to dry the tears she'd shed in private during those years in D.C. when she had become the brunt of bullying from other, more successful students. When she was scared or uncertain, it was him she always thought of.

Now was the most delicious dream yet. He was there in her room, stripping off his clothes in the dim light of the moon filtering through the window. He stood next to the bed, looking at her with an expression that was both somber and searching.

As she always did in her dreams, Erin moved to the side, a silent invitation. The mattress shifted with his weight, and she smiled drowsily at how realistic this dream was. His weight and warmth enveloped her. His lips nuzzled her face and her neck, his breath faintly flavored with bourbon. Big, calloused hands pulled her against him, molding her to him. Why couldn't he be like this when she was awake? Why couldn't he like her in real life?

"Sammy," she said with a sigh against his mouth. "Make love to me. I want you, all of you."

Her dream hero kissed her deeply, seducing her so she never ever wanted to wake up. She looked into his dark eyes and saw heat and passion so intense it burned straight down to her sex. She ached for him, throbbed for him. She helped him as he pulled her baggy shirt over her head, baring her breasts to him.

"Beautiful," he murmured, and his lips and hands caressed her, making her whimper and moan. "So beautiful. I've dreamed so long of touching you. Touch me too," he whispered against her ear.

Erin's fingers trembled as she traced the contours of his beloved face, skimmed along his muscular neck and shoulders, and spread across the sprinkling of hair covering the muscles of his chest and stomach. Her dreams had never felt this real, this compelling. As her hands brushed along the rigid outline of his hips, Sam's breathing altered, becoming harsh and strained. Then his fingers untied the string at her waist and his hands brushed the material down until she was as naked as he was.

Erin sighed with pleasure and arched against his work-sculpted body. Never had her dream been this detailed, this realistic. Her whole body burned and tingled where skin met skin…her thighs, her belly, her nipples. She and Sam rubbed together, hard and soft, until they moaned with the pure, heart-pounding pleasure of it. He moved away for an instant. She heard a sound like ripping paper; then he was back, pressing against her, his heat nearly burning her.

"Oh, Sammy, yes," she whispered. "Don't stop. Please."

He groaned near her ear. Then his hand slipped lower, sliding between her thighs to the moist, bare flesh there, and his fingers did the most deliciously wicked things… Things she had never even imagined. She whimpered again as a second finger joined what the first one was already doing, and his thumb rubbed the bud of flesh nestled in her swollen sex. She had fantasized about this so often it seemed real.

"I want you," he whispered. "I want to feel you around me when you come for me, baby."

Her fog began to clear. In her dream, Sam always said he loved her, not that he wanted her. But before Erin could puzzle that out, his knee parted her thighs, and even as she whimpered, his fingers were replaced with the hard heat of his erection. He slid along her moist folds until he found the opening he sought, then thrust powerfully into her.

Pain burst like the crack of a log in a fireplace. Erin gasped. This was no dream. This was actually happening. And it hurt. No one had told her that. Maybe Sam was just too big. It felt that way. At last, she found her voice.

"Get off me! Get off me!"

"Erin?" Shock reverberated in Sam's voice, and he abruptly withdrew. The lamp next to the bed snapped on, and she heard his muttered curse before the bed shifted again. Erin opened her eyes and looked down at herself. She scrambled off the bed, snatched her shirt, and threw it over her head right before Sam stalked back into the room still gloriously naked and carrying a wet washcloth.

She backed away from him. The flush of embarrassment that had flooded her morphed almost immediately into anger.

"Get out," she yelled. "Get out of my room. I thought you were a dream. Get out!"

Sam's dark eyes were shadowed with concern. "Erin! We need to talk for God's sake."

"There's nothing for us to talk about. Nothing." Her voice rose to near hysteria, but she could do nothing to control it. "Leave me alone!"

"Talk to me!" he ordered. "Sweet heaven. How are you still a virgin?"

Erin looked at his confused, frustrated expression and lost it. The first thing that came to hand was the alarm clock, and she sent it sailing toward his head. Sam deflected it with his forearm.

"You…you…you jackass," she yelled. "First I'm not pure enough for you because you think I've slept with everyone and their brother… Now you're pissed because I *haven't*?"

Erin picked up a crystal dish that was sitting on the nightstand and threw that too for added measure. Again, Sam deflected it, but this time before she could gather anything else, he rushed forward to grab her and pin her tightly against him.

"Talk to me!" he growled once more against her hair. "You let everyone think…. Everyone assumed… What about Rick? And Matty? The way you dress…the birth control pills. Darn it, Erin! What was I supposed to think?"

"You were supposed to leave me alone." She struggled in his arms, arching away from him now with her entire body as stiff as a board until she could glare him in the eye. "Put me down, Sam!"

She wouldn't cry. She wouldn't. She never cried. She wanted her dream back. She wanted that fantasy where Sam looked at her and saw *her*, not who everyone thought Erin Richardson was. Sam would look at her, and he would know. He was her hero. He had to be the one to see her.

He had always been her hero. From the day when she was nine and he'd found her with her broken arm. He'd picked her up, put her on his horse, and taken her home. He was her knight.

* * * *

Sam stared at her pale face. She had said yes. She'd told him not to stop. The shadows below her beautiful eyes were dark enough to be bruises. Oh God! What had he *done*? His mind recoiled. She had gone limp in his arms now, and her face was ever so slightly averted.

"Please, Erin, baby, talk to me," Sam pleaded. Her head dropped forward, and he felt a tear hit his chest. Christ. A tear. He had done this. His heart was ripping in two. He wanted to howl. He had made her cry. Sweet Virgin Mary. When all he had wanted was to love her, he had brought her to tears instead. She must have felt it too, because she began to struggle, but Sam wasn't going to let her run away. Not anymore.

"I won't let you go, Erin," he told her, and he picked her up in his arms as easily as if she weighed no more than a feather. "And I won't let you hide. Too many people have done that with you."

As he sat with her in the chair next to the bed, he saw that, even crying, she would not release the control she exercised over every emotion except her anger. Her tears were silent, the mortification written plainly on her face that anyone should see her cry.

"I'm sorry," he whispered as he pressed her head against his bare chest. Erin's soft hair tickled his skin, and Sam leaned his cheek against the top of her head, pain tightening his jaw. He had to clear his throat before he could continue. "I would never have been that rough if I'd known it was your first time. Oh, baby, I'm so sorry."

He held her close and rocked her. Sam closed his eyes, feeling her body jerk with her silent sobs. His arms tightened and he rocked her harder, desperate to ease her, aching with guilt.

"I thought it was my dream," she choked.

It was the second time she'd said it. She dreamed of him that way? Dreamed of him in her bed, making love to her? He hardly dared hope. Maybe there was something they could salvage out of this. He cradled her head and let his other hand rub soothingly on her back. He needed to make it up to her, to show her that making love was pleasurable.

"Oh, baby, I can't give you back what I've taken," he whispered, "but I can make it better. Would you let me do that? Would you let me show you how it should be?"

She looked at him with tear-drenched eyes. He hated the wariness there, hated the knowledge that he had put it there through his own actions and his own ignorance.

"It hurt," she muttered against his chest. "Nobody tells you that."

Sam closed his eyes in shame not only at what he had done, but also at the memory of Jenny telling them they didn't know anything about her and they would be ashamed when they found out. She had no idea just how right she was. Sam felt like the worst kind of heel. It was obvious from her words she had never forgotten him, just as he had never been able to forget her.

"It won't hurt again, Erin. I swear to you. Let me show you how amazing it can be. I know I don't deserve it, but I'm begging you to trust me."

Trusting anyone, when her trust had been betrayed over and over, was a struggle. He knew that, could see it. He racked his brain trying to think of some way to win her over. Maybe it was time he confessed a few things of his own. Using two fingers, he tilted her chin, kissed her nose, her forehead, and leaned his cheek against the top of her head. "Ever since I saw you in my pond all those years ago, I've dreamed of you, Erin. You're so lovely. I want to hold you, touch you. "

"Then why do you always push me away?" she cried.

How could he tell her the real reason, especially when he'd ended up doing exactly what he'd feared? His face flushed. She was so perfectly formed, so pretty…and so tiny! Next to her, he felt clumsy and huge, but worst of all, old.

She watched him. "Sam? Are you blushing?"

He stroked his big thumbs over her cheeks and wiped away her tears as he gazed into her face. "I-I haven't been with many women, Erin. I've spent so much time thinking about you—then feeling so guilty. You were just a kid. It was wrong. Then you came back…" He paused and took a deep breath. "You're so tiny. I'm afraid I'll hurt you. Sure, you're an adult…but—you said it yourself—I'm old. I keep trying to convince myself you need someone closer to your age. You could never want someone like me."

Chapter 6

His face was shadowed, his brows drawn together with uncertainty. Erin touched his cheek. "Sammy? I can barely remember a time when I didn't want you." Feeling emboldened by his gruff confession, she twisted until she straddled his lap in the chair and put her hands on either side of his dear, dear face. She leaned in close to him, touched her mouth to his, and let her hands drift into his hair to pull him closer. This was Sam, her Sam. She wanted to touch him and taste him. She wanted to hold him and never, never let him go.

"I've never wanted anyone else but you, Sam," she murmured against his mouth, then brushed her lips against his. "I could never give myself to anyone. It's always been you. At first, it was hero worship, then somewhere along the line it changed. All it took was seeing you again, and I was right back to wanting you. Your age means nothing."

"Aw, babe. Put your arms around my neck." When she had done that, he cupped her bottom and stood. She automatically wrapped her legs around his lean waist. "You just have no idea how wonderful that feels," he growled in her ear.

When he laid her on the bed, he followed her down, holding her and soothing her with hands that caressed from her shoulders down her thighs. Patiently, gently, he kissed her and touched her breasts through the material of her shirt. After easing the material up, he bent his head until he pressed his lips to the broken heart on her breast and gently suckled her nipple, flicking it with his tongue so she gasped and knotted her fingers in his short, thick hair.

It was even better now. Knowing it was real, knowing that Sam wanted her, that he was touching her, sharpened and heightened her responses. As he trailed kisses lower across her belly and along the sensitive skin where hip met thigh, Erin arched upward and cried out.

"What—what are you doing?" she gasped.

"Shh. Kissing you, baby. Relax. I promise you'll enjoy it."

And she did. His tongue flicked where his fingers had caressed just moments before. Erin whimpered and when he added his fingers to what his mouth was doing, she arched against him. Heat suffused her entire body until she felt as if she were once again aboard the *Sprite* with the sun beating down on the deck. Her heart beat as fast as the first time she'd felt the ship crest a wave and slide into a trough. Ecstasy like she had never imagined rolled over her and she cried out, this time in pleasure. He held her close as she trembled in his arms.

"Oh, Sam!" she gasped in amazed wonder. "I never imagined."

He hugged her. Slowly, as her pulse evened out and her breathing returned to normal, she became aware of other things. The silken feel of the sheets beneath her back and the hard length of his erection pressed against her hip. She ran her fingertips along his lean cheek. "Can I touch you?"

His smile was sultry and slow, his dark eyes lighting with passion and pleasure. "Baby, you can touch me anywhere you want, any way you want."

She pushed him onto his back, then sat back on her heels to study the body she had only been able to imagine for years on end. He was heavily muscled and covered in a fine sprinkling of dark, downy hair that arrowed over his stomach, around the bold, hard flesh of his swollen cock before thinning once more along his well-defined thighs and well-shaped calves. His shoulders were broad, the prominent muscles molding sleekly into arms that were powerful and hands that, for all they were huge, were incredibly gentle.

Erin met his dark gaze again, and found him watching her curiously and cautiously. There was an edge of vulnerability apparent in his expression that she would never have imagined. She wanted to make him feel as wonderful as she did. "You're even more handsome than I fantasized."

His fingers feathered along the line of her cheek.

"Then touch me with your hands as well as your eyes. Touch me however you want. Whatever you do, I want because it's you."

She started at his head, slowly and shyly making her way down his body until he trembled with the effort to restrain himself. She sat back again and stripped off her shirt, and stretched out full length on top of him, savoring the way her softness met and molded around his hard body. She laid her cheek against his chest and felt the heavy beating of his heart. A deep wellspring of need nearly choked her.

"I want this, Sam. I want you inside of me, part of me, but it hurt last time."

He stroked her cheek. "Stay on top, honey. Then you can decide how much or how little, how fast or how slow."

Erin stared at his thick shaft, before slowly wrapping her fingers around as much of it as she could. Her wide eyes met his hooded gaze.

"Will it fit?"

His breath gusted out on a soft chuckle. "It already has, but you can keep doing that for a while if you want," he rasped. He reached over to the nightstand, fumbling until he came up with a condom package.

She stroked him until he begged her to stop.

"Now would be the time to put that on," she whispered, watching him as he did. Erin's breath came out in a sob as she straddled his hips and slid her body onto him, sheathing him and feeling his fullness within her. They both trembled with fear, with passion, with restraint, but as pleasure replaced what had gone before, relaxation followed.

He braced her hips with his broad hands. "That's it, baby. Are you okay? I'm not hurtin' you, am I?"

She laughed, and for the first time since she could remember, she felt carefree. Her body had stretched and remolded to accommodate him. They fit in every way. "I feel wonderful. You feel wonderful."

He smiled again, and his strong, white teeth flashed more brilliantly than she had ever seen. "Then let's make it even better." With his hands, he taught her how to move over him and with him until they both gasped with pleasure that tipped them beyond the edge of reason. Erin climaxed first, crying out again, then watching as his expression changed from passion almost to pain with the intensity of his own orgasm. He held her hips firmly as he thrust into her, crying out as he came.

When she moved, he held her close. "Not yet. Stay with me, right where you are." He stroked her and soothed her, his body still a part of hers. Erin laid her head on his chest, overwhelmed by the intensity of what had just occurred. Her fingers threaded through the silky hair of his chest, and she rubbed her cheek against him, as content as a cat.

She must have fallen asleep, because when she awoke, the covers were over them and they were lying on their sides. Sam had curled his powerful frame around her protectively.

"Sammy?" she whispered.

"Hmm?"

"I'm glad it was you. I always wanted the first time to be you."

His arm tightened around her. She thought she heard a slight catch in his breathing. "Go to sleep, baby."

"Will you stay with me?"

"All night," he rumbled and gently kissed the back of her neck.

* * * *

Sam held her, willing his body to relax as she relaxed against him. She felt even better there than he could ever have imagined, but sleep eluded him. His thoughts churned.

Something about the scene in the hotel room was missing. It didn't add up the way it should. He pictured the two men. The one called Rick was almost certainly somewhere in his early forties, though he acted much younger. He was tanned and fit, leaner and shorter than Sam, with a wiry kind of strength and a world weary expression. For all that he seemed to be in charge, the one who knew the score and what they were all about, something in the younger man's expression nagged Sam.

Where Rick made sense in a cynical, roll with the punches type of fashion, the other one—what was his name? Matty?—did not jive any way Sam figured it. He was certainly no older than Erin, and even though his bright blue eyes appeared open and guileless, there was something else there, something lurking. Erin appeared to trust them both from what he could see, but Sam just wasn't so sure. He thought back to his last eye contact with the one she called Rick. He'd met plenty of men like him over the years, and he had a feeling that in a pinch, he was probably a man to be counted on.

Sam's gaze swept Erin's sleeping form, curled so trustingly against him. His throat tightened with emotion and his arms tensed around her. He would do whatever he had to in order to protect her. If it meant taking a closer look at her friends, he would do that too. He had found her now, and he wasn't going to let anyone take her away from him. Not again. Not ever again.

He had walked away from her all those years ago because she had been a child. To do anything else would have been wrong on every level. But she wasn't a child any longer, and by some miracle she wanted him. He wasn't a blueblood like her family, just a redneck county sheriff, a washed up jock struggling to make a living with his family farm and his job as a cop.

He smiled slowly in the darkness and nestled his face in her short, dark hair. She was a perfect fit. He had worried about that, as big as he was and as small as she was, worried they might not be physically compatible. Worried he would be too much for her. He stroked his calloused palm along her arm. He would give anything not to have hurt her as he had that first time, but he was so relieved to find when they tried again that she was able to take all of him.

Sam's lips brushed her hair and he closed his eyes. Erin. His love. She'd waited for him. He found it hard to wrap his mind around that thought. She'd had a piece of his heart for so long. Now she owned him heart and soul. He wondered if she realized what she held. And he seriously doubted he had the words to explain it.

The next morning left him no time to explain anything. When he and Erin arrived at the barn to feed, they found one of his young Herefords having a difficult labor. Sam was able to get his hand in far enough to determine the calf was in the wrong position, but not far enough to manipulate it.

"Darn it!" Sam snapped as he tried to maneuver the calf struggling to be born. "My hands are too big to move that foot. See if you can get it."

"What do you want me to do?" Erin asked, her eyes wide as her gaze darted from him to the cow.

"Just bring that one front leg forward, and this baby should come on out."

Erin unzipped her coveralls and stripped down to a sports bra so her arm would be bare for reaching inside the birth canal. Sam stroked the cow to keep her calm while he watched Erin in wonder. Everything he'd thrown at her, other than filling out paperwork, she'd tackled without batting an eyelash. This was no different.

With her head next to the heifer's rump, she gently maneuvered her hand and arm in until she could bring the leg forward. Once that was done, the calf slipped out taking Erin with it, so she landed on her butt in the straw with a wet newborn in her lap. Her eyes rounded and her mouth opened and closed a couple times.

Sam tried hard to contain his amusement. Erin's temper could be somewhat unpredictable, but all he saw was a look of surprise on her face, and it was finally too much.

He started to laugh and she joined in. Sam squatted next to her and lightly kissed her on the lips.

"You're amazing," he whispered, pulling back just enough to look into her eyes.

She held his gaze for a second, then looked away, blushing slightly. Sam's heart beat heavily in his chest. The angry, rebellious woman who'd returned was disappearing, and this new Erin was irresistible.

"Come on, squirt," Sam teased as he helped extricate her from beneath the calf. "Let's let mama do her job before this guy imprints on you."

"I hope I'm not interrupting," Evan said from behind them. Sam turned in surprise, then automatically blocked Erin from Evan's view as she scrambled back into her clothing and zipped the heavy coveralls.

"Just helping a new mama a little bit," Sam said over his shoulder as he waited for Erin to finish putting her clothing to rights. He faced Evan and smiled slightly. "Erin's doing a great job. I haven't lost any calves yet, thanks to her."

She stepped around, under Sam's arm, and stopped, nestled against his side. Pride and possessiveness swelled in Sam as he put his arm around her.

Evan's gaze shifted between the two of them, and he smiled. "I see things are going very well indeed."

Sam tightened his arm around Erin. He wasn't sure exactly how much he wanted to share. What was growing between the two of them felt too new, too tentative. Some of that uncertainty was right square on him because along with his feelings were lingering doubts. "We're doin' all right."

Evan cocked one eyebrow. Knowing just how blunt his friend could be, Sam narrowed his eyes and stared hard at him. Just for once, he hoped Evan got the message to keep his sarcasm on a leash and keep his mouth shut. Of course, maybe Evan's amazement had more to do with why someone as young and vibrant as Erin would hook up with Sam.

Evan cleared his throat. "Actually, I came by to invite you to Dad's for dinner."

Sam felt Erin stiffen, but he ignored it.

With a smile, he asked Evan, "What time?"

Erin elbowed him. Sam glowered at her and she huffed.

"Six. Joe and Tabby are coming with Melodie, although Joe might be a little late since he's got evening service. Jake and Holly are going to be there too with Noelle and Tyler, so dress is casual with all those kids in the house."

Sam glanced at Erin and saw her suspicious look at Evan. "Is that a hint I should avoid the leather micro mini skirt and any desire I might have to expose undue cleavage?"

Sam gave her a warning squeeze with his arm and aimed another glare at Evan. The last thing he needed was the two of them fighting.

Evan, to his credit, refused to take the bait. "Erin, at this point, I don't believe Dad would care if you showed up naked. I had to all but tie him to keep him from coming over here himself just to make sure you were okay, and you know he's not off house arrest yet." He turned to Sam. "You need any more help around here?"

"We're good." He glanced at Erin again. "I'll clean up in here if you want to go inside and shower."

Laura Browning

She grinned. "I thought you'd never ask." With a nod at Evan she said. "I'll see you tonight." And she was gone.

Sam watched Erin until the screen door on the porch slammed behind her.

"Don't hurt her, Sam," Evan warned softly.

Sam jerked his gaze back to Evan. "Why on earth would you even say that?"

"I've always admired you, Sam," Evan began. "Got a ton of respect for you. But even you have to admit, you can be harsh. We've all seen that side over the years. You don't put up with any shit, and you've got a reputation in this state as being hard-nosed. Don't you think that gives me the right to be concerned?"

Sam glared at Evan. "Seems to me, I'm the last one around here you should be worrying about. We'll be there tonight, but so help me, Evan, if Stoner does anything to upset her…"

"A little protective all of a sudden, aren't you?" Evan queried tightly.

Sam stared at him. "No, just finally admitting what I've been too darn stubborn to admit to myself for more than a decade, Evan. The summer you went wild and took off, things got a little tense around here too. I panicked, so did Stoner. The upshot was he yanked Erin away from here. From what I can tell, it turned her life into a living hell, and mine into a routine of just gettin' by."

He turned his face toward the house and his expression softened. "I've had feelings for your sister since she was just a kid. I was ashamed of being so concerned because she was just a little thing, but I'm beginning to think now I did both of us more harm than good when I pushed her away. At least in the way I did it. The age thing was a problem. I knew it. Your dad did too and hated me for even thinking about her the way I did. So the bottom line was your dad and I both messed things up just by trying to do what we thought was right."

"So exactly what does that mean—you've got 'feelings' for her?"

Sam scowled. "I'm not a defendant, and this isn't a trial. Like I said. I've got feelings. It's new, and it's between me and her."

Evan extended his hand. "Sorry I questioned you. You're a good man, Sam. I know that deep down, and even though I think you'll be the perfect match for Erin, she's still my little sister, a little sister who's always had a tough time."

Sam met Evan's eyes squarely. "She won't anymore. I'll make sure of it. And the fact you can see it now, when you didn't before, says a lot for you."

The two men shook hands. "We'll see you at dinner." Evan grinned and pivoted to amble back over to the farm truck.

* * * *

Erin was curled on her bed with her laptop when she heard Sam come in. The pipes in the old farmhouse rattled as he started the shower downstairs. Just imagining the water sluicing down over his hard, bare body made her belly flutter. She set her computer aside. With a smile on her face, she raced to his room, pulled back the thick covers on Sam's bed, stripped her robe off, and slid underneath.

She swallowed with just a hint of fear. She had been here before, and each time he'd rejected her, but after last night, this time would be different. Her heart pounded as the bathroom door opened. Sam came in with just a towel wrapped around his lean hips, his face set in its usual scowl...until he saw her.

"Erin?" He sat on the edge of the bed, concern lining his face. "Hey, baby. You okay?"

For just a moment, she had an eerie feeling of déjà vu, but then he smiled, his whole face softening. "You hungry or do you feel like going back to bed for a while?"

The erratic beat of her heart settled into a deep, regular pulse. "Bed. Definitely."

He stood and let the towel drop at the same time she flipped the covers back. His mouth found hers, and he pulled her arms over her head, holding them there as he caressed her with his lips and his free hand until she whimpered and cried out for him. She bucked against his restraint, and he rumbled with laughter. When their eyes met, the laughter died and he kissed her deeply and passionately. He nudged her legs apart and released her arms so he could use both hands to lift her hips and cup her buttocks.

"You're on birth control, right?" Sam asked, his dark gaze hot.

"Yes."

A flush stained his cheeks. "I'm clean. Do you mind if we..."

"Forget the condom?" She kissed him in answer.

This time when he thrust powerfully into her, she met him gladly and openly. Sam was careful not to crush her as he rocked his hips against her.

"Wrap your legs around me, baby," he murmured and sat back on his haunches, pulling her with him. She twined her arms around his shoulders, arching backward as the shift in their positions brought her to a swift climax. Sam kissed her again, tumbling her backward until he once more knelt over her.

Working himself in and out, his breathing grew harsher. He was close, and so was she—again. What this man did to her was positively delicious. He lifted her hips and pushed deep as he came.

"Sweet, sweet, Erin." He nuzzled her and turned her so he could curl himself around her. It was like being wrapped in a cocoon. Everything about him felt right. She sighed in utter contentment and drifted off to sleep, knowing she had found the place at last where she belonged.

Thanks to Sam and Erin's afternoon of lovemaking, everyone but Joe was already at Richardson Homestead when they arrived. As soon as they walked in the door, Erin felt the gaze of the little dark-haired, blue-eyed girl standing next to Tabby. Erin smiled at her and received a small smile in return, but the little girl's brows drew together as if she were worried about something. She tugged at Tabby's slacks to whisper something to which Tabby shook her head.

Erin leaned toward Sam. "Who is the little girl with Tabby?"

"Melodie Matthews. Joe and Tabby are her guardians, but they've petitioned the court to officially adopt her."

"Her parents are dead?" Erin asked.

Sam nodded. "Murder-suicide. Her mother went off the deep end after losing a child that was full-term and stabbed her husband to death. Melodie was able to hide, otherwise she would have been killed too."

Erin's gaze swiveled to the little girl. She seemed remarkably well-adjusted for having gone through such a traumatizing experience. Erin felt new respect for her younger sister. Melodie sat across from an older boy while they played with Peter and a dark-haired toddler. "I've seen the older boy in Tarpley's. Who's he?"

"Jake Allred's brother-in-law, Tyler. The baby girl is Noelle, his niece. You remember Jake, don't you?"

Erin nodded. She did vaguely remember him, though he was five years older than her, like Evan and Jenny. "Is the very pregnant lady with him his wife?"

"Holly. Jake calls her his Christmas Angel. It's a long story that you'll have to get them to tell you sometime. In fact, I'd bet Evan looks at her the same way. She was kind of a catalyst to him getting back together with Jenny."

Erin looked at everyone gathered in the big family room and marveled. She had never seen the house so alive. More than that, everyone seemed happy. She looked at Sam and found him watching her with an intensity that made her just a bit nervous. When their gazes met, his hand tightened at her waist and he drew her closer to his side.

"I've never seen my parents like this, Sam. Things have changed," Erin said. For the first time that she could remember, she didn't feel threatened. Warmth kindled, not just for the man at her side but for everyone in the room.

Sam smiled softly at her. "They can for you too. All you have to do is open up and let it happen."

The warmth grew. She could be a part of this. All she had to do was let down her guard. Erin blew out a breath. That was easy to say. Doing it might be a whole different matter. Old habits were hard to break.

She thought about that a lot as she watched everyone interact and listened to the stories. A basic trust flowed among all of these people that she couldn't relate to. She realized part of it had to do with shared history. They had been through things together. Longing filled her to have what they did.

So she asked, and they told her how each of their lives had changed. There was the trauma of Jenny's gang rape when she and Evan were in high school. Erin had been oblivious to all of that, wrapped as she'd been in her own issues. She learned how Jake had helped Holly through the birth and kidnapping of her baby, and finally Tabby's arrival followed by the nearly fatal accident that had at last brought everyone together as a family. Erin had missed all of it. While they had been bonding as a strong family unit, she had been sailing the Caribbean.

She realized with a shock that out of everyone in the room, she knew Sam the best. Something had been forged between them when she was just a child, and he'd taken her up on his horse that day he'd found her with the broken arm. It had grown and changed since then, but in her heart was the knowledge that she could depend on him with her life. He would never let her down. Deep inside, she had always recognized that at some level. She wasn't honestly sure she could say that about anyone else in the room. With a smile on her face, Erin hooked her arm in his and met his faintly quizzical look.

Joe's arrival was the signal for dinner. This was hardly the formal affair of many other meals Erin had suffered through in the stately house. With a couple of high chairs for the smallest children and a booster seat for Melodie, Peterson had to relax his usual starchy demeanor. Tyler, Erin noticed, did his best to look cool and identify with the adults, but when he thought no one was looking, he made faces at Melodie to make her laugh and spit her milk.

Erin perked up when Stoner asked Joe if he would mind singing after supper. They gathered in the front hall, and Erin was even more surprised when Peterson and the kitchen staff came to listen as well. Joe's clear, melodic tenor filled the space from floor to ceiling, as pure as birdsong on a spring morning. Tears filled Erin's eyes as she listened. Tabby put her arm around her and hugged Erin against her side.

"Don't be embarrassed, Erin. He has that effect on me too, and I'm married to him."

Erin hugged Tabby back, but she still felt distanced from this tight family unit. Everywhere she looked, talent and success surrounded her. Erin didn't know what she had to show for her life or how she could fit in

Everything began to wind down. Jake and Holly were the first to go, since she was expecting twins, which were making it difficult for her to get rest. As Tabby and Joe gathered their belongings together, Erin was surprised to feel a soft tug on her hand. She looked at Melodie. The little girl's expression was earnest, her big blue eyes staring up at her.

"Aunt Erin," she said softly, and Erin leaned down to her. Melodie touched her cheek. "I'm glad you're here."

Erin looked at her, surprised and touched. "Why is that, baby?"

Melodie chewed her lip. "You know about me?"

Erin simply nodded.

"You have shadows in your eyes, like I feel sometimes."

Erin's heart stuttered. Like the Grinch, she felt her heart grow at the empathy shining from Melodie's eyes. Erin touched the little girl's cheeks. "The shadows in my life don't even begin to compare, but you have Joe and Tabby now."

Melodie nodded. "Be careful, Aunt Erin. Tabby says we have to keep the shadows where they belong and not let them scare us."

A frisson of alarm snaked along Erin's spine. She kept a smile on her face as everyone left; then she dutifully hugged her mother and father. Not until they were headed home did Sam finally take her hand in his.

"What is it, Erin? You've been quiet ever since Joe sang this evening."

She swallowed. It would be so easy to say something flippant and brush him off, but that was the old Erin. She was beginning to realize Sam was right. All she had to do was open up. "Is Melodie like Tabby?"

Sam glanced her way, then asked slowly, "How do you mean like Tabby?"

"Was she abused?"

Sam sighed. "Yes. Her mother physically abused her, which we've kept as under wraps as possible. Of course the horrific way her parents died couldn't be kept secret, but what Melodie experienced in the wake of her mother's rampage, shut in the house with them, that's what they'd really tried to keep quiet."

Erin looked along the fence line as they drove toward the house and shivered. "She said I had shadows in my eyes like her."

Sam stopped his truck in front of the house and turned to her in the darkness. His long fingers brushed her cheek, then cupped her neck and encouraged her to slide over to him. "I'm not sure any of us can understand the trauma Melodie experienced. All I can say is the man upstairs must have helped her hide from a mother who had gone over the edge, stabbed her father in the eyes with a pair of kitchen scissors, and was looking for her."

"Oh, God!" Erin couldn't imagine a child as sweet as Melodie witnessing such a horrific event. "It just spooked me, you know. This whole thing with the Delacroix family has me on edge."

"You sure about your friends? Sure they're on the up and up?"

Something in Sam's tone just increased her anxiety. Erin began to shake, her mind in turmoil. Matty and Rick were here. Were they involved? The only danger she knew of was from Andre, and he certainly wasn't a friend. Not even close. She just couldn't suspect Rick or Matty. After all, it was just a stroke of luck they'd gone on board another boat the night the *Sprite* blew up.

"I trust them."

Sam tucked her against his broad chest and held her. At last he whispered, "I'm taking two weeks' vacation, Erin. The calving is about to get into full swing, and I want us both here. You won't be alone, not for a second. I'll keep you safe, no matter what, baby. I swear I'll keep you safe."

His words and his tone melted her last reservations. Out of everyone she knew, Sam never said anything he didn't mean. The bottom line was she could trust him, so she would. The thought freed her in a way she never expected, making her feel lighter than she had felt since she was just a kid.

They hit the ground running the following morning. Sam had gone out early to check on the more experienced mamas. He left those in the pasture nearest the house. It was only the first-time heifers he kept in paddocks, run-in sheds, or the barn. By lunchtime, they had lost one calf, delivered a bull calf from Sam's best cow, and a healthy set of twins from another.

"Let's get some lunch," Sam said. "I don't think we'll have any more today. We'll take care of the barn and delivering more hay to the back pastures this afternoon."

Erin pushed the cap back on her head and grinned. "Suits me. I'm starving."

"You're always starving," Sam returned.

She winked. "Yeah, but not always for food."

She stepped over the bucket near the barn door and was slipping her way over the ooze of the barnyard when she heard a curse and a thud behind her. She spun around to find Sam flat on his back in the mud and the bucket she'd stepped over jammed on one of his feet. Before she could help it, she started laughing.

"Not funny, Erin," Sam bellowed.

She hurried back to him, pulled the bucket off his foot, and held out her hand. "Sorry, Sammy. Here, let me give you a hand."

She extended her hand and he engulfed it in his. As she braced, he pulled. Damn, he was heavy, she thought just as he released her hand and she tumbled back onto her butt in the mud.

"What the hell? Sam!" Erin screeched.

He sat up with a grin.

"You shouldn't have laughed," he said, then grunted as Erin nailed him on the chin with a big blob of brown goo. She howled, but seeing the way Sam's eyes narrowed, she scrambled to her feet to escape. Before she could get more than ten feet away, Sam tackled her from behind. Air whooshed from her lungs as she sprawled face first into the mud.

"You are dead!" Erin sputtered as she wiped mud off her face and rolled over before snatching his cap off with one hand while she slapped a handful of mud on Sam's head with her other. They were wrestling in the cold mud and laughing when the sound of a truck pulling into the yard sent them both scrambling to their feet.

* * * *

Stoner couldn't believe his eyes. Sam Barnes, the somber, taciturn Castle County Sheriff, was covered head to toe in mud, and the pint-sized mud blob next to him was none other than Stoner's own daughter. As he slowly exited his truck, he forced himself to maintain a serious expression.

"Just what," he asked in a deadly even voice, "are you doing?"

Sam started to put his cap back on his head, had to run fingers through his hair to get the mud out, and simply stopped and stared sheepishly at the former senator. "I could ask the same thing," Sam said. "What are you doing off your farm? Aren't you off your leash?"

"Don't try to change the subject." Stoner looked at his mud-caked daughter. "Erin, I presume?"

She grinned lopsidedly, showing white teeth between black muck. "Hi, Daddy."

Stoner grinned as he looked back and forth between the two. "The judge suspended the rest of my sentence. I came over to let you know."

"Oh, Daddy!" Erin laughed. "That's great!" She rushed forward, but Stoner backed up.

"Whoa!"

She stopped and laughed again. "Sorry! We were just going in for lunch."

"Well, that's why I came by. Your mother and I would like you both to join us. Kind of a celebratory meal. But, uh… Why don't you take some time to clean up first?"

"Give us an hour, if you don't mind," Erin said with a look over her shoulder at Sam. Stoner's eyes narrowed. He watched the silent communication between the two and realized their relationship had definitely changed. He sighed. Stoner couldn't help the regret that washed through him. Oh, not because Erin and Sam appeared to have found each other, but because he finally felt he'd gotten back the girl he remembered from so long ago, and she was looking at another man with those stars in her eyes. However, if she was going to have a man in her life, Stoner was beginning to see that Sam Barnes was the right one… Maybe he always had been.

Stoner nodded. "See you in an hour, then." And he got back into his truck. He managed to make it to the end of the driveway before he had to stop and give in to the laughter that overwhelmed him when he recalled the mud covering the two of them from head to toe.

* * * *

The next week passed in a haze of work, between calving and a late winter storm that meant hauling more feed out to the other pastures. Sam and Erin worked from sunup to after dark. After cleaning up and eating dinner, they spent their evenings and half their nights locked in each other's arms, often too tired to do more than sleep.

Sam watched Erin blossom. Her moods evened out and he saw once again the same bubbly personality emerge that he had first seen when she was just nine years old and following him around like an irrepressible puppy. She ran full tilt from the time she rose until she dropped into bed at night. She was amazing and exciting, and he loved every minute he spent with her.

More than anything he wanted to make their arrangement permanent, but he held back. He still couldn't get past the idea that he was nearly forty and she was just in her mid-twenties. She deserved someone closer to her age. He was too old, too grumpy, and as Evan had pointed out, too hard-nosed. He would nearly have himself convinced he should ask her to go back home; then she would touch him, kiss him, or simply curl up on his lap while they watched a movie in the evening, and he would melt.

He discovered something else about both of them, a nearly insatiable appetite for each other. In one week they made love nearly every place imaginable: the bedroom, the bathroom, the couch, the recliner, the floor, the barn, the truck, against the wall of the mudroom and even on the kitchen table. After a particularly vigorous session on the living room floor, they lay curled near the woodstove. Sam stroked her hair and kissed the soft skin of her temple. Feelings didn't even begin to describe what he had for this woman. Sam finally admitted he was so in love with Erin he couldn't imagine ever being any other way.

And still he couldn't say it to her.

What a chicken shit.

* * * *

"Sam," Erin called through the barn door Friday morning. "I need to borrow the truck to go into town."

"Wait!" Sam said. Erin tapped her toe as she waited for him to appear in the barn door. "Erin, you're supposed to be here for your protection. Taking off for town whenever the mood strikes you is not a good idea."

She glared at him. "I've been on the farm all week long. I have some errands to run."

"Like what? If you'll wait a couple hours, I can go with you. I should have the tractor fixed by then."

Erin blew out a frustrated breath. "I'm just going to Tarpley's. I wanted to pick up food to cook us both a nice dinner. Come on, Sam. We've had a back-breaking week."

She could see he was weakening, so she pressed her advantage. "I'll go straight there and back, no stopping along the way. I promise." She crossed her hand over her heart."

"I just don't think it's a good idea," he muttered, casting a frustrated look over his shoulder to where his tool box sat next to the tractor's PTO.

"I'm going to make pork chops with apple chutney and roasted potatoes."

Sam sighed. "Go there and come straight back. I'm going to call Jake and tell him to keep an eye out for you."

She grinned at him. "Deal."

After the week they had experienced, she was going to pull out all the stops to cook him a meal to knock his socks off. It was more than just a way to say thanks. It was one of the few ways Erin knew she could give Sam something that was hers alone. Sure she'd thrown some breakfast together, same thing with dinner. But it was time to show him what she could do. There were few things she could truly number among her talents, but cooking was one of them.

After parking the big truck at the side of the building, Erin hopped down and hurried toward the store. She had promised Sam not to take any chances. Before she could get inside, though, the sound of someone calling her name made her stop.

"Erin Richardson?" Betty Gatewood, the wife of the mayor and one of the biggest gossips in town, waylaid her.

Erin turned. While she kept a smile on her face, inside she worried. This woman was the unofficial ringleader of that gaggle of church ladies she'd waved to outside the computer store the other day. Mrs. Gatewood had never had anything nice to say to her when Erin was younger, but Erin would be polite. After all, she had to think about Sam's reputation as well as hers. She blinked as the thought settled into her brain. The thought of her and Sam as a couple. It didn't scare her at all.

"Good afternoon, Mrs. Gatewood."

"I had heard you were back in town."

Erin just bet she had. No doubt from her gossip girls, or maybe Facebook. Erin had heard the town had a public page that posted some pretty nosy comments. Mrs. Gatewood smiled, but it didn't appear to go all the way to her eyes.

"Weren't you working as a hostess or something at one of those singles resorts in Florida?" the woman asked with barely concealed contempt.

Erin's gut tightened. "As a cook on a sailing vessel. And it was in the Virgin Islands, not Florida."

"Oh, well. All those places kind of blend together, don't they, dear? With all that loose living and drinking and drugs?" There was a pause and Erin started to feel the throb of a headache in her temples. "That must be difficult for you to be around all that, what with your past and all. I remember…"

Erin glanced away, desperately, but no one else was headed her way who might rescue her, and for the life of her, she couldn't think of an excuse to get away on her own. And get away she definitely needed to do before she lost her temper.

"Sheriff Barnes has to be so careful, him being an elected official. It would be a shame for any scandal to damage *his* reputation."

Erin froze. She and Sam hadn't been anywhere together. This was one of the facets of small town life she'd hated. Everybody was always in everybody else's business, and how news got around was anyone's guess.

"What kind of scandal would that be Mrs. Gatewood?" she asked, for once trying to keep a tight rein on her temper.

"Well you are living with him, aren't you?"

It was tempting to lie or just tell her to mind her own business, but Erin remembered all too well how stories got around. While it might not hurt Erin in the long run, it could have an impact on Sam's job where respect was such an integral part of it. If Betty Gatewood was even bringing this up, then she had to already know something.

"I'm staying at his house, working on his farm," Erin finally admitted, then kicked herself. No doubt the old biddy had just been fishing, and now Erin had confirmed it. Shit. She would have to tell Sam. He would be so angry.

The older woman shook her head. "You should think about it. You might flit away again, but Sam has to live and work here. Folks might think twice about re-electing a sheriff who has a young woman living with him. He doesn't have a powerful family ready to gloss over *his* mistakes."

Erin was livid, but she knew giving rein to her anger like she wanted would only hurt Sam that much more. Swallowing back the furious response that sprang to her lips, she simply smiled. "Thank you for sharing your concerns, Mrs. Gatewood. I'll keep those in mind."

Betty Gatewood patted her arm, and it was all Erin could do not to cringe. While the older woman sailed off to her car, Erin stood rooted to the spot, her hands fisted inside her pockets. She wanted to ignore everything that woman said… But she couldn't. No matter the motivation, there was some truth in words she knew weren't truly motivated out of concern for Sam.

But Erin was concerned. She didn't want to hurt Sam's career.

"Erin?"

Lost in thought, she jerked slightly, and looked up to see Holly carrying Noelle. Erin stepped forward. "Can I help you? I mean, should you be carrying her as far along as you are?"

"She normally likes to practice her walking, but she's a little pooped, and I'm in a bit of a hurry. I'm meeting Jake for lunch."

"I could carry her for you. Are you going to Mercer's?"

"Yes." Holly handed her the girl. Noelle grinned and patted Erin's cheek. "Thanks. She likes you."

Erin rubbed her cheek against Noelle's. "I like kids. They just accept you for who you are, you know?"

Holly touched her arm. "Are you okay?" Erin pasted a smile on her face, but before she could say anything, Holly continued. "I saw Betty

Gatewood out here talking to you. I tried to get here sooner, but I wasn't quite in time, was I?"

After adjusting Noelle on her hip, Erin grimaced. "I don't guess she said anything that I didn't already know."

Holly stopped her. "Jake threatened to punch her in the nose when she came to talk to him right after Noelle was born. I think you showed remarkable self-control."

Some of her tension eased. Erin even managed a smile. Noelle suddenly squirmed. "Da-dee!"

Erin looked over her shoulder to see Jake striding along the sidewalk toward them. While Noelle waved her hand and bounced up and down on her hip, Erin studied the man coming toward them. His dark hair lifted in the light breeze, and a smile lit his face. Like Evan, Jake was a man obviously happy with his life. She only noticed the dark uniform and the cap in his hand as he drew near.

From spending most of her life trying to avoid anyone in uniform, Erin now found herself surrounded. It hadn't struck her before. That she, of all people, should find herself in love with an officer of the law, was the ultimate in irony. She had been doing everything she could since she became a teenager to flout any type of authority, and had found herself skating on the wrong side of the law on more than one occasion.

Jake kissed Holly on the cheek, then reached for Noelle, who leaned toward him with a giggle. "Daddy, Daddy, Daddy!"

He grinned. "Hi, pumpkin." He hugged her close and gave her a smacking kiss on the lips. "Hey, Erin. Sam called a little while ago. You joining us for lunch?"

She shook her head. "No. As I'm sure Sam mentioned, I'm on my way to Tarpley's to buy ingredients for dinner. Sam and I've been working pretty hard this week with the calving, and I thought I would cook him a nice meal."

Jake grinned. "Whatever you cook, make it a lot. That man puts away more food than…"

"Jake!" Holly said. "That's not nice."

Erin laughed. "It's true. Hmm, and I thought it was because he was working so hard with the calving going on. Y'all have a nice lunch."

"I'll just keep an eye on you until you get there," Jake said.

As she walked back toward Tarpley's, Erin realized her dark mood was gone. Between Holly's comments and the happiness that just seemed to ooze from her whole family, Erin was once again back on an even keel.

Seeing the expression on Sam's face that evening when she set the pan seared chops, apple chutney, roasted new potatoes, and green beans in front of him lifted her spirits even more. He dug into the meal with hardly a word, but when it was over and she started to clear the table, he pulled her onto his lap.

"Thanks, baby. You're good for me."

Erin caressed his cheek. She hoped he was right. Betty Gatewood's words echoed in the back of her mind, but Erin tried to shove them firmly away.

Chapter 7

"I'd like you to go with me to church tomorrow," Sam murmured as they snuggled together on the couch Saturday night. "Joe's a great preacher."

"Wouldn't that blow my keeping a low profile?" Erin asked, swallowing around the sudden flutter in her throat. She remembered how the matrons of Mountain Meadow looked at her. She had felt it every time she visited the town. Then there was her brush with Betty Gatewood. Erin was always too something for them: too busty, too haughty, too wild, too stupid. Some of them had been her teachers; some of them had been the classmates who taunted her. They'd all left her feeling raw, and the whole idea brought up that conversation with Mrs. Gatewood. Maybe she should avoid being seen with Sam. She didn't want to damage his career.

"That cat's already out of the bag, baby. Check Facebook if you don't believe me. So will you go?"

"I—I don't know…."

Sam tilted her chin. "What is it?"

Erin rubbed her face against his bare chest. "Oh, Sam, my life here was almost as miserable as it was in Washington. The only time I was happy was out here, wandering the Homestead or your farm. Then I ran into Betty Gatewood yesterday when I drove into town."

"Nosy old bi…"

She put her fingers over his mouth. "Don't say it. She's a voter. She had valid points. I could hurt your career."

Sam's frown was fierce. "Bull."

He kissed the top of her head, then ran his hands down to knead her bottom and press her against his rapidly hardening cock. "So you want to hide? That doesn't sound much like my feisty, in-your-face Erin. Baby, you couldn't ask for much more support. Your brother-in-law will be preaching, your sister, your brother, and your parents will all be there. Hell, you'll even have the city police chief there, all in your court. Don't let a few cats scare you. Between the Richardsons and the Allreds, I think this town has learned a few lessons over the last year and a half. Jake and I will both be carrying, if that's your concern. We won't be sitting ducks."

"Okay. I'll go." Erin crawled up his body until she could straddle his hips. She didn't want to talk about this, so she smiled flirtatiously at him and leaned down. "Since you're my knight in shining armor, can I play with your sword?"

Sam laughed. "Baby, you can do anything to my sword your little heart desires."

Erin raised her brows, then bent over to take him into her mouth.

"Especially that," he groaned and tangled his fingers in her spiky hair.

* * * *

Sam jingled the keys in his pocket impatiently as he bent his head to look at the watch on his other wrist.

"Erin," he called once again. "Come on or we'll be late. Joe makes the latecomers sit up front, after he stops the service to say hi to you by…name…." His voice trailed off as she walked into the kitchen. She was dressed in a form-fitting navy wool dress that ended just a couple of inches above her knees. With it she wore a short, matching jacket and heels. A single set of pearl studs that matched the strand around her neck adorned her ears. She'd tamed her inky hair and toned down her makeup so that he could hardly tell she wore any. She took his breath away.

Erin stared at his raised brows for just an instant and looked at herself in disgust. "I look like shit, don't I?"

Sam shook his head. "You look beautiful. It's just so…so…" He stopped at a loss for words.

Erin wrinkled her nose. "So just like the rest of my family."

Sam chuckled. "Well yes. For you, it's almost like camouflage. My little stealth bomber. I can't wait to watch everyone's faces."

Erin laughed as she glided gracefully over to him and stretched on tiptoe to kiss him. Thank God. He'd said the right thing.

"Come on, Sammy, let's knock 'em dead!"

On impulse, he grabbed her and kissed her again. Obviously the doubts from yesterday had disappeared. "That's my girl."

And as he watched, heads did indeed turn. From the moment he helped her out of the truck and in the front door, until they sat in the pew with Stoner and Catherine. The older woman smiled serenely at Erin as if she would expect nothing less; then Stoner leaned forward and arched one brow in such a wicked way that Erin nearly laughed out loud. Sam smiled at her.

During the opening hymn, he whispered, "Why aren't you singing?"

Erin raised her nose into the air and hissed, "Because I don't want to ruin my image with a voice that sounds like a scalded cat."

Sam did laugh then, and several heads turned to stare at him with either disapproval or disbelief. He smiled at all of them and slung his arm around Erin's waist. She had awakened a whole new side to him, and it was all he could do to resist caressing her shapely little bottom. Lord. They were in church and he could barely keep his hands off her.

As they sat, Evan leaned forward from behind them and whispered in Sam's ear. "Down boy! I saw that hand start to wander south."

He was painfully aware of her. After so many years on his own, trying to date other women but comparing them all to Erin, the woman of his dreams finally stood at his side, and he wanted everyone to know she was his. He glanced at her during Joe's sermon. As if aware she was being watched, Erin tilted her face to his. Her beautiful eyes searched his as Joe made a point about forgiveness. When she smiled, just a gentle curving of her generous mouth, Sam's heart turned over. He reached for her hand and tucked it in the curve of his arm.

At times like this, it was easy to forget the difference in their ages. He could believe there might be a future for them. He wanted there to be.

* * * *

When the service ended, Erin found herself the center of a group of people. In addition to family, Mr. Tarpley from the general store stepped forward to shake her hand and kiss her cheek. Sam kept her tucked into his side, and made it more than obvious to everyone who stopped to greet them that he had staked a claim. Erin glanced at him a couple times and realized she didn't at all mind his possessiveness.

Evan grinned at her. "Okay, I can believe Sam twisted your arm and got you to come to church with him, but I can't believe you dispensed with the leather mini skirt and the commando boots."

Erin tilted her chin. "Sam says I'm in camouflage. A sneak attack on nosy church matrons."

Evan threw back his head and laughed, drawing stares from more than one person as they filed toward the door.

"Come on over to our place. We're going to do brunch."

Erin glanced at Sam who nodded imperceptibly. When her eyes caught her father's, just over Sam's shoulder, she found him watching with a thoughtful expression on his face. For an instant, she flashed back to that awful summer when she'd tried to sneak into Sam's bed. She could only pray her father wasn't trapped in all that history between her and Sam. She was an adult now. What she felt was no longer a girlish crush.

In no time at all once they reached Evan and Jenny's home, Erin took over in the kitchen. When Jenny and Catherine protested, Erin looked at all of them with her hands on her hips. "Look, until a few weeks ago, this was my job. It's what I do for a living…cooking, and usually for a bigger crowd than this. Now, Jenny, what did you have in mind?"

Jenny ticked off on her fingers what she had planned while Erin nodded. Finally when she reached the last dish—grits with a creamy shrimp sauce—Erin shook her head.

"I'm not familiar with that dish."

"Oh that's okay. I have a…recipe." Jenny glanced from Erin to Catherine. Erin shook her head imperceptibly. "Mother, why don't you start the coffee? Erin you get started with the other things, and Tabby and I will gather the ingredients for the shrimp dish."

"That sounds great!" Erin smiled gratefully at her sisters and pulled on the apron Jenny offered. Setting to work, Erin soon had a potato casserole sharing space with biscuits in the lower oven. In the upper oven, she kept a large platter of bacon and sausage warm. She stirred the grits while Tabby chopped onions, celery, and peppers.

"Mother, would you help me take the coffee into Evan's study? I think they're all in there discussing some investments they've been talking about for months."

Erin's ears perked up. For just an instant she wanted to leave the kitchen and join them. No, better to leave it alone. It was probably better all around if they didn't know about her avocation, even if she had made herself and Captain Rick a bunch of money. If she had to explain, then everyone was bound to find out about her reading disability.

"You should tell them," Tabby said quietly.

Erin dropped the spoon back into the grits with a plop. "How do you do that?"

Tabby shrugged. "Sorry, but your expression's been a dead giveaway ever since Jenny mentioned the recipe. Besides that, you were mumbling to yourself too."

Erin spun on Tabby with her fists braced on her hips. "Just how much have I managed to share with you while I've been talking to myself?"

Tabby glanced toward the door and back at Erin before she began quietly. "You can't read well enough to decipher a recipe… That's okay. I'll walk you through it, and you're a wizard with money. Who's Captain Rick? You mentioned him while you were mumbling."

"*Shit!* You know you are really annoying, Tabby. If I had to have a little sister, couldn't it have been someone who didn't have ears like a bat and look as perfect as a cover model? And to make it even worse, you're nice. Just swear you won't tell them."

"Tell them what?" Stoner stood in the doorway watching them.

If Erin's face looked half as guilty as Tabby's, they were cooked. She stared at her younger sister and Tabby stared right back, her golden eyes narrowing.

Erin blew out her breath on a heavy sigh. "Oh damn it, all right. It's just now is not the time. I-I'll tell everyone after breakfast."

Stoner walked farther into the room. He stopped by the cream and sugar, and turned back to Erin, his expression a mixture of curiosity and concern.

Erin felt his uncertainty.

"Are you all right, honey?" he ventured.

Erin grimaced at the cautious way he asked the question, as if he expected her to bite his head off. And she guessed in the past that would have been exactly her reaction. "Yes, Daddy."

"If it's Sam…" he began, his tone growing thunderous.

"If it's Sam, what?" the man in question drawled challengingly from the doorway.

Tabby and Erin both watched, jaws agape as Stoner and Sam glared at one another like male lions getting ready to challenge for dominance.

"Just how long does it take to get…" Evan paused in mid-sentence, "cream and sugar." He stared at the other two men with narrowed, gray eyes. "What's going on?"

Erin was completely exasperated. She rolled her eyes and stared at Tabby. "You might as well call everyone in here. There will be no peace until this is out in the open." She spun around to work on the cream sauce and realized she'd sent out the person who was supposed to read the recipe to her. With her patience at an end, she turned and glared at Sam.

"Come over here and read this recipe to me while I add everything in." It never occurred to her to question the fact that he did so without any comment or remark. A couple of minutes passed as she added the ingredients and adjusted the heat according to his instructions. By the time they were done, everyone was in the kitchen either seated or standing.

As Erin started to turn, Sam muttered under his breath. "You don't have to do this. You don't have to tell them."

Her eyes widened as she stared at him. "You know?"

He swallowed and nodded.

Laura Browning

So many questions popped into her head, but in the end all she finally managed to whisper was, "How long?"

He flushed. "Since a couple of days after you moved in."

"How?"

"Your computer set up."

He'd snooped in her room? Before Erin could demand to know what he'd been doing, Sam hastened to explain. "You'd left it on that night you pulled the calves. I went in to shut everything down. That's how I figured it out. I didn't say anything. I guess I hoped you would tell me."

Erin studied his expression. She didn't see pity or any of the other things she always feared she would see. Sam looked at her in just the same way he always had. Her throat tightened with emotion. She had always been so afraid of others finding out. When she turned around to face everyone else, Erin reached behind her and found his strong, callused hand. He squeezed hers reassuringly.

"Erin?" Stoner prompted. "What is it Tabby and Sam seem to know that the rest of us don't?"

She swallowed but felt Sam's hands settle reassuringly on her shoulders, giving her confidence to admit what she'd always dreaded putting into words. "I can't read… And I can barely write."

Catherine reached for Stoner's hand and he grasped it. "Is this a joke, honey?" her mother asked faintly. "You attended college. How could you not be able to read or write?"

"I—I found ways to cope." She spread her hands and grinned uneasily. "I'm good in math, so I would trade favors with other kids. You know, do their math work if they would write papers for me." Her chin rose defensively. "I am also an accomplished cheat, and even paid some students to take exams for me."

Stoner looked thunderous; Catherine looked appalled. As Erin looked at Evan, she realized Jenny must have dropped some hints, because he looked the least shocked.

"How… How could this happen?" Stoner finally asked.

Erin closed her eyes for a minute. "Oh believe me, a lot easier than you might think. It wasn't any one thing. Your political career bounced me around to a lot of different schools, and I managed to stay in trouble enough that I got bounced around from teacher to teacher and nanny to nanny. You were both busy between campaigns and other social engagements. By the time it started to become a major issue, Evan was all wrapped up in being a teenager, and I was so ashamed I didn't get the whole reading thing that I got better and better at hiding it."

"There are literacy programs…" her mother began, but Erin cut her off.

"It's not that simple. It was never just a matter that I didn't learn, or that I was lazy." She paused and frowned as she remembered how many times she'd heard that. It was so much easier to blame it on her than take the time to properly assess and identify her problem. "I'm profoundly dyslexic. Sam's seen it. I-I can barely even read the Sunday comics, for God's sake."

"But you send us e-mail and read ours," Catherine continued, still puzzled.

Erin bit her lip. "My roommate in college helped me. In return, I helped her ace her statistics course. Then, if you'll recall, I didn't contact you much until just a few months ago, when I began working on the *Sprite*. Rick figured out what was going on. He helped me get a voice recognition program that reads everything to me, and I can talk to it, so it will write for me as well."

"Rick?" Evan questioned. "The guy…"

Erin flushed. "Yes."

Catherine was still shaking her head as if she couldn't take it all in, but Stoner stood. Haltingly, he approached her. His gaze slithered from Sam's glowering expression, to Erin's shuttered one. "Forgive us, Erin. Forgive *me* for being too busy, for not noticing." He stretched his hand out. "I remember how happy you were as a little girl. You were so excited when you started school, but then as the years passed that changed. I guess it was just easier to think it was the normal disenchantment most kids develop for school, but it wasn't, and we didn't see."

Erin ducked her head. "I should have told you."

Stoner shook his head and sliced his hand through the air. "No. You were a child, for God's sake. One of us, any of us who were around you—Catherine and me, your nannies, your teachers—someone should have noticed, should have done something."

His hand trembled as he touched her cheek with his fingers. "I'm so sorry, honey."

Erin leaned into his gentle touch for just a moment, but then grasped his hand and held it away from her face. "Don't, Daddy. Don't pity me. I've found ways to get along. I do okay."

Stoner frowned. "As a cook? As farm help for Sam?"

Erin's gaze shifted. She didn't want to talk about the rest of it. It was a lot easier for them to continue thinking of her as a screw up than it was to go into the explanation of how and how much of a success she had managed to become. Her biggest fear, if she ever shared it, was seeing the looks of disbelief they would no doubt have on their faces. Cooking was much safer. "Yeah. Speaking of which, my cream sauce needs stirring. If everyone will set the table, we're almost ready to eat."

"Erin…" Stoner frowned.

"Later," Sam said.

The two stared at each other for a moment; then Stoner nodded. Erin turned her attention back to the sauce. After turning off the burner, she transferred it to a serving bowl. Sam and Stoner still hovered, so she glared at them.

"Shoo! Get out of my way and let me finish." She was back in her element. "Tabby, if you'll take the dishes out of the upper oven, I'll get the biscuits and the casserole."

Even as she tossed out orders, Erin was scraping the grits into another large serving bowl and putting the pot in the sink to soak. Jenny placed the bowls with the shrimp and grits on the table, which Evan and Joe were setting while Catherine took drink orders from everyone.

Erin smiled as she bent to retrieve the casserole and the biscuits. The noises of home. For this moment at least, she felt she belonged here. In this, at least, she could make a valuable contribution.

"Here, I'll take that for you," Sam said quietly from her side. Erin looked at him and smiled.

"Thanks, Sammy."

He looked uncomfortable. "It's just a casserole dish," he muttered, deliberately misunderstanding her.

Erin punched him in the arm. "Don't be dense. You know I mean more than that."

Sam glanced over his shoulder before he gently rubbed the back of his hand over her cheek. "I know."

Erin's breath caught at the look on his face. Was she reading too much into what she saw there? Because to her it looked like a whole lot more than a you're-so-hot look.

"I think we're ready," Jenny said, interrupting her thoughts. "Ev, have Melodie bring Peter in, and Joseph can say the blessing."

The meal was filled with chatter. Sam and Stoner began discussing the calving season, while Evan and Joseph talked basketball. To Erin's right, Catherine helped Melodie with her plate and kept one eye on Peter who sat in his high chair gurgling and playing with toys that he inevitably carried straight to his mouth. Tabby and Jenny discussed how Holly was doing carrying her twins.

"You should talk to Rachel Hastings," Catherine said to Erin out of the blue. "I don't know why I didn't think of it sooner."

Erin tilted her head. Where had she heard that name before? Hastings. "The kid at the computer store mentioned her when I bought the reading software."

Catherine brightened. "So you're working on it?"

Erin nodded. "I—I have a voice recognition program embedded in the computer, but I practice with the reading program."

"Is it helping?"

Erin shrugged. "Sometimes I think so. Then there are some days the words just seem to jumble in front of me."

"You *should* talk to Rachel," Tabby said. "I met her last fall before I quit teaching. She teaches Freshman English and a reading intervention class. She's a certified reading specialist, and I know she did her dissertation on dyslexia intervention strategies. Besides that, you'd like her." Tabby's grin turned mischievous. "She's tiny, just like you and Jenny."

"So speaks the Amazon woman." Jenny laughed.

"Are you talking about Rachel Crawley?" Sam asked from the other end of the table.

Catherine nodded. "Yes, I believe that was her maiden name. Do you know her?"

Sam chuckled. "Not that well. She was a freshman in high school when I was a senior. A real nerd—two years ahead of herself and complete with coke bottle glasses. It always seemed like Luke—Jake's older brother— had to run interference for her."

Erin gaped at them all. "You want me, the class idiot, to hook up with a freaking genius? Oh yeah, that will make me comfortable."

Tabby frowned. "Rachel's not at all like that. And she could help you, Erin."

"I wish I'd known," Joseph commented. "She was in church this morning."

"Oh I hate I missed her," Tabby remarked. "That would have been perfect."

"That was always part of the problem, as I recall," Sam said. "Rachel was easy to overlook, except for those eyes of hers. Purple as pansies. Luke Allred sure noticed 'em."

"Not enough to stick around," Evan commented.

Sam shrugged. "Things change. Jake says Luke's veterinary practice is very successful. We were really close up until he got married. Then we kind of lost touch. You know how it is. You get busy. Life happens."

As the conversation drifted back again to finances, Erin absently munched on her food and listened. The conversation turned toward a prominent pharmaceutical company, and her interest perked up.

"I wouldn't invest in that company right now," Erin interjected after a few minutes. Four pairs of male eyes turned to stare at her. Erin grinned. "Their flagship drug is about to go generic, so you can expect them to take a big hit in the market in the next couple of weeks. Of course, you could wait for their stock price to bottom out, then buy. They're expected to make an announcement within two months of a breakthrough on a new drug to substantially reduce the length and severity of common cold symptoms. At that point, I would expect their stock to double and split at the very least. So if you'll be patient enough to wait for the price to tank, you could see an enormous ROI down the road."

Her father stared at her as if she had suddenly grown a second head. "How do you know all this?"

Erin set her silverware down and looked at her father. Sucking in a deep breath, she realized she might as well get it all out. "It's what I do when I'm not cooking, pulling calves, or shoveling sh…" Her glance landed on Melodie's interested expression. "…poop."

Sam coughed. "Actually, you listen to the financial news on the radio while you cook and clean stalls like most people listen to music."

Erin grinned. "You're right. Habit, I guess. Look, Daddy. I might not be able to read, but I can listen. So I do, and now that I have the voice software on my laptop, I read that way. Captain Rick urged me to get the computer set up after I gave him a couple of tips, then turned his portfolio over to me to manage along with mine."

"You have a portfolio?" her father inquired in a stunned tone.

"And how has that worked out?" Evan asked curiously.

Erin shrugged. "I do okay," she mumbled.

Everyone stared at her. For several seconds, the only sound in the kitchen was Peter chattering to himself.

"Dare I ask how okay?" Stoner ventured.

"Daddy!" Erin flushed. When everyone continued to stare, she shifted. "I tripled Rick's portfolio in six months. It's worth about one point five million right now."

"Holy sh…Toledo," Stoner finished with a glance at his granddaughter. "And you?"

"Mine's worth more than that," Erin admitted. Maybe this was something that should make her feel special, but Erin wasn't at all comfortable standing out in a positive way. That came with expectations, and she had a long history of failing to meet anyone's expectations.

Stoner's silverware clattered. "You're a millionaire?"

"On paper," Erin protested.

"Will you take on more clients? Like all of us?" Evan asked quietly into the silence.

Everyone was watching her and nodding. Erin gulped. It was one thing to play with her own money. She had made extremely high-risk decisions that could have left her broke. Rick too, though she had been more conservative with him. The thought of handling her family's investments made her quake. It was a game, not something serious. No expectations and no pressure.

"I…I…" Erin jumped up from the table and fled. She had gone from being an idiot freak right to the other end of the spectrum and didn't know how to handle it.

* * * *

Sam threw down his napkin in disgust. "Now look what you've done!"

"Me?" Evan snapped. "All I wanted to know was if she'd look at our portfolios."

Tabby set her silverware down. "Sam's right. We all need to back off. Look, she's confused and upset right now."

Evan arched one brow. "And that would be different, how?"

"Evan!" Jenny said. Sam had already come halfway out of his chair. He was sick and tired of Erin being the Richardson family joke.

"Oh all right. I'm sorry," Evan said.

"Maybe you should try saying that to her some time," Sam suggested, his tone nearly as cold as he felt.

"You just don't understand how much she left out of what she told you," Tabby said.

Sam thought back to the little nine-year-old who had tagged along behind him wanting so desperately to please, and of the luscious teenager who'd thrown herself at him. Even then she'd been crying out for help, but no one had listened. No one had bothered to look beneath what they saw on the surface: a teenager hell-bent on making life miserable for everyone within range.

He stood. "I'm going to find her."

"Sam," Stoner started to protest but abruptly halted when Sam glared at him.

"Of all the fools in this room right now, Stoner, you and I are the biggest." He stomped out of the kitchen and down the hall. Sam found

Erin curled on a loveseat in the living room, staring out the front window. She turned her head when he stepped into the room.

"Is it time to go?"

Sam sat next to her and leaned forward, resting his elbows on his knees as he raked his hands back through his hair. He studied her from the corner of his eye. She hadn't cried, but then he had only ever seen her do that one time. So much miscommunication had transpired among all of them he hardly knew where to start. And he was so afraid he might screw things up beyond repair.

"You kind of threw everyone for a loop, squirt."

Erin snorted and turned back to staring out the window. "And you weren't?"

Sam chuckled. "Well maybe by the fact that I've been making love to a multi-millionaire, but I've gotten used to your ping-pong personality. It keeps me on my toes."

He saw her mouth twitch. "Are you trying to say I have mood swings, Sheriff?"

"No. I don't believe there was any try in that. I believe it was quite clear." He leaned back and waggled his eyebrows. "Nobody will dare to come in here for a few minutes. Wanna take advantage of me?"

Erin's eyes widened, and she laughed. "You are so bad. What's even worse is everyone thinks you're such a paragon of virtue and sober morality."

As soon as she relaxed, Sam snatched her across his lap and started running his hand up her thigh under her skirt. His hot gaze lingered on her lush lips and the fragile column of her throat. "We know better, though, don't we?"

His hand glided to her inner thigh until his searching fingers were less than an inch from where he wanted to be.

"Sam," she breathed. "We can't. Not here."

Reluctantly he removed his hand from under her skirt and smoothed it back down. "A few kisses. We can do that."

He nibbled at her lips and wrapped one arm around her shoulders. With his free hand, he cupped her jaw and held her still so he could plunder her mouth. When they were both breathing just a little hard, Sam leaned his forehead against Erin's.

"Take pity on them, squirt. First you show up in church with me, dressed like you're ready for tea at the country club. Then you slap them with the double whammy of your dyslexia and your financial genius. Their brains are still bouncing with aftershocks."

Erin giggled, then pulled away to search his face. "And you, Sammy?"

He smiled at her tenderly. "You're still an annoying little squirt, baby."

She touched his face. "Come on, Sam. You know what I mean. The reading, the money. Does it make a difference?"

"Erin, I'd already figured out you had a reading issue, so no. As far as the finances? I'd be pretty darn foolish to be anything other than ecstatic." He paused and grinned at her. "And if you don't want to work for me, you don't have to."

"I like it," Erin admitted. "I wasn't sure at first, and I almost just wrote you a check to pay for everything, but it's been wonderful."

"All of it?" he asked with an arch of his brow.

She blushed and he laughed.

"Miss Richardson, I was talking about delivering baby cows. What were you thinking of?"

She stroked his cheek and stared into his dark eyes. "Oh, Sammy, you're good for me. You haven't asked what I'm worth. Don't you want to know?"

Sam shrugged. "You'll tell me when you're ready. In the meantime, as you would say, I do okay."

She held his dark gaze. "I love you."

He swallowed, humbled by the simple honesty of her admission. Sam pulled her tight against his chest. "I know you do, baby. I know you do." But he was frowning again. Say it! Just say it. But he couldn't make the words come out. Couldn't take the step he knew would tie him to her…a woman more than a decade younger than him. The bottom line was he feared he would be tying her down just when she was learning how to stretch her wings.

Chapter 8

"Are you ready to face everybody again, squirt?"

Erin fluffed her fingers through her short hair and sighed. "I guess. I'm just so tired of being a freak, Sam. Do you know I think you're the only one who's ever looked at me as just Erin?" She bit her lip as she stared into his eyes. "I wish..."

"What do you wish, baby?" he prompted quietly.

"I was going to say I wish I'd been older when we first met, that I hadn't been such a kid."

He cradled her cheek in his palm. "We could sit here and work through a whole truckload of might-have-beens, but we are who we are because of everything we've gone through just the way we are. I could wish I'd never been sidelined from my football career, but then I might never have been around here to meet you."

She leaned her head against his shoulder. Feeling her there, so trusting, made him feel like he could do anything. She made him better than he was.

"Let's go finish the meal. Then I'm going to show them what it is I do."

"That's my girl." He patted her butt and winked at her, loving her just as she was. His Erin.

Less than an hour later, Sam sat back in Evan's study, one shoulder propped against the wall as he watched. Erin sat on the couch with Evan and Stoner on either side of her as she breezed through her explanation, looking happy and confident like none of them had ever seen her look. The defiance and anger they all associated with her were missing because she was finally in her element. He wondered if she fully realized it.

"It's a matter of weighing certain risk factors against a list of qualities that all successful companies have in common. Then I apply a formula I developed to predict timing, partially based on widespread investor interest which can balloon a company's worth..."

"Whoa!" Evan said with a laugh that sounded vaguely overwhelmed and made Sam want to howl with laughter. After spending so many years feeling like she was their intellectual inferior, it was clear her father and brother were scrambling to keep up with her. "Can you show me?"

She looked doubtful. "Well, if you can work the computer for me. It will take me too long without the voice software."

Sam watched her in wonder. As she talked about money and investing, her eyes lit with an interest he had never seen her show in anything before, except maybe this past week in helping him with the calving, and she thought she was *stupid*? It appeared to him that the tiniest of the Richardsons might be the most singularly gifted of them all.

Evan sat at the computer, and Erin talked him into her investment account. When her brother and Stoner saw the amount of money in it and the percent increase in the last quarter, their jaws gaped.

"Good God, Erin! Can you do this with my money? With Daddy's or Sam's?"

She looked a little dumbfounded. "Well yeah, I guess. It's not hard. It's a question of the amount of risk you want to assume. I mean, I do some pretty risky investments because I still have lots of time to recoup if I blow a hunch, but Daddy might not want that same level of risk."

Stoner chuckled. "Because I'm old?"

Erin blushed. "You know what I mean…."

He squeezed her shoulder. "Yes, honey, I do. I have a lot of my funds in fairly stable investments, and those I won't gamble with. But I do have a higher risk portfolio I play with, and I'd be happy to put that in your hands, especially seeing what you've done with your money."

She flushed with pleasure, and Sam sucked in a breath. A line of praise from her father. Such a simple thing was all it took to give her pleasure. "Thanks, Daddy. You have no idea what that means to me."

Stoner looked over at Sam. "Sheriff, maybe you should let her handle your finances too."

Sam smiled slowly as he caught Erin's eye. "We'll see."

* * * *

Erin and Sam had finished the morning feeding and mucking out. There were just a few cows that had not yet dropped their calves, but to Sam's practiced eye, none of it was going to happen today. As they walked back toward the house, Sam tossed an arm companionably around Erin's shoulders.

"I've been thinkin' about what Tabby said about Rachel Crawley…I mean Hastings…you remember, the English teacher over at the high school, her being a reading specialist. I thought I might give her a call if you'd be interested in working with her."

He waited, a little uncertain as he felt Erin's shoulders go rigid, but then she relaxed. "I'd like that, Sam. You know I'll always be dyslexic. It's not something that goes away, but I've heard about some things people can do to help."

"You want to talk to her?"

"Yeah. If I could even learn to read well enough to read stories to Melodie or Peter...."

Sam scowled as he felt his throat tighten. He had a sudden vision of her sitting with a dark-haired, dark-eyed little boy on her lap while she read him a story. Not only did he like the picture, but it made the difficulties she'd faced her entire life all too real. It was nearly impossible for him to imagine not being able to pick up a book and read a story to a child.

"Come on, baby," he murmured, his voice husky, "let's get some breakfast, then play for a little while."

She grinned at him. "In the tub? I like that."

Sam growled. Breakfast could wait. He grabbed her once they hit the mudroom. After they stripped off their coveralls and boots, Sam carried her into his bathroom.

"I thought we were getting breakfast?"

"Later. I'm hungry for you right now." He set her butt on the counter next to the sink and ran his palms from her hips, up her arms, and on to the straps of her bra. As he followed the lace with his fingertips, she sucked in air. He brushed across the swell of her breasts until his fingers met between the twin globes. Her soft skin trembled at his touch.

"Sam." It was just a whisper of sound, but it made him shiver with anticipation.

Her beautiful eyes had gone dark with passion, her mouth full and pouting. Just looking at her, touching her, made him swell to an aching, tumescent fullness. Her fingers hooked into the waistband of his boxer shorts and tugged them down, springing his erection free.

"See what you do to me? I spend half the day in pain, wanting you. Can you tell me what the heck I'm going to do when I have to go back to work next week?"

She laughed, a low sultry sound that made his cock twitch. "I could stop by at lunchtime and we could eat together in your office."

Instantly, he pictured locking the door of his office, setting her on his desk, and sliding his hands under that micro-mini leather skirt she'd had on last fall.

"Have mercy on me, Erin. I don't think I can wait for the bathtub to fill." He pushed her panties aside with his fingers, and when he felt how wet she already was for him, he lifted her hips and plunged inside of her, his hips rocking back and forth.

Erin clutched him with her fingers and her femininity, her cries muffled because she had her mouth buried against his chest. Would it always be like this? Would he always be able to make Erin glow and her whole body vibrate with the need he saw in her expression? Heaven help him, he hoped so. When his fingers slid between them to caress her, she arched back and cried out.

"That's it, baby," Sam coaxed hoarsely. "Come for me."

Erin shattered. She was so limp in his arms he knew she couldn't move on her own. Sam picked her up and took them both to the oversize tub and sat in it. As the water splashed around them and onto the floor, they both laughed. Erin traced her fingers down his stubbled cheek. Sam grinned at her.

She'd changed him since she'd first arrived in Mountain Meadow. He laughed and smiled much more often, like he had when he'd first met her so many years ago.

"I love you, Sam." She leaned back against him, smiling in enjoyment as his hands moved over her slick, wet body. She didn't seem to want or need a response from him, one that Sam was still unable to voice, though he felt it. He loved her to the soles of his feet, but just couldn't find the words—or the nerve—to tell her.

He could show her. And he would, every day in every way until he could tell her. Sam knew what caused his hesitation. Neither of his parents had been demonstrative. It simply wasn't their way. So Sam had never learned to be comfortable with putting his emotions into words. But he wanted too. Soon.

* * * *

They agreed to meet Rachel Hastings at the library that afternoon. The whole way in to town, Sam went over the importance of her staying inside the library, of being aware of who was around her. By the time they pulled into the parking lot, Erin's palms were sweating. She wiped them on her thighs and chewed on her lower lip. Smart people had always intimidated her, but to hear Sam and Evan talk, Rachel Hastings was beyond smart. She had skipped ahead grades and graduated from college early. Erin had dropped out. What could she possibly have in common with someone like that?

Sure, everyone kept reassuring her how great Rachel was. She sounded like the embodiment of everything wondrous and helpful, and that just made Erin's case of nervousness that much worse.

As they got out of Sam's truck, Betty Gatewood stepped up to Sam with a frown on her pug-like face.

"The town Facebook page says you got her living with you, Sam Barnes. What are you thinking, taking someone like that underneath your roof? Just because she's a Richardson doesn't mean she's any better than anyone else. Your mama would roll over in her grave if she knew. And I already warned *her*. Lot of good it did."

Sam's expression was tight. "What I choose to do in my personal life is just that, Mrs. Gatewood—personal. I believe I'm old enough to make my own choices and have been for some time. Erin is also a responsible, intelligent woman fully capable of making her own decisions. If you'll excuse us? You have a nice day."

His grip when he took Erin's arm was just a little stiff. She glanced at the woman who pursed her lips disapprovingly before stomping off to her mid-size sedan. Erin had noticed the looks yesterday at church. As they strode toward the building, her legs pumping to keep up with Sam's longer strides, she glanced over her shoulder.

"Sam…"

"Betty Gatewood is the nosiest old gossip in the whole town."

Erin tugged her arm from Sam's grip. "Sam! I know we talked about it before, but tell me the truth. Is having me at your house going to hurt your reputation? People are posting things on Facebook about us. I mean, you're an elected official…."

He halted, turning his nearly black gaze on her. His dark eyes snapped angrily. "You think I care about that? You're at my house for your safety, Erin. The Betty Gatewoods of this world do not matter."

Ouch. For her safety. Not "because I want you there" or "because I love you."

She ducked her head and nodded, hiding her gaze from him. How many times would she tell him she loved him and get no response in return? Erin swallowed. It was familiar territory. She'd walked it as a teenager. He had kept pushing her away then too.

When Sam took her elbow again to guide her inside the library, Erin resisted the urge to shake him off. The feeling of inadequacy that had faded in recent days came roaring back as loud as a Harley at a church service.

A few people inside were looking for books or using the computers. Sam guided her past them to a table in the back corner of the library. As they approached, a slender, almost boyishly-figured woman stood. She wasn't any taller than Erin, but standing next to her, Erin felt like a cow. This was absolutely not going to work. The woman already intimidated her. She looked like a brain and was built like an elf.

"Hi, Erin. I'm Rachel." Her voice flowed like warm syrup over hot pancakes. The elf stuck her hand out.

Erin took it and reluctantly met her gaze. Why her eyes *were* just like pansies, just like everyone had said. But it was more than that. As soon as Erin looked into Rachel's eyes, she felt warm and welcomed.

"Hi." She smiled.

"I'll leave you to it," Sam rumbled from the stratosphere above them. "I want to check in at the department. I'll be back in an hour. Will that be okay?"

"That will be enough for today." Rachel nodded and took Erin's hand. "Sit down. Let's get started."

Sam weaved his way out of the library, and Erin felt an almost overpowering urge to run after him. Her gaze shifted along the racks upon racks of books. She couldn't remember the last time she had willingly stepped inside a library. Seeing thousands of books that were largely hieroglyphics to her was more than intimidating, it was terrifying.

"Erin?"

She swallowed and jerked her head back to Rachel who was already sitting. Her smile, just a tilting of her lips, soothed some of Erin's nerves. How did such a tiny, delicate-looking woman handle a room full of rambunctious teens?

"Sit down, honey. Let's just talk for a few minutes."

Talk. She could do that. Erin sat, tried to smile but felt it came across as just a grimace.

"Sam tells me you've been a huge help to him during calving season, and that you even pulled a calf on your own." Rachel's pansy purple eyes were bright with interest. It helped Erin relax just a little

"Yes. I found out how to do it on the Internet."

Rachel smiled. "That's what Sam said. He said you've got your laptop set up so it talks to you and you can talk to it. That's a great coping strategy for a person with dyslexia. So you've already learned one of the most important points for being successful in a world that relies on the written word."

Erin laughed without any amusement. "Yeah. I wish they'd had that while I was trying to go through school."

Rachel nodded. "Well, the technology is out there now. You know, Erin, you're not at all alone. Conservative estimates put the number of people with dyslexia in our country between five and seven percent. Some experts say the reality could be a whole lot higher, maybe even as high as twenty percent. So many people develop their own coping mechanisms, or are just never diagnosed, that the higher figure could easily be more accurate. It doesn't mean you're stupid, slow, or lazy. It simply means your brain is wired differently."

Erin snorted. "Well I've always felt different."

Rachel's dark eyes softened. "We'll work on some things to help change that, give you some more coping skills for when you don't have access to your laptop."

Erin felt a faint stirring of hope, but she had struggled for so long. "Can you still teach me to read, even though I'm an adult?"

Rachel covered Erin's nervously tapping fingers.

"The good news is intensive intervention works with children and adults. Plenty of research backs that up. You may never be the world's fastest, most fluent reader, but I can help you become more competent and confident. The other thing you need to accept is that there are many more definitions now of what it means to be literate. It's more than being able to read. You are literate through the use of technology and text to voice programs. We're going to work on strategies to help you with the old-fashioned kind of literacy now."

Erin blinked, nearly overcome at the idea of being able to read, even if it was just well enough to complete a job application or read the Sunday comics without agonizing.

"I'll work really hard."

Rachel smiled again at her. "I know you will. I have plenty of students at the high school who are there because they have to be. Sometimes they're a challenge to motivate. But the students who come to me because they want to? That's a huge leap ahead already. It's one of the reasons I volunteer my time outside of school."

"You like what you do, don't you?" Erin gazed at her with wonder. It was difficult to imagine actually enjoying teaching, especially when it involved reading and writing.

Rachel laughed. "Most of the time. Now, let me show you some text...."

* * * *

Sam returned to the library just under an hour later. As he approached the building, he scanned the area out of habit. Absolutely nothing out of the ordinary. Maybe her coming back home had been enough. They hadn't heard anything more from her friends either. Maybe it was time to relax a bit.

When he walked inside, he immediately spotted Erin and Rachel. They sat next to each other, their heads bent over material Erin had in front of her. He could see the concentration on Erin's face in the way her brow was furrowed. She spoke quietly to Rachel. As she finished, Rachel said something to her, and a quick flush of pleasure brightened Erin's face.

Something twisted inside him at that moment, seeing not only the satisfaction but the sense of accomplishment in her expression. Sam stopped, afraid for a moment that he might weep for the pain it was now obvious she'd suffered her entire life, believing she was stupid, that she couldn't do what seemed to come so easily to others. And somehow everyone had missed that, not just her parents, but everyone. Her whole life she'd been crying out for help, unable or too embarrassed to put it into words.

Like him. Unable to tell her just how much he adored her.

He saw the determination on her face and knew what he'd only partially acknowledged before. Erin Richardson was beautiful, intelligent, determined, and unconquerable—and he loved her as he had never loved another human being in his life.

As if she somehow sensed his presence, Erin caught his eye and beamed at him. Her gaze was so bright, and her face so alight with joy, he laughed from sheer happiness. As the deep sound rumbled out in the quiet library, several folks looked up disapprovingly. Seeing it was him, their eyes widened in surprise.

But he ignored them, weaving his way back through the tables to the one where Erin sat with Rachel.

"How's it going?" He could see, but he wanted to hear it.

Rachel smiled. "She's doing beautifully."

Sam looked at what they were working on. It appeared to him to be simply letters and blends of letters, not actual words. He looked quizzically at Rachel. "Can I help with this on the days you don't meet with her?"

"Sure. We're working on training her brain to associate the sounds she knows with all the possible spellings of that sound. For example, the sound 'shun' at the end of a word can be spelled t-i-o-n, s-i-o-n, or c-i-o-n. Since many dyslexics don't automatically translate the sounds in language to spelling or reading a word, I'm trying to tap into another part of her brain. It's a little like rewiring a car or an appliance."

Erin laughed. "Yeah, now I'm a toaster."

Rachel laughed softly, a rich almost sultry sound. Sam truly looked at her, realizing she was far prettier than they had thought in high school with her delicate frame and her large doe eyes. Too bad Luke had moved away before he had the chance to see her transformation. Maybe it would have kept him around here. Sam missed the friendship they'd shared. Occasional phone calls just didn't do it.

He turned back to Erin. "You ready, baby? It'll be dark soon, and we need to get back so we can feed and bed everyone down for the night."

Erin impulsively hugged Rachel. "Thank you."

Rachel blushed as she smiled. "There is nothing more rewarding for a teacher than to see a student make progress. I'll give you some material to work on, and let's meet again day after tomorrow, okay?"

"Yes."

Sam helped Erin on with her jacket and guided her out to the truck. As he opened the door for her, he waited for her to climb onto the seat before he stepped in and kissed her lingeringly.

"What's that for?" Erin's expression was bemused.

"Just because, baby, just because." As he walked around the truck, Sam decided he would take her out to dinner the next evening. Someplace special where he could finally tell her how he felt. He blew out a breath, still nervous at the idea.

* * * *

Erin yawned as she stepped inside the back door. Who'd have thought just working on learning letters and sounds would be so exhausting. "Sam, I'll go ahead and start dinner," she said. "Do you need help with the barn?"

He shook his dark head as he pulled his coverall on over his jeans and flannel shirt. "No. You go ahead. I'm starved."

She grinned at him. "I'll make it something quick and simple. How about steak and salad?"

He caught her chin in his hand and brushed a kiss across her lips. "Sounds great. I'll be back in just a few minutes."

She heard the door shut followed by the slam of the screen porch door. Erin pulled the steaks from the fridge, whistling as she began working. She was on a real emotional high. Sam seemed different, more attentive, and he'd stuck by her to begin with; then there was her session with Rachel. That had gone so much better than she could have imagined.

Even better, Rachel was a fascinating lady. She'd recently left her husband and purchased a small farm she was in the process of fixing up. It was the old Crawley place, and Rachel had been able to buy it only because she had family ties. If Erin remembered correctly, old man

Crawley had hung on to the place for years, unwilling to sell it, but also unwilling to fix it up in any way. Go figure. What a waste of an asset. At any rate, Rachel had bought it, moved in, and was rehabilitating animals.

Now there was a woman she could admire—someone who was independent along with being super intelligent. Erin grinned. She really hoped they'd be friends. She hadn't stopped long enough to have many friends, especially other women, but she thought someone like Rachel would be perfect.

As she washed the produce in the kitchen sink, Erin's eyes drifted to her reflection in the window. Darkness lay beyond, but for just a second, she could have sworn she saw a flash of something. That was silly. There was nothing in that direction but pasture and the woods off in the distance. Probably just her imagination. Still, it gave her a bit of a chill and reminded her just how isolated Sam's farm was.

At least at Richardson Homestead there were servants in the house and the farm manager not too far away, but here, acres of pasture, woods, and hills separated them from the lights of her parents' home. The nearest thing besides that was a couple of double-wides on the opposite side of the highway, but even those were a half mile away.

She swallowed, sudden uneasiness creeping along her spine. It was a little too spooky for someone who'd always been firmly grounded in reality. The whole woo-woo thing was more along Tabby's line, what with her artist's imagination and all. When Erin finally heard the slam of the screen door and the familiar tromp of Sam's feet in the mudroom, she sagged against the counter with relief. He entered the kitchen on stocking feet, and she ran over to him and wrapped her arms around him.

"Hey!" He pulled her close. "What's this? You look like you've seen a ghost, squirt."

Erin shook her head and buried her face against his chest. When Sam's arms tightened around her, she relaxed against him.

"What's up, Erin?" Sam's tone turned serious, concern edging his voice.

She shook herself and sighed. "I don't know. I got weirded out there for a minute. It's nothing, Sam. I guess it's just the excitement today. I mean, I'm not high strung, but I kind of lost it. I'm sorry."

He ducked his head to her level and grinned. "Well anything that lands you in my arms is fine by me."

He cupped her butt and drew her into him. Erin wrapped her arms around his neck and tilted her face for his kiss. She loved the feel of him against her, the roughness of his jeans and the scratchy softness of the wool flannel shirt. When his tongue teased her mouth open, then plundered inside, she moaned against him and pressed her breasts into him.

"Sweet heaven," Sam groaned. "How long until dinner's ready?"

"The salad's in the fridge. I was just getting ready to put the steaks on."

He lifted her and urged her legs around his waist. "Hold off on them. I've got the biggest hard-on. Sure hate to waste it."

Erin giggled. "Do you want to take care of it here or someplace more comfortable?"

"I might be able to make it as far as the couch, but that's about it."

He carried her through the doorway into the family room before letting her feet slide to the floor. In seconds, they had stripped off their clothes. Erin's eyes widened as she saw the way his cock stood flush with his muscled stomach.

When he caught the direction of her gaze, he said. "I told you."

Gently he pushed her down to the couch before going to his knees next to it. Slowly, despite his previous impatience, he began to kiss and caress her, his lips and tongue sliding from her mouth along the column of her throat to her breasts. While he kneaded her with one hand, he drew the nipple of her other breast into his mouth and suckled. Erin stared at his dark head, watching his lips on her. It was such an incredible turn on. The heat between her legs became unbearable.

"Touch me, Sam. I need to feel you."

His fingers found her, teasing her until his mouth could join them. Twisting her hips, he threw her legs over his broad shoulders and cupped her bottom in his hands so he could bring the wet, swollen heat of her to his seeking lips. Erin arched and whimpered as his tongue laved her. He drew her sensitive nub into his mouth at the same time his fingers thrust inside her, and it sent her over the edge.

"Sam!" she writhed against him, wanting him closer and at the same time needing a respite to catch her breath. "Let me touch you."

He rose to his knees next to her, and she drew him into her mouth. As she caressed him with her hands and lips, Sam groaned.

"Yes, baby. Oh yes." His big hands caressed her head and shoulders, and Erin felt the fine tremble that shivered through his big body. "Gotta be inside you."

He sat her up and drew her hips forward until he could guide the tip of his erection to her opening. Erin watched him, her breath panting through kiss-swollen lips.

"Wrap your legs around me," he growled.

When she did, Sam held her with one arm and braced the other on the back of the couch as he thrust forcefully. Her heart pounded and heat swept through her as her climax built. She clung to him for dear life as they both hurtled over the top. They fell back against the couch cushions, panting and laughing.

"Sweet, Erin. Some things just get better and better," Sam rumbled. "Wanna shower together? Then I'll set the table while you sear the steaks."

She smiled. "If you'll carry me, it's a deal. I don't think my legs will support me."

Chapter 9

The buzz intruded into her sleep. Erin reached over to the nightstand and began to blindly slap the alarm clock until it quit making noise.

"Don't kill it," Sam mumbled. "Just tranquilize it."

"Snooze."

"Mmm."

He pulled her back against his broad chest and curled around her. Snuggling against him, Erin smiled sleepily. She loved the way he felt when he cuddled close. It made her feel protected and cherished, like being tucked inside a big bear rug.

"Mmm," he mumbled again. "Keep that up and we'll never get out of bed."

She smiled in the darkness and wiggled her bottom against him. One thing she had discovered about Sam, he loved lazy, sleepy, morning sex as much as she'd discovered she did. When the alarm sounded a second time, Sam was the one who slapped at it at the same time he thrust gently in and out of her. It was vastly different than their lovemaking the previous evening, but just as enjoyable in its own way.

Erin hated when they finally had to get up. Showering and breakfast would come later. Work first. Once the animals were fed, they would return to the house for a meal, but a cup of coffee now was a must. While Sam fired up the woodstove in the living room, Erin put on the coffeemaker. She handed Sam his mug and they both leaned against the kitchen counter to quietly sip the flavorful brew in the dim light from above the stove.

"How many more calves do we have to go this week?" she murmured between sips.

"Five. All experienced cows out on pasture. We'll ride out and check on them after daylight." Sam set his mug aside. "You ready?"

"Yeah. I hope it's warmed up some. I'm ready for spring."

"Me too, baby."

Sam tucked his small pistol into the ankle holster he wore. He was the first one out the door, leading the way across the still muddy farmyard to the darkened barn with Erin just a couple of steps behind him. He hadn't gone far enough for the motion to trigger the security light over the barn door when she heard him grunt and stumble. A split second later, the crack of a rifle punctuated the air.

"Sam!"

"Run, Erin!" he gasped. "Take the truck. Hurry, baby. Keys in it…"

She turned and made a dash for it, slipping in the darkness as her breath escaped in harsh sobs. Behind her, Sam groaned. Over her shoulder she watched him struggle to stand. There was another crack. This time he fell with a dull thud.

"Sam!" Her scream was hoarse. She knew she should obey him, knew she should get to the truck and get out of there, but how could she leave him? Erin stopped. Even in the darkness, she could make out the outline of his body, sprawled in the mud, unmoving.

Oh, God! *Sam!* She started to take a step toward him, but when she heard someone running toward her from the direction of the barn, Erin spun and made a break for the truck again. She had to get help, and whoever was sprinting toward her wasn't it. She yanked open the truck door and was halfway inside when she was abruptly jerked back by the collar of her coverall.

"Not so fast!"

Cold seeped through her. Matty. The freezing cold of betrayal. She felt immeasurably old, as if someone had sucked the life from her. She turned and glared at her captor.

"How could you?"

Another voice came out of the darkness. "You simply don't understand the immense motivation of money, darling, but then you've always had it, so why should you."

Erin focused on the slender figure now moving toward her, and realized her entire escape from Andre Delacroix had been just an illusion. When one of her closest friends was so ready to betray her, she'd never had any chance at all. Her gaze slid to Sam's still form. *Why didn't he move?* She swayed, afraid for a moment she was simply going to faint.

"You won't get any help there. Lover boy is gone," Andre said callously.

No! Erin denied it with every breath in her body, but before she could scream it at Andre, he stepped up and jerked her arm, pulling her toward him. "You're in luck, though, because I'm willing to take you on, even if you are used goods. And so magnificently used. You and your stud were entertaining, to say the least. Watching you last night made me realize just how well you and I might get along."

Fury and grief roared through her, making her feel as though her sanity teetered on an edge so fine she had no hope of regaining her balance. He talked as if Sam was dead, and if he was, Andre Delacroix had also soiled one of her last moments with Sam. Erin spit in Andre's face. His fist cracked into her jaw, rocking her head back and making her see stars for a moment.

"Hey! There's no need for that," Matty protested.

Andre laughed. "Shut up, and drive us back to the hotel. I'll stay with our guest in the back seat."

Erin tried to look over her shoulder at Sam, but they were dragging her away too fast. She had to get back. Desperately, she yanked against Andre Delacroix. She had to get to Sam. The cold steel of a gun barrel pressed against her temple. Erin quit struggling.

"That's right, bitch. It's only a question of time. Do I kill you now or later? Show me enough reason not to shoot, and I might even let you live for a while."

Even with the pain in her jaw and her heart, Erin somehow gathered her strength around her. No, she wouldn't let him shoot her now. She wanted to live long enough to make both men pay for what they'd done. Somehow, she'd find a way, no matter how long it took. She struggled to catch one more glimpse of Sam, but Andre's hold blocked her view.

As they bundled her into the rental car they'd brought with them, dawn lightened the sky. Erin craned her head over her shoulder. She could see him. Her breath caught in her chest, but she managed to keep the scream she felt building inside her silent. Sam lay in the mud unmoving. He couldn't be dead. Not Sam. Never Sam. He was too vital, too strong. She kept looking over her shoulder as they pulled away from the farmyard.

Get up, Sam! Get up, damn you!

But as they started down the hill, he still hadn't moved and Erin doubted he ever would. She closed her eyes. It wasn't pain she felt, it was…hollowness, as though she were eroding from her heart out. She was empty inside. All the lonely spaces Sam had touched and filled began to bleed out until she felt like the Erin who had first come back last fall, the Erin who had arrived a few weeks ago, not caring, not feeling.

Sammy. She willed her tears away. She would cry for him later, after she'd found a way to get revenge.

Erin tried fighting when they reached the hotel, but Andre clamped a hand over her mouth, half covering her nose as well until she could barely suck in any air. With his free hand, he dragged her toward the door of the motel room.

"Open it. Get her inside. I need to make sure she'll stay quiet for a while. Did you load that syringe?"

Erin twisted, her eyes widening as she tried to see what they were doing. Drugs? No. No matter what had happened, she didn't want to be there again, didn't want to feel that lost, drifting despair. She needed to be able to feel whatever was left of Sam. If they drugged her, she would forget him. She didn't want to forget him. She kicked backward and caught Andre in the shin. Satisfaction surged through her when he grunted in pain, but then he took it out on her with a crack to the side of her head. It knocked her through the door and to her knees at the edge of the bed. Erin twisted defensively at his approach, her eyes widening again as she saw the syringe in his hand.

"No!"

"Grab her and shut her up," Andre snarled.

More arms, the arms of *her friend*, confined her, immobilizing her so Andre could drug her. The needle pinched, and he pushed the plunger. Whatever they'd used, it was powerful. The buzzing in her ears grew steadily until it was like being inside a beehive with every angry insect hissing around her head.

* * * *

Sam's leg and arm burned like the seven levels of hell, but it was the crack on the head that hurt the worst. He clamped his eyes shut against the pain and the nausea roiling inside him. He slowly opened his eyes. *Please don't let her be lying there dead*. He could deal with anything but that. The farmyard was silent and empty, the door to his truck open so that the interior light cast only a faint glow in the increasing light of morning. She wasn't there. The house was dark and quiet. Relief and fear filled him. As long as Erin wasn't lying there already dead, hope remained.

He studied the house. They could be inside, waiting to finish him off. From this angle, he couldn't see what, if any, footprints, led that way. He tried to get to the gun at his ankle, but his injuries wouldn't let him.

He had to get up, had to get help. Sam lurched to one knee, but the pain in his other leg made it useless, and now the nausea was worse. Braced on one arm and one leg, Sam heaved, the retching making his head pound even worse.

Sweet heaven. Erin. He had to get help. He'd promised he'd keep her safe. Sam sucked in a hoarse breath. He had to tell her he loved her.

With sheer will, he dragged himself forward. His phone was in the truck. If he could just make it there. The burning in his arm and leg intensified as he forced them to at least support some of his weight while he inched his way across the farmyard. Blood trickled into his eye, but he couldn't even wipe it away for fear he might fall. If he collapsed again, Sam was afraid he wouldn't wake up.

He had almost made it to his truck when he heard the rumble of another vehicle rolling up the driveway. Sam pulled himself into a sitting position, his weight leaning against the truck tire. If it was Erin's kidnappers, there was little he could do. His service revolver and his hunting rifles were all inside the house. Even the pistol he carried in his ankle holster would be of no help. His right arm was dangling uselessly by his side, and he could feel the slow trickle of blood still oozing from the bullet wound. He could shoot left handed. He just couldn't reach his backup because of the wound in his leg.

The truck slid to a gravel crunching halt next to him, and two doors slammed.

"Sam! *Shit!* It looks like he's been shot. Call 911, Carter." Stoner bent over him, grasping his shoulders carefully. Even through the haze of pain coating his vision, Sam saw how pale the older man's face was. "Erin? Where's Erin, Sam?"

"Gone, I think. Haven't been able to check the house. Be careful." Through the pain, he fished in his memory for something to tell him. He'd heard footsteps and voices. "At least two men. Don't know how long ago. Before sunrise."

"Carter!" Stoner yelled. "Get the rifle out of the truck. Erin's been taken. Sam looks like he's been shot twice, also has a head wound of some sort. I'm going in to check the house."

Sam grabbed Stoner's sleeve with his uninjured arm. "Take my gun. Don't worry about me. Find her. Find *her*, Stoner!"

Sam's eyes squeezed shut, but he couldn't hold back the tears. Their moisture tracked down the drying mud on his face.

Stoner cupped his hands around Sam's neck. "I will. We will. Hang in there, son. We're going to get you help, then find her, you hear me?"

Sam grimaced against the pain that surged through him, and sobbed. He was mortified. To cry was bad enough, but to cry in front of Stoner? When the other man put his arms around him, Sam stiffened for a moment in surprise, then relaxed.

"It's all right. We'll get her back. Erin's tough. Remember that."

Sam nodded slowly and painfully. Stoner released him, took Sam's gun and disappeared. Sam had no idea how much time passed before he heard Stoner say the house was empty. Shortly after, the wail of sirens split the morning quiet. With pain dulling his awareness, Sam watched what looked like the entire world show up. While the EMTs cut away his clothing to get to the bullet wounds, deputies as well as state troopers crawled over the farm, sealing off the area and searching for evidence.

The staccato shouts of voices and radios and the rumble of diesel engines all mixed together in his pain-fogged brain. There was only one thing that remained clear. Erin. They had to find her, had to find her before it was too late.

A young EMT bent over him. Sam recognized his face, but couldn't think of his name. "Okay, Sheriff, we're going to move you to the stretcher. One, two, three. Lift."

The movement made his stomach roll, but Sam clenched his jaw and stared at the pink of the morning sky. In his peripheral vision he watched the movement around him, listened to the hum of the paramedics' conversations.

"Both bullets traveled clean through."

"Just missed the brachial artery."

He tried to turn his head, but they had immobilized it.

"Saw one," he croaked.

In an instant, his lead detective was next to him.

"Sheriff. You saw one of them?"

Sam pulled at the memory trying to escape his fogged brain. "Friend of hers. Try hotel. Truck stop. Rick or Matty."

"Can you give me a description?"

"Evan can."

Everything around him dimmed as the roaring in his ears grew louder. Sam struggled against it. He had to stay awake. Had to be able to help Erin.

* * * *

Stoner stood to one side, not sure what he was supposed to be doing, but feeling like he should be doing something. His daughter had been kidnapped. That much was clear, and whoever had done it thought they'd left Sam for dead. The fact the kidnappers would gun down the county sheriff without any apparent second thought was terrifying. If they would do that to Sam, what would they do to Erin? She'd feared the people she suspected were drug dealers would come after her. Guilt gnawed at him that once again he'd let her down. Had they thought they could just put

Erin at Sam's place and she'd be hidden? They had all gotten too relaxed, too casual. Now his daughter was missing and the man she loved was seriously wounded.

His phone vibrated. Stoner reached for it and saw it was Catherine.

"Katie…" He tried to keep the tension and fear out of his voice, but they'd been married far too long for that.

"Whatever it is, Stoner, just tell me. Don't soft pedal it."

"Sam's been shot."

"Erin?" He heard the plea in his wife's voice.

Stoner swallowed. "Missing. Kidnapped. Sam's got a couple of wounds. They're getting ready to transport him right now. Call Evan and Tabby. Let's get them both to the hospital. I just"—he paused to take in a deep breath—"I need to see them, pick their brains about anything Erin might have said."

"Oh dear God. I'll call right away." No hesitation. No fear. It was what had always fascinated him about her. She took everything in stride, stepping in and stepping up to do what needed to be done.

"I'll come get you, Katie. I need to clean up before we head to town."

He ended the call and leaned against his truck. For the first time in a long while, he felt every single one of his years. In six months' span, this was the second time he'd stood covered in the blood of someone dear to him. They'd been able to save Tabby, and it looked like they would save Sam, but the thought he might lose Erin when they'd only just gotten her back was almost enough to drive him to his knees.

"Senator? Can you answer a few questions?"

He opened his eyes. Sam's lead detective, an older, burly man he'd known for years, stood in front of him.

"Sure, Jim. How could I do anything else?"

"Sam mumbled something about seeing one of the kidnappers. Said it was a friend of your daughter's."

Stoner frowned. "She doesn't have any friends around here that I know of. She's been living in the Virgin Islands until recently, and Detective, I have to tell you she left there and came back here because she overheard arrangements for a drug deal. She was afraid someone might come after her."

The detective's eyes narrowed. "Sam *knew* this?"

"Yes. He and Evan were checking things out. We were trying to keep it quiet. As I'm sure you know, anything involving our family always seems to get into the press. Erin didn't want that. Neither did Sam. We were afraid it would lead them directly to her. So Sam moved her in with him to provide protection and what we hoped would be a safe place to hide."

Jim raised a brow. "That's a little difficult to do when everyone in town's seen the two of them together."

"Sam was taking precautions," Stoner said in Sam's defense.

"You know who these people from the Virgin Islands might be?" Jim asked.

"Not the dealers, but she did have two friends who showed up, also trying to lay low. But I only know first names. Rick, he was the captain of the *Sprite*, the boat on which Erin worked. And Matty, one of the crew."

Jim looked thoughtful. "Where did they sail out of? I can probably chase down names that way."

"Saint Thomas, I think." Stoner stared after the departing ambulance and swallowed. There'd been bad blood between him and Sam over the years, but any idiot could see Sam was head over heels in love with Erin. The connection that had always existed between Sam and his daughter had only grown stronger. Stoner was afraid what would happen to either one of them without the other. He knew probably better than anyone just how far back their attraction stretched. Twelve years ago, it had infuriated Stoner and shamed Sam, but now he couldn't think of a man he'd rather see with her.

"I need to find Evan. Sam says he's seen the two guys."

Stoner nodded. "He'll be at the hospital. Sam's a close friend."

* * * *

Erin hated the foggy, floating feeling that sent her mind spinning off in several different directions at once. She wanted to keep her eyes shut, but she was so dizzy. Hoping the spinning kaleidoscope behind her eyelids would go away, she carefully opened her lids.

Her face felt tight. When she tried to rub it, she realized two things. Her hands were bound behind her, and tape covered her mouth. Her eyes popped all the way open, and the light from the bedside lamp sent a jolt of agony to her visual cortex. As quietly as she could, she shifted, hoping to see where she was. It appeared to be a suite of some sort. Not many hotels had those. She listened carefully, and in the distance detected the low rumble of big trucks. The truck stop.

She closed her eyes again as the arguing from the other room filtered back to her.

"He's supposed to come back today. I either have to be there or make it look like I've checked out and left him."

"I need him…and you too. You can both help with the girl."

"Looks to me like she's pretty quiet right now. You didn't overdose her, did you?"

Cruel male laughter rippled over Erin's nerve endings.

"If I did, you're the one who loaded the syringe."

"According to your instructions."

"Let it go. She's fine. She'll be out for a while. Let's make sure the place you found is ready so we can move her."

Erin tried to speak around the tape. She wanted to warn Matty not to trust Andre, but the only thing that came out of her mouth was garbled.

The door shut behind them. Erin strained her ears, but she could no longer hear anyone. Had they left her alone? Fat lot of good it did her, with tape over her mouth, her hands bound, and her ankles taped together. Maybe she could still get to the phone, dial 911 with her toes, something. Erin tried to shift her body on the bed, but it was much harder than she thought. Her legs felt heavy and unwilling to obey her commands. Finally, she managed to roll from side to side. Just when she thought she'd made it, she fell off the bed, cracking her head against the night stand.

Now she lay on the floor, feeling blood trickle down her forehead, and knowing she was stuck. With an exhausted, defeated sigh, Erin pressed her head to the floor. The tears she had held back for years trickled from the corners of her eyes. What happened hardly mattered anyway without Sam. His name spiraled through her brain over and over. Despair crept along her veins, as cold as trailing an ice cube down an arm.

Chapter 10

"Sam! Can you hear me? Come on, Sam. Open your eyes for just a moment so I can see you're still there."

"Donshoutjenny."

Light feminine laughter floated over him, disturbing his peace as effectively as her voice had. "You are one lucky guy, you know that?"

"Erin?" His heart pounded as he waited for an answer. He couldn't bring himself to open his eyes, fearing what he would read in Jenny's expression.

"No. That's not what I meant, though everyone's out working on it from Jake's guys to your deputies. Even Evan and the state guys."

Sam opened his eyes, staring at the ceiling. He shouldn't be lying here in a hospital bed. He should be going out to help find Erin. He tried to throw back the covers, then realized he had all sorts of tubes and wires stuck to him.

"Whoa, big boy!" Jenny gently pushed him back. "You can't go anywhere right now. You've been in surgery for the past few hours. While you were lucky both bullets shot through and didn't do any major damage, we still had to clean things and repair what we could. You're down a leg and an arm right now, so you're out of commission, Sam."

He stared at Jenny. "Have to find her."

His stomach knotted and his heart ached as much as his wounds. He'd sworn to protect her and failed. He'd taken precautions in town, but an attack in the dark on the farm hadn't crossed his mind.

She touched his forehead. "I know you have to find her, Sam, but for once you're going to have to rely on the men you've trained and the other men in her life. Evan has already given everyone an excellent description of Rick and Matty. He and Stoner are working closely with everyone involved. But you have to rest. In addition to the bullets, you took a nasty crack to the head. You're damn lucky to be alive, Sam."

With a reassuring touch to his shoulder, Jenny left him alone.

He didn't feel lucky to be alive. He closed his eyes, but he couldn't shut out the thoughts that tortured him. Where was she? Was she even alive? And worst of all… How could he have been so incredibly naïve? He should have put additional protection on her and the farm. Should have done something other than carry his backup gun. He had allowed his ego and libido to get in the way of the basics of sound police work.

Several hours later, Sam was staring out the window when he heard the noise at the door. Evan and Jenny entered the room with Stoner and Catherine right behind them.

"A little crowded for ICU, isn't it?" Sam's voice was a hoarse rasp.

Jenny came forward. "I'm making an exception. Besides, I'll bust you out of here tomorrow morning to a regular room."

He scowled. "I'd rather go home."

"That would be an option if it were only the arm wound, but for two bullets and a concussion, you have to serve extra time."

Sam turned his head away from them. He appreciated Jenny's effort, but he couldn't forget what loomed over all of them. Erin was gone.

"Any luck?" he asked softly.

Evan stepped to the foot of the bed. "Not yet. Jim and a couple state guys have a room at the hotel next to the truck stop staked out. Your man Rick was registered there, but no one's been there all day, so we're keeping an eye on it."

Sam ground his teeth together in frustration. He knew how these things played out. The longer a kidnap victim was gone, the smaller the chances were of survival. His brain thrust a picture at him of life without Erin. He closed his eyes against the desolation.

"I have to get out of here." He started to move.

"Whoa!" Jenny's voice cracked like a whip. "Sam, you'll be of no use to her dead."

His eyes swiveled to her. "And if I don't go, she could end up dead."

Catherine gasped. Sam's gaze darted to her. He turned his face away in shame. He wasn't the only one in pain in this room. "I'm sorry," he choked.

He felt lost, empty. Just at the point where he'd finally realized the difference in their ages didn't matter, that she didn't care that his farm wasn't Richardson Homestead, she was gone. He had planned to ask her to marry him. They should have been curled up on the couch. He would have given her his grandmother's ring. It had sat in the box on his dresser where he kept his most personal possessions for years. He'd never questioned why. Now he realized he'd been waiting for her to grow up, to come back. He could almost see her eyes light up. His vision blurred, and Sam blinked the moisture away.

At the touch on his arm, he found Catherine standing next to the bed. She leaned over and hugged him gently.

"It's all right, Sam. I share your feelings. As soon as we can persuade Jenny to let you out of here, I want you to come to our house."

"Why?" Sam couldn't help asking and blinked in embarrassment. The animosity between Stoner and him had been so longstanding, it was still difficult for Sam to adjust to the change that had made him almost a part of the family rather than the older man trying to take Stoner's daughter.

"I...my farm," he protested, trying to dig his way out.

"All taken care of," Stoner finished as he entered the room. "Carter and my hands will get your herd and your horses tended. I also talked to your hired man. He's about cleared with his doctor. The neighbor kid said he can help out extra too."

Sam looked at Stoner.

"I don't know how to thank you."

"Just get better so you can find my daughter, Sam," Stoner rumbled. "She needs you a whole lot more than she needs the rest of us."

Sam swallowed. It eased some of the guilt he'd been feeling. That Stoner would even make that kind of statement was an admission of just how far his relationship with Erin had progressed.

Sam didn't want to admit it, but he was tiring. Everything on him ached abominably. He knew he needed to rest, but he was afraid that would never happen. Images of Erin tormented him every time he started to relax. The thought she might be injured or frightened tore at him. As tough as she was, she was still no match for a gun. And the idea of someone shooting her made his nerves crawl with impatience to be up and out of bed. He had promised to protect her, but he hadn't.

Evan was going through what they had discovered about her two friends to update him, but Sam was having a hard time concentrating.

She was so feisty, but she was also tiny. Someone with any size could hurt or break her so easily, and she was too assertive not to fight back. Then there were her emotional reserves. Sam wasn't sure how deep those ran yet. He recalled the brittle young woman who'd shown up at the country club last fall. She had been more than halfway to having a serious addiction problem, but she'd overcome that. Sure she'd changed a lot, but it wasn't that long ago that she'd stood in that guesthouse too scared to go into dinner with her own family. Just how much pain or temptation could she stand?

"Sam? Did you hear me?"

He looked back to Evan and passed a hand over his eyes. "I'm sorry… Lord, Ev, I can't get her out of my mind."

"Do you know if she'd heard anything more from the guys from her ship…Captain Rick and Matty?"

"No, she hasn't heard from them."

"Are you sure?"

Sam glared at Evan. "I'm positive."

Evan's phone vibrated and he pulled it from his pocket. When Jenny frowned at him, he shrugged.

"Yeah. This is Evan."

He listened for several minutes, then jammed it back into his pocket.

"Jim caught up with Rick Nelson at the hotel where he and Matty have been staying. Jim's just finished questioning Rick. They're checking his story right now. He claims he'd gone to the coast to talk to a charter captain there about buying a boat, and he just got back into town tonight. Said Matty was supposedly checking out some late season skiing in West Virginia, but should have been back today. There's no sign of him at their hotel room, and his belongings are gone."

"Matty's who I saw." Sam's voice was grim.

"You're sure?"

"Positive. I didn't see anybody else before I blacked out, but I heard another voice. Someone else was with him."

"You think it was Rick?"

"No. The voice was different. Colder. Didn't have that smoky quality Rick's voice has."

"You think it was the drug dealer?"

Sam sighed. "I can't come up with anyone else, Evan. Erin was scared of the guy. Damn… What was the name? Delancey…Delacourt. Delacroix. That's it. Delacroix!" Sam tried to sit up. Now that he'd remembered the guy's name, there were so many things they needed to follow up on.

"Whoa there," Jenny barked, moving in to ease him back against the bed. "Sam, you've got to get some rest. Evan can make sure everyone follows up on the guy. If you continue to show improvement, I'll move you out of ICU in the morning, but tonight, I want you to get some sleep."

How the hell was he supposed to do that? His mind was in turmoil and he couldn't calm himself.

"You want me to give you something?" Jenny arched a slender blond brow, as if she sensed where his thoughts had gone.

"No." The last thing he wanted was to be drugged up if something developed. "I'll settle down. That's all I can promise."

After she ushered everyone out, Sam closed his eyes. He had seen the fear and concern on all their faces and knew it was echoed in his own. His uninjured hand clenched the covers. *Oh Erin, baby, I'll find you. Just hang on!* Sam glared at the tubes and wires attached to him. They were as effective as handcuffs. If he even attempted to remove one of them, it would set off alarms and bring nurses running.

He would wait until they moved him. He could wait for that, and then he was outta there. He didn't care if he had to walk out in a hospital gown with his ass hanging out in the breeze. He was going to find Erin and bring her home. No matter what had happened, he would bring her home where she could be safe with him.

He swallowed thickly. He wouldn't fail a second time.

* * * *

"I see you've decided to come around."

Erin opened her eyes. Andre sat on a chair nearby. She was in a heap on the floor, but not the same floor as before, and the tape was gone.

"Go to hell." Erin glared at her captor.

He grabbed her hair and pulled her into a sitting position. "You're in a bad spot to take that kind of tone. It's a shame. Guess I could put the tape back over that mouth, but I can think of so many better uses for it. Besides, we've moved accommodations, so even you screaming won't help you now. My resourceful companion found this for me." Andre paused to cast an arm around the room. "Not my taste, but then trailer trash has never been my thing. Still, this will do until I can get everything settled. Then we will discuss your future."

He paused and smiled at her, his pale eyes cold despite what she was sure was meant to be a pleasant expression.

"You should thank me, you know. Originally I intended to simply kill you and rid myself of the inconvenience of having someone who had heard too much about my family's business. However, the little show you and your lover put on last night has convinced me you have some other, more useful purposes. That was a magnificent blowjob you gave him. I look forward to getting one."

Andre smiled again, and Erin's stomach rolled. He had seen her with Sam. Just the thought he had watched her and Sam make love was bad enough, but that he imagined she would ever touch him in the same way was insane.

"Ah... I see you think you would never do that, but you will darling, because you're about to develop a serious drug habit, and with me as your only supplier, you're going to find you'll do anything for a fix, including sucking my cock or anything else I dream up. And I can promise you I'm endlessly inventive."

"You're crazy," Erin spat at him. He was even sicker than all the rumors she had heard, and there had been plenty of talk in some of the dives Rick and his crew frequented. Erin had heard tales of Andre's penchant for roughing up women, not to mention the fact she was fairly certain Andre had been branching out recently. "Besides, what do you need me for? You've got Matty. Did you let him suck you last night?"

The crazy light in Andre's eyes hardened into something even uglier. He slapped her hard enough to snap her head sideways. "You will have to learn to keep your mouth shut. It's you who may go back to St. Thomas with me, bitch, not him. But only if you learn to keep quiet and do what you're told. Otherwise, there are plenty of dense woods behind this place where no one will find your body for a long, long time."

Erin ducked her head. The sheer force of his reaction told her a lot. She had suspected something more had gone on aboard the *Sprite* than just Andre riding as a passenger. She had heard them on deck late one night after she had gone to bed, heard the moans of passion, and guessed what was going on. Rick and the rest of the crew had always thought it fun to seduce men, especially the ones who so vehemently insisted they were straight. Matty, in particular, always laughed afterward that the ones who protested the most also moaned the loudest.

If Matty wasn't going back to the island with him, what was he going to do? More importantly, what did Rick know about all of this? Erin felt as if her heart were breaking. Rick had been her best friend, almost like a father, though she never would have said that to him. To imagine he knew was enough to crush her spirit. But how could she think otherwise? Matty obviously did, and she couldn't imagine him doing anything without Rick telling him. When tears clouded her vision at the idea of such a betrayal, she shook her head to clear them. She would not let them see her cry. Not ever again.

She lifted her head to glare at Andre. "I will never thank you. You're scum."

He hit her again, this time drawing blood when the blow split her lip. He put his face close to hers and snarled, "You'll thank me, and you'll beg me."

Erin started to snap something back, but instead kept her mouth shut. She already felt like a punching bag, her lip split and her cheek swollen from his blows. In addition, there was a throbbing where she'd hit her head when she fell.

Her thoughts slipped to Sam, but she forced that picture away. Sam was dead. She'd seen it. Oh God. Erin felt the emptiness again, a vast chasm with no bottom. How could she handle that huge hole?

You're about to develop a serious drug habit.

Andre's words came back to her. It wasn't as frightening as it first seemed, and probably not as frightening as Andre intended it to be. In some way, she'd been self-medicating most of her life. Not relying on anything was the novelty. Falling back on her old habits would fill the emptiness of a life with no Sam in it. If she never had to think or feel again, then maybe she could forget Sam was dead. Maybe if they calculated wrong, she'd overdose. Good-bye, Erin. Good-bye pain.

"Where's Matty?" Erin finally asked after Andre shoved her into a chair at a scarred kitchen table.

"Gone. You don't need to worry about him anymore."

"What do you mean gone?" Her heart tightened. Sure, she knew Matty had betrayed her, but he had been a friend. She wouldn't put anything past Delacroix. He'd already shot Sam in cold blood, so getting rid of Matt and Rick was logical. Erin sucked in a shaky breath. She didn't want to be next. As long as she was breathing there was hope she could get away, and when she did, she would make sure Andre paid.

Andre popped the lid on a can of beans and pushed it in front of her. Erin kept her expression impassive even though the cold beans made her want to puke.

"Did you kill him?" She tried to keep her tone nonchalant, as if she didn't care one way or the other, but she wasn't sure she'd managed it.

"Shut up and eat. Like I've already told you, you'll be a whole lot better off, darling, if you'll learn to keep that mouth of yours shut other than when I tell you to open it. I've got plenty of uses for it, none of which involve you talking."

Erin looked at the room temperature beans in front of her and forced back the bile rising in her throat. He had untied her hands, but had one of her arms cuffed to the table leg. Knowing she would only make him angry if she didn't eat something, she picked up her spoon and shoved a mouthful of beans inside. Andre watched her like a hawk.

"I've got a little dessert for you after dinner."

At first she thought he meant sex, that he would force her into some of the kinky stuff she'd heard he liked, but then she realized he had a syringe sitting on the counter just behind him. Erin didn't want to plead. She'd done so well getting clean. As easy as it would be to give in to the oblivion of getting high to help her forget what had happened to Sam, she didn't want to do that. She had worked too hard to crumble now. After two more shaky attempts to eat, she tossed the spoon down.

"I'm not hungry."

Andre smiled. "Then it's time for dessert. You'll really love this. I promise."

She tried to fight when he came at her with the needle, but with one hand chained to the table, it was easy enough for him to grab the other and jerk it behind her. She knew the drug he was using. It was a popular one in the club scene, and there was no need to find a vein. Ketamine in the muscle was just as effective. If he used enough, it was effective as a date rape drug. It could also be addictive.

"No," she whispered. "Please don't." She hated to beg. Hated it. She tried once again, to jerk away, but succeeded only in wrenching her shoulder. Andre laughed. With the ease of long practice, he pushed her sleeve up and plunged the drug home.

"You'll like it, baby," Andre breathed in her ear. "You won't give a shit what happens once you've been high a couple times. You'll just want more. Then we'll play."

She stared unseeingly at the paneled walls of the trailer. As the drug took effect, she felt unreal, as if she were no longer a part of her body. The pain was gone and she was floating. He was right. This was all right.

None of it seemed real to her any more, and if it wasn't real, then that meant Sam was still alive. Soon, they would eat dinner and curl up on the couch together. She would burrow under his shoulder and lean her head against his muscular chest. His arm would curve around her shoulders and his hand would stroke her arm. They would stay that way for a while until he kissed her. Then as their kisses deepened, he would take her clothes off. They would touch each other.

"That's it, baby," a voice came from a distance. "Touch yourself for me."

That wasn't Sam. Erin bumped back to earth with a jolt, found her hand between her legs, and Andre staring at her. When she noticed the bulge in his trousers, she began to scream. He slapped her, but she hardly felt it. Rage and frustration made her thrash against the cuff on her wrist. The chair tipped out from under her and Erin slammed to the floor.

"Bitch. Just wait. A few more times and you won't be able to pull out of it. And you'll crave it. You'll crave that feeling that you're on the outside looking in. Nothing can touch you. I can wait until then. I don't trust you otherwise."

She knew better by now than to antagonize him. He enjoyed inflicting pain. It made his pale eyes sparkle with sexual heat. Erin closed her eyes as he dragged her back to a room and cuffed her hands through the metal headboard on the cot there. A part of her, a part she'd hoped was gone forever, wanted the oblivion the drug promised. Right now it was still a whisper, not a shout. With almost every other fiber of her being, she wanted to kill the man now turning on his heel and leaving her handcuffed, kill him for what he'd done to Sam.

* * * *

As Jenny promised, they moved Sam the next morning. He had worried he wouldn't sleep at all, but exhaustion had finally taken over. Now they wheeled him to a different floor, and he felt the stares of the other hospital personnel. Pity. He didn't want their freaking pity. He wanted to be out where he could find Erin. He snarled at the nurses and bit the head off the deputy who stopped by. By the time Jenny came into to check on him, he was already sitting on the side of the bed attempting to walk.

"Samuel Barnes! You stop right there, and don't you dare move another muscle."

"Then get me out of here," he snapped. "And don't use that I'm-your-mother tone with me. *Damn it*, Jenny. He'll kill her."

"And killing yourself will prevent that how?" She stomped over to his side, but laid her hand gently on his broad shoulder. "Sam. You have capable men, the state has capable men, and even Jake is working this. They'll find her. Let them do their job while you concentrate on recovering. Why won't you understand? Another half inch and the bullet in your arm would have severed an artery. By some miracle, neither of them shattered bone, but you're not invincible. This is a major trauma."

Sam looked deep into her golden eyes, pleading for understanding. "I love her, Jen. This guy's a drug smuggler. Even if he doesn't kill her, he could be feeding her all sorts of crap. She's not like she was last fall. It took me a little while to see it, but she's trying to change her life. She's clean."

He was embarrassed his voice shook, but he couldn't control it, and at least it was Jenny, not Stoner or Evan. She squeezed his shoulder. "Can I compromise with you?"

He blinked the moisture from his eyes. "How?"

"I'll have a portable two-way radio moved in here along with your phone. You can keep up with what's going on, and I promise if anything breaks, I will personally take you out there. In the meantime, you'll agree to stay here and take it easy until that happens."

As Jenny laid out her deal, Sam's throat tightened until he wasn't sure he'd be able to speak, but he had to. When she finished, he laid his usable hand against the side of her neck. "You are special, Doc. If I wasn't nuts about your sister-in-law, you'd be it."

His voice caught at the end, and his smile felt shaky, at best. Her golden eyes shone with sympathy.

"I'll take that as a yes, you accept. Now lie down, Sam, while I get you what I've promised. You should know, Jake headed out this morning on a body behind Crawley's old tire store at the edge of town."

Sam's stomach twisted in a knot. A dead body showing up was unusual enough, but if it turned out to be a murder? Sam ground his teeth. "Could you hurry up with that radio and my phone?"

"Yeah. Be right back."

A dead body. It wasn't Erin. He was sure of that. He would know. Somehow, he would know if it was her, but he also had a sinking feeling there would be a connection. He tuned the radio to bring in Jake's town frequencies. They'd located a white male, mid to late twenties with a gunshot wound to the back of the head, base of the skull. Looked like an execution style killing. No ID, but the description matched the one for Matty Davis given by both Evan and Rick Nelson.

Sam flopped back against the pillows, his mouth tight with frustration. He couldn't generate any sympathy for the dead Matty. He simply viewed it as a link to finding Erin that had just been shattered...and a warning that Delacroix would stop at nothing, even her death. If he'd wiped out all those links, what hope was there now of finding her? He picked up the phone and called Jim.

"Sam! How are you doing, man?"

"I'd be a whole lot better if they'd let me out of this place. I just heard over Jake's radio frequencies that they may have found one of your suspects—Matty Davis—shot execution style."

"Hmm. Hadn't heard that. I was on my way back to the hotel where Rick Nelson's staying. You want me to put him in protective custody?"

Sam squinted as he stared out the window. He had to gamble that Delacroix wanted to hang on to Erin for some reason. Why else go to the trouble of coming over here himself when it would have been so simple to have Matty Davis simply kill her? No, if he was going to come out to kill anyone else, it was probably Rick Nelson.

"Don't bring him in. I want you to call me back when you're with him. Can you put me on speaker so we can all talk back and forth?"

"Sure thing, Sam. Give me five minutes and I'll call you back."

He raked his good hand through his short hair and tugged at his ear as he waited for Jim to call back. He was going to bank on the concern he'd seen in Rick the day Evan and he had plucked Erin out of the captain's hotel room. Rick had stopped Matty that day from revealing things about her that were private, and Erin had spoken of the man as being responsible for helping her find a way to read and exercise her talent for investments. Sam hoped that meant Rick Nelson was not a part of this and would be willing to lay himself out there for bait.

When his cell phone rang, Sam grabbed it.

"Sam, I've got you on speaker. Rick is here with me."

"Hi, Rick. I'm the guy who punched you in the nose."

There was a gravelly chuckle from the other end of the line. "Trust me, I remember. I also remember you're the same guy Erin used to mumble about in her sleep, and the same man it was obvious to me, would do anything for her. In that, we share something. The only difference is my interest isn't a physical thing. She's like my kid sister."

"I need your help, Rick."

"Name it. I'll do it. No matter what."

Sam felt some of the tension leave him for the first time since the first bullet had ripped through his flesh and he'd realized Erin was in danger. He outlined the plan to both Jim and Rick. They listened, asking questions every now and then.

"I think it fair to warn you, Captain, the town's police chief has spent the morning investigating an execution style slaying on the edge of town, and the victim looks like your friend."

There was a long pause on the other end, followed by a shaky sigh. "Delacroix's already killed two of my friends. I'm pretty positive he was behind the explosion of the *Sprite*. You think he'll come after me now?"

Sam looked out the window at the leaden sky. "You're a loose end. It's a logical assumption."

"So was Erin, but you think he's left her alive?"

"I'm banking on it. There was no need for him to come here otherwise. He already had Matty who could have taken care of you and Erin if his only intent was to kill. Delacroix could have dealt with cleaning up Matty as a loose end when he returned to the Virgin Islands.

"Now the game has changed. For some reason, he's decided he wants Erin, and you and Matty became the dispensable ones. Can you think of some reasons he might keep Erin?"

"Two. Sex and greed. He fixated on Erin while he was aboard the *Sprite* and wanted me to arrange things so he could have her in his bed. My refusal set a lot of this in motion. There was an additional sexual reason, though. Andre's been getting a little too friendly with the gay and bi community in the islands, something his father wouldn't tolerate. He's looking for a smokescreen, and thinks Erin will provide that since she's spent so much time around me and my crew."

Sam's brows rose. "He's bi?"

"He's experimented," Rick clarified, "and he's afraid daddy will find out. The second reason he would want Erin, though, is for her financial talents. The whole Delacroix family is looking for a way to launder money, some legitimate businesses they can use to conceal their drug trade. Erin could provide them with that, along with the cachet of being a former senator's daughter, if she'll cooperate."

Sam felt a deadly coldness slide through his veins like ice water. Erin's stubbornness was legendary. Would she try to defy Delacroix? He swallowed thickly. When had Erin been anything but defiant, especially when she was frightened?

While that thought made Sam even more uneasy, from one issue at least he drew comfort. Delacroix wanted her alive, not dead. They could use that and his desire to kill Rick to their advantage.

"If she won't cooperate, Rick, what's he likely to do?"

There was a long pause on the other end. "He might drug her. That would be the best case scenario."

"And worst case?"

Again a pause that only served to increase Sam's concerns.

"Andre likes inflicting pain, especially on women. He's got a reputation around some of the sex clubs and brothels."

"Then we need to be ready to act if he makes a move."

He could only pray that while everything unfolded, they would get some lead on where Delacroix was holding her. It might be the only way to save her. He silently cursed the injuries that kept him from getting out there on his own.

Chapter 11

"Get up, you stupid cow!" Andre yanked Erin to her feet. She was still floating, once again under the influence of the Special K with which he'd injected her. Erin no longer fought it. So much easier to just accept the feeling that she was somewhere watching this happen instead of actually being a part of the horror.

Andre shook her, forcing her to focus on him. "I have to go, and this may take a while. No way am I leaving you in here where anyone could look in and see you. I have a special place for you, Erin. Come on."

She tried to pull herself back to reality enough to realize what he was doing, but couldn't comprehend where he was dragging her. She followed him, stumbling over the rough ground behind the trailer. Then he shoved her down and inside somewhere dark and cold, following her in and pushing her along in front of him.

While Erin was still trying to wrap her mind around where she was and what he was doing, Andre snapped one of her wrists to a metal rod above her head and shoved a canteen next to her before he retreated and closed the entrance behind him.

Just the faintest light trickled in through chinks in the material covering the place he'd tossed her. As if the sound were being filtered through water, she heard the roar of an engine coming to life followed by the sound of the car leaving. One glance around her and Erin realized this wasn't a place she wanted to be. Closing her eyes was so much easier. She could slip back into the drug fog he'd kept her in. Here she could pretend Sam was still out there somewhere—alive. He would come for her and take her home. He would hold her and never, ever let her go again.

She shivered. Andre had taken her coveralls and her shoes. Her jeans and sweatshirt were some protection, but not nearly enough. Spring might be bursting already at lower elevations, but here in the mountains winter hadn't quite relinquished its hold. The days warmed nicely, but the nights often dipped below freezing, frosting the ground in the early mornings until the spring sun could melt it away.

She eyed the canteen, her thirst penetrating the fog surrounding her. Stretching as far as she could, Erin managed to grasp the shoulder strap of the canteen and pull it toward her over the rough dirt of her prison. Struggling to get her hands on it cleared her head to some degree. Balancing the canteen between her up-drawn knees, she used her free hand to unscrew the top and tilted the steel container to take a deep swallow. She'd already swallowed a couple of gulps before she realized it had a faintly bitter taste.

He'd drugged it.

Erin screwed the lid back on, nearly throwing the canteen in frustration, but giving in to anger or despair at that point and throwing the canteen beyond her reach or pouring the water out was something she couldn't afford to do. Both because he might come back and see, or because he might not. If he showed back up and saw she'd wasted it, there was no telling what he might do. And if he didn't show…? That thought scared her most of all. She would need the water, even drugged, to live until she could figure a way out. Like the kid who refuses to even look under the bed in case monsters really do live there, Erin refused to think there might not be a way out, and yet the idea still nagged at the edge of her consciousness, making her heart pound.

Her eyes narrowed as she studied the fine dust motes dancing in a shaft of light falling through the chink. They sparkled and shimmered in front of her eyes as if they had a life of their own. She shook her head. Focus! She had to find something to focus on. Her anger at Andre was the easiest target.

"You are a dead man, Andre Delacroix," she mumbled. "When I get my hands on you, I'll find a way to make you rue the day you fucked with me and mine. If Sam is dead, I swear I'll kill you."

She yanked at her wrist to see if she could budge the metal pipe the handcuffs were attached to, but the pipe wouldn't move even a fraction of an inch, so the only thing she succeeded in doing was to send a sharp, stinging pain along her wrist and arm.

Erin screamed until she was hoarse, but realized there was absolutely no one to hear her. Just like Andre had told her. She was completely alone with no idea when or if her captor even intended to return. Was that was he had planned? Would he simply leave her hear to die a slow death? Erin tried to beat back her panic.

* * * *

It was nearly dusk before Sam got a call. He had been half asleep and fumbled for his phone, grabbing it just before it slipped off the edge of the hospital bed.

"Yeah."

"Delacroix's just made contact with Rick," Jim, Sam's lead detective, said. "Wants to meet Rick for dinner." Sam realized the fluttering in his belly was the faint stir of hope.

"Okay. Make sure it's someplace public. Can we wire him?"

There was a moment of hushed conversation on the other end of the line. Rick had already agreed to helping however they needed him to, but Sam was sure Jim was just double checking.

"Yeah. Rick says he's fine with that. We'll fix him up so we can monitor and record what they discuss. Right now we don't have any hard evidence unless we can find Erin. Jake's guys couldn't find any usable prints at his crime scene. If we can get something on tape, or an attempt on Rick's life, then we can arrest him. We'll set it up. One way or another we'll get something."

"We need to have men close enough to ensure Rick's safety. And, Jim, I'll be there too."

"Sam… Are you sure?"

"Yeah. Doc promised she'd spring me if anything started to happen."

After hanging up with Jim, Sam called Jenny who agreed to let Evan take him, but when they were done, she wanted him bedded down at Stoner's. She would be there to check on him later to ensure he didn't do any further damage. Sam paid her only half a mind, but as he began to ease around his room and dress in the clothing she had brought him, her warnings about how injured he was nagged his every move. He had to stop several times to catch his breath while getting ready. By the time Evan and Jenny arrived, Sam was dressed and trembling like a leaf.

Jenny arched a brow knowingly. "So how are you feeling, Sheriff?"

Sam met her gaze steadily. "Like I owe you an apology."

"You sure you want to do this?" Jenny asked. He saw the concern in her expression and knew she was letting him out against her better judgment only because it was Erin involved.

He nodded. "I have to. It might take a lot out of me, but lying here when I know she's out there somewhere, probably hurt, is driving me insane. I can't do it, Doc."

Jenny crossed her arms and stared at him. "Okay then. Here's the deal. Evan stays with you, no matter what. If you feel any bleeding start or have any increased pain or dizziness, you're to call me right away. No playing hero, Sam, or you could end up doing damage you'll have to live with the rest of your life. Is that clear enough?"

He nodded, but when an orderly pushed a wheelchair through the door, Sam protested.

"Come on, Doc. You can't be serious."

Jenny didn't even crack a smile. "As a heart attack. I can't control what you do after you leave this hospital, but while you're in here, you will use the wheelchair. If you want out of here, then this is your ride to the door. I'm surprised you could even move around well enough to get dressed, quite frankly."

Sam glared the entire way down the hall, into the elevator, and out the front doors. Not a single person dared speak to him. Evan waited there with the passenger door to the Tahoe open. Sam twisted his hips and used his left arm and his right leg to lever himself onto the seat. It hurt like hell, but he kept his face carefully expressionless. No way would he give Doc any ammo at this point to stick his butt back in that hospital bed. He was going to find Erin, come hell or high water.

They drove to the restaurant where Rick had agreed to meet Andre Delacroix. Evan pulled the SUV up next to the surveillance van, and the tech inside handed a set of earphones across the space to Sam. After slipping them on, he heard the conversation between the two men while the rest of the restaurant noise remained a buzz in the background. He growled in frustration. Delacroix was giving nothing away. He kept the conversation on what had happened to the *Sprite* and mutual acquaintances. Rick tried to lead him a couple of times, but Delacroix wasn't biting.

"Does he know he'll need to lure him back to the hotel room?" Sam asked his detective.

Jim nodded. "Yes. He's prepared to do that. We've promised him backup, and Rick's no slouch. He's spent enough time around some pretty rough ports that he won't be the easy mark the younger guy apparently was."

Sam balled his hand into a fist over the wound in his thigh. He had to temper the impatience he felt, fight the desire that made him want to walk through the restaurant and snatch Delacroix by the collar to demand he tell him where Erin was. Better yet, Sam wanted to beat it from the man slowly.

Evan's hand came down on his shoulder and squeezed.

"Easy, Sam. I feel what you're going through, after all Erin's my sister, but jumping the gun won't get either one of us what we want.

We both need Erin back, but I also need enough for an air tight case against this asshole."

Sam glared at Evan, needing him to understand the impotent fury that twisted like a snake inside him. "How would you feel if it were Jenny instead of your sister?"

Evan's mouth tilted. "I'd be right where you're at, and I'm nearly there as it is, Sam. In the past few weeks I've seen her change so much, largely due to you. We'll get her back, bro. We're not going to lose her now."

Sam stared back at the front of the restaurant. "It can't be any other way. I won't accept any other possibility."

* * * *

Erin had gotten used to the slivers of light that filtered into her prison. They brought at least some reassurance that there was a world out there beyond the dirty, cramped space in which she was chained like a dog, but now with the setting of the sun, her light faded and the temperature plummeted like it often did in the mountains. As much as she was able, she huddled into a ball to preserve her body heat. What she wouldn't give to have on the insulated coveralls she wore to work around Sam's farm. The dirt in the crawlspace was loose enough she scooped as much as she could around her, covering her feet to try to give them protection from the cold. She refused to think about what might be in the dirt. This was survival. Nothing more, nothing less.

She thought about the previous Sunday, going to church with Sam and listening to Joseph preach. She hadn't spent much time sitting in a church or even praying for that matter. But she said a prayer now. *God, don't leave me here.* It wasn't much as prayers went, certainly not elaborate or long, but it got the point across. God probably appreciated that.

Surely Andre wouldn't have kidnapped her just to leave her to die chained underneath an abandoned trailer. Erin yanked again at the pipe she was handcuffed to. *Son of a bitch that hurt!* She knew she was making her wrist raw, but she was desperate to get away. The fingers of the hand caught in the cuff had grown numb with cold, and she moved them, clenching and unclenching them in the hope of keeping some feeling and some circulation going. The pain reassured her that she still felt something.

The last light of evening faded, leaving her in an endless, stygian silence where the only thing that touched her senses was the unrelenting and increasing cold of the night. Her breathing was shaky as she rested her face against her knees.

Oh Sam! I know if you could, you would be here. If there was any way, you would be. So the only thing I can figure is what I saw was the truth. You must be dead.

She hadn't thought she could still feel pain, but she felt it now, screaming along every nerve ending and wrapping like a garrote around her heart. And when the pain lessened, despair replaced it, crushing her spirit into dust. It beat her down, bowed her until she was afraid she would break after all. Even her determination to seek revenge for Sam wavered. Without him, Erin was unsure if she had a desire to live let alone avenge him.

The constant fighting she had done against her dyslexia was like nothing to this. This was bigger than anything, and she wasn't sure she could overcome the loss. She had loved Sam ever since that day he'd found her with her arm broken. He'd cradled her close against his lean body while he took her home.

She remembered tilting her head to stare at him, so tall and broad, and thinking God must have sent him just for her. She had fallen in love with him that day, and never stopped loving him she now realized. Her feelings had only grown and changed over the years from hero worship to a mature passion and respect for him. He had laughed at her childish infatuation, then distanced himself from her teenage puppy love. But despite that lack of encouragement, Erin had never forgotten him. Never found another man who quite measured up to her heroic image of him.

She'd realized last fall when she came back, intent on disrupting her family's recognition of Tabby as Stoner's daughter, that Sam had been the one trying to run interference. But she hadn't been able to stay, hadn't been able to process the changes in him. He was even sterner than he had been before. Not the heroic image she carried in her memory, and no longer just the ex-soldier on the neighboring farm. He was now the Castle County Sheriff, a person people looked up to and respected. He'd want nothing to do with her.

But he had. Miracle of miracles, he had wanted her. He loved her. He didn't need to say it. He showed his love every day. Because of that, she knew he would never leave her in a place like this if there was any way he could get to her.

Her throat closed and her chest ached, and finally in the lonely, silent dark of night she wept with her face buried on her knees and her shoulders shaking with grief and cold. She didn't weep for herself. She wept for the dark-haired, dark-eyed man who might turn a dour, taciturn face to the rest of the world, but had always been a refuge for her. She thought of how he'd helped her with the calving, defended her against her family, and how securely he'd held her through the night. A world without Sam wasn't a world she wanted to think about. It wasn't a world she even wanted to inhabit.

As Erin shifted position, her foot brushed the canteen with its drugged contents. If she drank it all, would it be enough oblivion? Somehow she doubted it. A shiver worked its way down her spine. In her heart, she had always believed Andre would return. He had plans for her. He'd said so. Now, the first niggling doubt wiggled through. What if Andre didn't come back?

* * * *

Rick and Delacroix were going to drive back to the motel. Sam stripped off the earphones and handed them back to the tech. He nodded his thanks when the man shut the passenger door for him. Just a few seconds later, the SUV shifted as Evan opened the door and hopped behind the wheel.

"So now what?"

Sam stared at the front of the restaurant. "We let them get back to the hotel room. Jim's got men already posted there, and the guests in the rooms adjoining Rick's have been moved to other areas so we could move our men in. We'll stay in your vehicle and keep at least a little distance."

"And what are you going to do, Sam?"

He met Evan's quiet, serious expression before looking at the sling on his arm and the thick bandage bulging beneath the material of his slacks. "As much as I wish it was different, I'm going to stay out of the way. I'm no use to anybody like this, but at least it's easier to take seeing it go down firsthand. I'm hoping once we get him in custody we can get him to tell us where Erin is."

Rick and Delacroix exited the restaurant at that moment, both getting into separate cars for the short trip back to the hotel. Evan kept his distance, cruising past the parking lot the first time around so that it would give the impression they weren't tailing them. When they pulled back in, Sam saw Rick outlined in the light of the open doorway to the room. Delacroix was just getting out of his car. There was a quick flash of something in his hands.

"*Shit!*" Sam blurted. "Delacroix's armed."

Evan stopped the SUV. All thought of remaining only an observer fled. Sam was already fumbling with the door latch, seeing his chance to find Erin slipping away as he spotted a sharpshooter on the balcony, his rifle trained on Delacroix. Everything seemed to happen at once. He heard someone shout "gun!" as he shoved the door open, grimacing as pain shot through his injured right arm, and half fell from the passenger side.

"Delacroix!" Sam yelled almost simultaneously. "Drop it!"

If the man didn't surrender, the sharpshooters would take him out. One bullet could wipe out any chance Sam had of finding Erin, and if that happened, his sniper might as well take aim at Sam's heart.

Delacroix turned, the gun swiveling from his intended target to Sam. The black bore of Delacroix's weapon yawned. For just a moment, Sam saw the other man's eyes widen with startled recognition—surprised Sam was still alive?—but before he could pull the trigger, the sharpshooter fired two times in quick succession, and Delacroix dropped with a short, sharp grunt.

Sweet merciful heaven! Delacroix was the only one who knew where Erin was. Sam sobbed as he lurched across the parking lot and fell to his knees next to the bleeding man. He snatched the lapel of Delacroix's suit coat into his fist and jerked the man half off the ground.

"Where is she?" he snarled. "Where the hell is Erin? What did you do with her?"

Delacroix's lids fluttered and his pale eyes weren't quite focused. Sam could swear he saw the man's lips twist into some semblance of smile as he rasped, "Fuck. You."

Delacroix jerked once or twice with involuntary muscle movements. Sam looked at him in disbelief. He was dead. Delacroix was dead, but not before already killing the only other man who might have had any idea where Erin was. He shook Delacroix's limp body with both hands, oblivious to the pain lancing through his right arm and the sobs racking him.

Others gathered around, trying to pull him away. Sam shook them off like a wounded grizzly. All he could picture was Erin lying somewhere, cold and hurt. He remembered the first time he'd looked into her deep blue-gray eyes. They had been filled with pain then, and he was sure they were now. But this time there was no one there to pick her up, hold her, and make the hurt and fear go away. He had failed her. Again.

Sam roared.

"Sam!"

Evan's firm, quiet voice broke through the turmoil in his brain. Sam yanked his hands away from Delacroix as if he had suddenly realized he was holding a rattlesnake.

"Snap out of it," Evan continued. "You're an investigator. There are always clues. It's just a matter of finding them."

Sam stayed where he was for a minute, fighting for control over the emotions overwhelming him. This wasn't getting it done. This wasn't helping Erin. That's what he had to focus on. Finally, Sam allowed two of his deputies to help him to his feet and back to Evan's vehicle.

"You're bleeding," Evan told him. "I have to call Jenny. You understand me? I'm taking you back to the hospital."

"Wait." It might have come out as only a hoarse croak, but Evan stopped.

Sam looked at the officers gathered around him waiting for the leadership he had never failed to provide, and he wouldn't fail now. "Gentlemen, we have a whole new problem. Our dead suspect is the only one who knew where Erin is. I want Delacroix and everything he's touched gone over with a fine-toothed comb. Nothing is insignificant. We need to know every move he's made since he arrived here."

The sharpshooter wiped his hand over his face. "I'm sorry, Sheriff. I had no choice. It was him or you."

"I know," Sam said, thinking it might as well be him if they couldn't find Erin, but he had to offer some reassurance. "You did the right thing."

As he waited for Evan to get behind the wheel, one thought truly remained. Delacroix was dead, and time was running out for Erin.

Chapter 12

Her mind dulled by exposure and hunger, Erin stared at the sliver of light. She had watched it brighten, then march slowly across the area in front of her. Now as another day passed, it began to dim again.

Don't go.

Had she spoken out loud? She didn't want the light to fade. It was almost like a friend to her now, the dust motes dancing in the glowing golden ribbon of afternoon sunlight. There were other reasons she didn't want it to fade. As muddled as she felt, she knew time wasn't just passing, it was running out. Right now, time was more of an enemy than Andre. He wouldn't just leave her here. He would want to kill her himself, see her die. He had been gone too long. He should have been back by now, at least she thought so, but she couldn't be sure.

Erin stared at the canteen. She was so thirsty. People could survive for a while without food, but not water. Her eyes roved over the canteen possessively. If she took just small sips, maybe she could prevent enough of the diluted drug mixture from making her high. Her fingers crept over the dirt to the strap, and she pulled it toward her.

You're admitting defeat. You're admitting no one's coming back for you. Why not just go ahead and drink the whole thing? Maybe you'll freeze to death while you're stoned and never know when you die.

She gave a short bark of laughter, the hoarse, cracked sound startling her. How appropriate would that be, to die of a drug overdose? It was exactly what a lot of people expected of her. Former Senator Stoner Richardson's troubled daughter dies of an overdose while chained like a dog to a sewer pipe underneath a rundown mobile home. It was a headline on par with any from her past exploits.

Erin laughed until she couldn't stop, and if there was an edge of hysteria in it, it didn't matter. No one could hear her. She could scream as long and as loud as she wanted, and no one would hear. She knew that for certain because she'd already tried it. That was how she knew. She was in the middle of no-fucking-where.

No! She could hear herself, the defeated negative self-talk, and she would not give up. She would get out of here alive and make sure Sam hadn't died in vain. With her free hand, Erin frantically pulled at the pipe holding the opposite end of the cuff. She crawled along its length, sliding the cuff along it as she tried to find some weakness in the pipe, but there was none. She managed to get close enough to the trailer's rusting water heater that she was able to pull the plastic-coated blanket insulation off of it. Mice had eaten holes in it in several places, but she could still use it to give her some cover.

No matter what she had to endure, she wanted to live. Resolve hardened inside her. Although there would never be another man like Sam, all this time to think had helped her realize there were other people in her life who cared about her—her parents, Evan and Jenny, Tabby and Joe, Melodie, Rachel—Erin realized the list was much longer than she'd ever imagined. She could live for them, even without Sam. And she would remember him. She'd never been a quitter and she wouldn't quit now. Sam wouldn't want her to. Even when he'd pushed her away or been exasperated with her, he'd still been her most ardent champion. Now she would become his.

With the insulation around her shoulders, Erin once again piled dirt around her legs, trying to get ready for the night to come. She glanced again at the canteen. She would drink. Even if she risked being drugged, she had to have liquid, and maybe it would make the night pass faster, if not dreamlessly.

* * * *

Sam awoke and stared at the ceiling above him. The soft cream color and the elaborate light fixture just off to his right were definitely not a part of any hospital he'd ever seen before. So just where the hell was he now?

"You're finally awake, I see."

He turned at the sound of the deep, mellifluous tones that had once rung through the US Senate chamber and saw Stoner seated casually in a chair near a tall, narrow window. Maybe casually wasn't the right word. Upon closer examination, tension had settled on the older man's shoulders like an ox bearing a yoke. Sam took in the opulent surroundings, the sun streaming through the sheer curtains at the window.

"Your guest, I presume," he rasped in a voice that sounded even rougher than he'd imagined it might.

"Mmm." Stoner set aside the magazine he'd been reading and leaned forward. "You put up such a fuss last night Jenny finally brought you here."

"What time is it?" Sam's gaze strayed to the window again.

"About three-thirty."

His eyes widened. He'd slept until three-thirty in the afternoon? He needed to get up, but when he looked around the room, he didn't see his clothing.

As if aware of Sam's intentions, Stoner continued "She sedated you, Sam. You were combative and bleeding."

Dimly, in the back of his brain, he recalled agreeing to that, as long as she didn't make him go back to the hospital.

"Erin?"

Stoner's expression turned haggard. "No word yet."

Sam's mouth tightened. "I need to get up, see what's going on." Stoner was shaking his head. "You don't understand...."

One look from the older man's stormy gray eyes stopped him.

"She's my daughter, Sam. I understand. Exactly. Now if you'll let me finish...?"

Sam's mouth tightened and he nodded. Their relationship had never been easy. It wasn't just about what had happened with Erin when she was a teenager. No, it went back even further to when Sam was a teen and had discovered exactly what was going on at the cabin between their two farms. Although Sam had never breathed a word of it, the fact he'd known of Stoner's lover—Tabby's mother—was enough to make him if not an enemy, certainly unwelcome. Sure, that secret had all come out in the open, and the two men had an uneasy truce, even a friendship of sorts now, but Erin's disappearance was straining everyone's relationships.

"Evan invited them to set up shop downstairs, so the combined task force is down in the front hall. If you'll stay put, I'll send Jake up here. He can update you."

Sam blinked. This was now the staging area for the search? As Stoner stood, Sam put his hand on his sleeve to stop him.

"Stoner, what day is it? I mean, I haven't missed any more than a day, have I?"

The gray eyes warmed slightly. "No, son, you haven't."

"Thanks." Sam laid his head back against the pillows, relief flooding through him. It was bad enough that he could do so little, but the time was already going by so quickly. *The longer she's gone...* He couldn't complete the thought.

Jake would be here any second. He would be able to tell him what was going on. Sam wiped his eyes with his fingers and brushed his hand across his unshaven cheek. It hadn't been that long ago that Jake had been in a similar situation. Holly's ex-fiance had stolen Noelle when she was just a newborn. Since Jake had delivered the baby, it was like his own daughter had been kidnapped. So Jake would understand just how impotent Sam felt, and his injuries only made matters worse.

He looked up when Jake walked in and tried to smile, but he knew it was a weak effort at best.

"Hey, man. Stoner said you were awake."

"You making any progress?" Sam tried to keep his tone cool, but his voice cracked at the end and he glanced down, embarrassed he couldn't keep it together.

"Some," Jake responded as if he hadn't noticed anything out of the ordinary. "You want to hear it all?"

"Yeah. Don't leave anything out, even if you think it will upset me." He needed the details. It was the only way he could feel he had some control over trying to find Erin.

"Well, we discovered several things in the car and on Delacroix, which lead us to believe he didn't plan to kill Erin." Jake sat in the chair Stoner had only recently vacated. "In his glove compartment, we found a vial of ketamine. It's been used as an anesthetic for people and animals, but it's also had some popularity as a hallucinogenic in the drug culture. There were syringes, and the vial looks like doses are gone. I've got someone checking on dosages and how much has been used."

That was promising. Rick had said Delacroix might use drugs. "What else?"

"Keys to handcuffs in his pants pocket. We also found what looks like a door key. A paper tag hooked to it had Matty's name on it."

"A hotel key?" Some of the smaller mom and pop hotels still used keys.

Jake shook his head. "No. Looks like a deadbolt like you'd find on a house."

"There's something else, Jake. What?" Sam stiffened because he doubted it was anything he really wanted to know.

"Her coveralls were in the car along with her boots and socks. Wherever he has her, she doesn't have any protection from the elements. It was mighty cold last night."

Sam's jaw clenched. "She's tough."

He said it to reassure himself, but it did little good. While some of his anger had faded—hanging on to being angry with a dead man was just plain stupid—fear they wouldn't find Erin gnawed at him like an insatiable hunger. As tough as she was, there was only so much any human body could take. And this time of year, no one could be certain what the weather would do. It could be nearly summer-like one day and snow the next.

"We've set up a search grid," Jake said into the silence stretching between them.

"On what criteria?" Sam forced himself to think logically, keep his mind on the investigation. If he could just step away from the emotions, just for a minute, but it wasn't possible. Not with Erin in danger.

"According to Rick and Jim, Delacroix wanted to meet at the restaurant as soon as possible. Between his call to Rick and his arrival at the restaurant, only an hour and ten minutes passed. Using the restaurant as a center point, we drew a circle around it to encompass what would constitute that amount of drive time."

Jesus! That was huge. Sam ground his teeth. "It will be nearly impossible to search an area that size within a realistic timeframe for finding Erin alive."

"I realize that, Sam, but we don't dare cut it down geographically and risk that she really is that far away, so we've also got deputies contacting realty and rental agents around the area. Matty's name on the deadbolt key doesn't match his handwriting, Delacroix's, or Rick's."

"So you think it might be the key to a place they rented specifically to hold Erin?" Sam felt the first small flare of hope.

"That's what we're going on right now." Jake's words just helped to cement that.

Sam wrapped his fingers around the back of his neck and massaged the aching muscles thoughtfully. The panic faded. His brain began to kick into gear, and his years as an investigator shoved themselves forward. "I wouldn't stop with realtors and rental agents. Have someone start going through the area papers and their classifieds. They would have wanted something cheap, something that could be rented quickly and without a formal lease of any sort. Plot everything you find on a map. If it fits in your grid, check it out."

Jake nodded. "We've got assistance from other counties and the state. We're gonna find her, Sam."

Sam ran his hand over his untidy hair and sucked in a deep breath, the first time he really felt like he'd gotten any oxygen since he'd realized Erin was gone. They could do this. For the first time since her disappearance, he began to actually believe they could find her. Now the next step was to get his ass out of this bed and downstairs so he could help.

"I need to get cleaned up."

Jake grinned. "I'll see what I can do."

* * * *

Her light was coming back. Erin shivered, hoping that with the light would also come warmth. She was so cold. The insulation had helped, but her left hand, the one hooked in the handcuff, was numb. She had scooted to a place where the pipe was closer to the ground and had tried to cover it as much as she could, but it wasn't enough. As the light grew, she crept back to where some of it might fall on her if she stretched out a little bit. To actually feel the sunlight on her would be nice. She dragged the canteen along with her.

Drinking some of the water last night had given her a high, but it had also helped her sleep. She didn't want that now, but she was so thirsty. Two nights, nearly forty-eight hours. She had to believe Andre wasn't coming back. Whether he'd deliberately left her here to die or something had happened to him. He wasn't coming back, and if he wasn't coming back, then no one was.

As the sunlight strengthened, she realized that even though the temperature was warming—she wasn't. Surviving another night might not happen. There, she'd admitted it. Erin seriously considered her options for getting away. She remembered stories she'd listened to on the radio and over her computer about people who'd been stuck places, out in the desert after a car accident or hiking in the mountains, and the extreme measures they'd used to get free. She looked at her cuffed hand. Even trapped animals sometimes chewed off their captive limbs in order to free themselves.

Her stomach rolled, but there was nothing for her to throw up. *Sever her own hand?* She hadn't reached that point. Yet. If the choice was that or death, she would have to decide if she could go to that extreme. She would have to make a decision before she became too weak to carry it out. But not yet. Please, God, not just yet. For now, while the sun shone and the crawlspace warmed ever so slightly, she would keep hope alive. She had to.

The day wore on. Her sliver of light continued its creep across the crawlspace. Erin felt in the dirt while she scooted along on the ground. Sometimes people left things behind, tools, a rock, something she could use to try to knock the pipe loose. When her efforts turned up nothing more than a discarded cat food can, she growled with frustration and scooted back to her spot. It would be time to start digging in again for another night.

Her glance slithered to the canteen. After picking it up and shaking it, she realized about half its contents were gone. At best she had about two more days, and that was only if the temperatures didn't drop as low. Then she would have to get free or die. Her choices were narrowing almost as quickly as her body was weakening. But whatever her options, she was on her own.

Erin unscrewed the top of the canteen with fingers that shook and tipped it to her mouth. She would swallow half the water now and save the rest for tomorrow. When the drug began to work on her this time, she welcomed it. Her body craved food and water, but more and more it demanded sleep, and the drug helped. She pulled her plastic insulation cover around her curled up form, resting her head on her knees as she slipped into a state somewhere between drug-induced unconsciousness and sleep.

* * * *

By the second morning after Delacroix's death, Sam was slowly inching his way around the room again. Desperation drove him. The passing of time now had a new meaning. Each minute that ticked by was one less minute Erin had to live. He didn't want to think about it in those terms, but that was the reality…and what drove him. He was able to move more freely and didn't feel like every shift was going to rip something back open again. By the time Jenny arrived to check on him, he had showered, shaved—somewhat inexpertly with just one hand—and dressed in the clean clothes Catherine had brought for him the previous evening.

Jenny's attitude was all business. After checking him over, she smiled. "You can come downstairs, but take it easy."

Those were some of the sweetest words he'd heard. He squeezed her shoulder. "I love you, Doc," he rasped.

Jenny grinned. "Sorry, big guy, I'm already spoken for, but if you'll let me, I'll accompany you down the steps."

Sam felt himself flush. "Yeah. Thanks."

Stoner's front hall and study had been converted into a high-tech crime lab. When Sam raised his brows, Stoner said, "I have money. Erin is my daughter, so I see no reason not to use it. A few other people have kicked in too."

"Like who?"

"Her friend, Rick, Evan and Jenny, Jake and Holly, Catherine…"

Jake walked out of Stoner's study at that point. "Welcome back, Sam. We've got a list of places we're going to check out today. The realty companies were a bust, but I found several promising places through private ads. I'm sending your deputies out to check most of the list…the places where we actually spoke to someone, and it's probably not a hit, but still worth putting eyes on."

Sam leaned on the cane Jenny had pressed on him. "That sounds like you've saved a few to check out yourself."

Jake's grin was a quick flash of white teeth and dimples. "Yup. I've got four places here, a little spread out, but within our search range. We haven't been able to get a phone contact other than leaving messages. Wanna come?"

Sam turned to look at Jenny and raised his brows inquiringly. As anxious as he was, he couldn't afford another incident like the night with Delacroix. She rolled her eyes.

"Go ahead. Nothing I say stops you unless I shoot you up with drugs, but I don't want to hear one word tonight if you're in pain."

"Thanks, Doc." Sam relaxed the tight hold on his jaw.

"Don't mention it. And Sam?"

"Yeah?"

"You better call me if you find out anything."

"You know I will."

When Jake started to help him into his pickup, Sam swatted at him with his cane. "Get the hell away from me. I am not some damn cripple."

"Language, language! Holly would be so disappointed in you for such backsliding. And besides, you let Jenny help you."

Sam scowled. "I can get in the truck by myself. And Jenny's a whole lot cuter than your monkey butt face."

Jake laughed. "That's more like the Sam I know and love."

After Jake slid behind the wheel and buckled his seatbelt, Sam asked, "Where to first?"

"I figured we'd start the farthest away and work back in toward the middle."

Sam stared out the window as they wound their way along narrow, twisting state roads. A little divine intervention would certainly be nice. His eyes narrowed on the road as he tried to think of every conceivable angle to finding Erin.

Jake glanced over at him, then back to the road. "I ran into Tabby and Melodie at Tarpley's this morning. Tabby wanted you to know Joe's got Erin on a prayer chain. Of course, he's also volunteered to help with the search."

Sam knew he should make some positive response. "That's thoughtful."

Jake glanced his way again. "Melodie told me to remember to look under everything because that always helped her when she was trying to find something she'd lost."

Sam rubbed his eyes. "She's a good kid, especially considering everything she's been through."

"Yeah. Well, her advice isn't bad either."

It was just over an hour to the first location. When they arrived, they were greeted by a little old lady who was so hard of hearing she'd missed their call. She told them she had rented the place out about a week ago to a nice young couple who were both away at their jobs. Did they want to wait?

Sam crossed that off Jake's list as they bumped back down the drive. After the second place was also a bust, Jake suggested stopping by Mercer's and grabbing a couple of sandwiches before they headed to the last two. "It's getting late, bro. I'm hungry."

Sam had no appetite but knew he had to eat. The sun had shifted toward the mountains to the west. Once they were back in the truck, Jake sipped his coffee and set it back in the drink holder.

"The next place is only about five miles from where we found Matty. No one could remember any structure on the property, so we might have to look around. There must be something, otherwise why run an ad to rent it?"

"Hunting rights? Not the right time of year, though." Sam frowned. Great. This was probably a bust too. Jake turned off the highway to bump down a narrow gravel road that barely had enough room for two cars to pass each other. Trees overhung the road from both sides, casting it into deep shadow.

"Hell, this is almost as bad as Mistletoe Lane, that goat path where Holly was living when I first met her."

"It's worse. Mistletoe Lane at least makes a pretense at being a road. I'm not sure this even qualifies. Are you sure there's anything back here?" Sam's brows drew together. They couldn't afford to waste time on wild goose chases. He felt time ticking off Erin's life clock with each beat of his heart.

"I was about to say cattle, but judging from the gaps in that fence, any self-respecting steer would already be long gone."

"Whoa!" As Jake was speaking, Sam had spotted what looked like tire marks angling off to the right.

"What is it?"

"There's an old road bed that heads off here... Mainly grass, but it looks like it's seen some traffic recently, too much of a coincidence not to check out."

Jake braked and backed up until he could make the turn in. They spotted an old shed with part of its roof missing and were about to turn around when Jake abruptly stopped again.

"Hmm." His eyes narrowed as he peered out through the windshield.

"What?" Sam snapped. It had been a long, frustrating day after such a hopeful start.

"You see anything back there among the kudzu vines?"

Sam squinted a little bit. At this time of year, the tangle was still dead looking and minus the leaves.

"Yeah," Sam acknowledged slowly. "Let's keep going. Of course how anyone thought someone would want to rent this kind of crap, I don't know."

Jake grunted. "Probably some absentee landowner who hasn't bothered to check the condition of their property in years, but if someone did rent it, let's hope it was Delacroix."

They pulled into what once might have been a front yard. Now it was littered with creeping vines. The trailer appeared abandoned, but not in total disrepair. Windows and doors seemed to be intact and the roof looked solid.

"Looks like it's still habitable," Sam murmured.

Jake snorted as he eyed the kudzu. "I hear the owners only moved out last week."

Despite the situation, Sam chuckled. The speed at which kudzu grew was a running joke all over the southeast. "That can't be. I'm sure the kudzu would have been strangling the roof vent by now."

Jake shook his head and sighed. "I don't know, Sam. This looks like a dead end, man."

"Let's check it out anyway. It's nearly dark, and we won't get to anything else today." Sam rubbed the back of his neck, not sure if the feeling creeping over him was legitimate or just wishful thinking because in the back of his mind, he knew Erin was about out of time.

The slam of their truck doors echoed in the deserted area. Both men snapped on latex gloves, and picked their way to the front steps.

"You brought the key, didn't you?" Sam asked.

"Yeah."

"So try it, Cinderella. Let's see if it fits."

Jake slid the key in the front door. While it slid all the way in, it wouldn't budge a single tumbler. He pulled it back out and shook his head. Sam leaned to the side of the narrow front porch to peer through one of the front windows. A beat up couch sagged along one living room wall and a cheap table sat forlornly in a kitchen bare of appliances. As he squinted, he saw a glass on the counter and next to it, a hypodermic needle. His heart thudded heavily.

"Jake, someone's been here recently. There's a syringe on the counter. Try the back. You know how some of these places are. Different keys fit different doors, and I can see a door off the kitchen."

"Wait here," Jake suggested. "I'll try the back door. If it works, I can let you in."

Sam watched through the window, saw Jake's shadow at the back door, then the shaft of afternoon sunlight as it opened. This was it. Now where was she? Everything was so silent. Were they too late? Had Delacroix moved her somewhere else? Fear clawed at him, so when Jake finally opened the door, Sam almost knocked him out of the way to get inside.

"Erin!"

"Easy, bud. Check the bedroom on this end. I'll go the other way."

Sam turned to the small bedroom next to the front door. One glance told him there was nothing in there to be concerned about. Jake approached from the other end. He shook his head.

"Nothing."

"The key fits. It's the only lead we've got, Jake. We've got to keep looking. Maybe this was a red herring. Maybe he's stashed a key somewhere to the real place." Sam glanced back at the hypodermic. It could be just some addict looking for a place to shoot up, but the key had fit, and there was just something that bothered him about the whole deal. He shifted his eyes back to Jake. "What was it Melodie said?"

Jake frowned. "Look under everything."

They returned to the bedrooms and the bathroom, checking in closets and inside cabinets, calling Erin's name as they searched. Nothing. They rifled through the drawers, searched cabinets with their fingers, feeling for keys. Sam stood in the middle of the kitchen, still reluctant to leave even though the light was fading. He glanced back over to the cabinets under the sink. Jake had left them open, and he could see the pipes leading from the sink through the bottom of the cabinet…to the crawl space under the trailer. He looked up slowly and found Jake's eyes following the same path his had.

"Under the house."

They both said it at the same time. Jake with an air of anticipation, and Sam with cold dread. If she was under the house and alive, she should have made some noise or responded when they called her name. They clambered down the back steps, Jake much faster than Sam, but Sam wasn't far behind.

Like many rural trailers, this one had only cheap aluminum skirting to hide its underpinnings. An area just to the right of the back stairs looked like the metal had been recently moved, the ground around it disturbed by both footprints and signs of something being dragged or scraped. Sam reached it first, snatching it back, and once again feeling a jangle along his right arm. Both men bent low to peer into the dimness, but they neither heard anything nor saw anything other than disturbed dirt.

"Fuck!" Nausea rolled through Sam. He straightened and leaned against the house, closing his eyes in sudden pain. God in heaven. Had Delacroix killed her and buried her here? Sam started to shake.

Chapter 13

"Hold it together, Sam. No matter what we find, you gotta keep it together, man." Sam heard Jake's attempt to bolster him, but there was no comfort.

"You got a flashlight?" Sam snarled.

"Yeah." Jake pulled it off his duty belt and flipped the switch before pointing it into the dimness. "Looks like just some trash, the water heater, and some wadded up insulation."

Sam bent over, braced on his cane. "Shine it up along the bottom of the trailer."

As soon as Jake raised the beam, they both saw the glint of metal and a limp hand protruding from the insulation.

"Erin!" Sam cried, then roared right on the heels of that, "*Bastard!*"

"Jesus!" Jake exclaimed at the same time.

As Sam started to dive into the confined space, Jake stopped him. "Get real, Sam. You can't do this. You're in no condition to bring her out. I've got the handcuff keys. Use your cell. Call it in and call an ambulance. I'll get her."

Sam's breathing was as heavy as if he'd just run several miles. Fury nearly clogged his thoughts to the exclusion of all else. Impotent fury because the man who'd done this was already dead. Get a grip. They had to get Erin out of there. Get her out where she could get help because God only knew what kind of shape she was in by now. Tough as she was, no human was meant to go through what she had.

Jake touched his arm.

"You hear me, bro? Don't wig out on me. I'll bring her out. You're in no shape for that. You call. Now!"

Erin needed him. He might not be able to crawl underneath and bring her out himself, but he could make sure that this time she had the help she needed. He wouldn't fail her again. Sam pulled his cell phone out, relieved to see he had a signal, and tapped 911, all the while keeping his eyes trained on Jake as the big man crawled through the dirt toward Erin. Sam would have recognized her hand anywhere.

"This is Sheriff Sam Barnes, I need an ambulance and detectives sent to thirty-one, six-twenty Branch Road, a mile off the Shady Valley Church Road."

In the background, he heard Jake call over his shoulder, "She's breathing."

Sam had to lean hard on the cane as he swayed with relief. She was alive, and the euphoria flooding his every pore made him lightheaded.

"We've found Erin Richardson. She's unconscious." He paused for a moment to regain his composure. "Have someone tell her family."

He jammed the phone back into his pocket, watching as Jake carefully unhooked the cuffs holding her wrist. Jake uttered a muffled curse.

"What is it?"

"Her wrist is raw, looks like from trying to get loose, but that's not all. Sam, this sleep isn't natural."

She could simply be exhausted, but if that were the case, surely releasing her wrist would have roused her.

"Can you wake her?"

From beneath the trailer, he heard Jake's urgent voice. "Erin! Erin, can you hear me, honey? It's Jake Allred. Sam's with me...no, nothing. She is breathing though."

Sam forced himself to breathe evenly, to think as he'd been trained to so he could get past the emotion. "Is there anything lying nearby? If she's ingested something toxic, we'll need to be able to give them an idea of what." Frustration made him clench and unclench his fingers. He should be in there, not looking on while Jake pulled her out.

"Just a canteen. Appears to still have something in it."

"Bring it." Hurry, he wanted to yell. His whole body shook with the need to see her, to put his hands on her, and reassure himself that she really was alive.

"Okay. I'm putting her on my back so I can crawl out. She appears to have some contusions to her face along with the injuries to her wrist."

All Sam could see at this point was the flashlight bobbing as Jake crawled back to the opening with Erin on his back. When he reached the gap in the aluminum, Jake held the canteen and the flashlight out for Sam, who took them even while his eyes devoured Erin. She was filthy. Her wrist was raw and bruised. Through the dirt and tear tracks on her face, he spotted a fading bruise along her cheekbone, a cut near her hairline, and a scabbed-over split lip.

Anger, like acid, rose in him until he thought it would eat away his insides. If Andre Delacroix hadn't already been dead, Sam would have killed him for the tear tracks alone because he knew just how much it took to make Erin cry.

"I'll carry her out to the truck," Jake murmured gently.

Sam wanted to hold her, wanted to be the one to carry her out of this hell hole, but he pushed his pride aside. It was all he could do to walk on his healing leg, and there would be no way at all he could support even a portion of her weight with his right arm. One thing he could do, though. He could stay with her. Sam was not going to leave her now that they'd found her. Not ever again.

Jake laid her on the back seat. "Go around to the other side, get in there. Talk to her. Maybe you'll have better luck getting a response from her."

Sam's leg throbbed. He hoisted himself into the back and leaned over her recumbent form, stroking her dusty hair. She'd told him she loved him. Maybe that would give his words and his voice more weight. He cleared his throat before he spoke, but his voice still sounded choked to his own ears.

"Come on, Erin baby, wake up for me. You're safe now. No one will hurt you, baby, not again, not ever again."

He continued to talk to her, croon to her. They were nonsense words, but he just wanted her to hear his voice in the hope it would give her something to reach out and hold on to. He brushed his fingers along the edge of her hair, along her cheek, and down her neck. His hand trembled. Weakness or relief, it didn't matter. All that mattered was being able to touch her again. She felt thinner, but then he knew she had eaten nothing at all for two days and wasn't sure about the days preceding. For all he knew, her last meal might have been dinner the night before he was shot.

In the distance, he heard the wail of the ambulance. Thank God. "Help's almost here, baby."

Jake stuck his head in the window. "I'm going to walk out to the end of the farm road and flag them down to guide them in."

Sam looked her over. "You have a blanket in here? She's got to be suffering exposure at the very least."

Jake reached behind the seat and handed him one. "Here, put this over her. I've jacked the heater up, but she probably needs even more warmth."

Sam took the blanket and spread it over her before touching her hair. It ate at him. He curled himself around her as best he could. With his arm and his leg screaming in pain, Sam still needed to touch her and reassure himself she was there. She was breathing.

"Please wake up, Erin." Sam's voice broke. Jake was right. This sleep wasn't natural. Delacroix had to have done something to her. Sam thought back over everything Erin had told him about the scumbag. If Delacroix and his family had been heavily into transporting drugs, there was no telling what type of concoction he might have forced on her.

Sam picked up the canteen, unscrewed the lid, and sniffed. There was no obvious smell that would indicate anything in the water. He tilted it to his lips and put a little of it on his tongue. Bitter but not metallic. Even the nastiest well water around here didn't have an aftertaste like that. The most logical conclusion was that Delacroix had somehow spiked the water. God only knew for what reason. It seemed unlikely it would be enough to kill her, but maybe enough to keep her docile…or passed out. Sam screwed the lid back on, set the canteen within easy reach, and once again stroked her cheek.

"Erin, baby," he whispered, his voice cracking. "Come back to me. I swear to God I'll do a better job of looking out for you this time. Just come back to me."

She shifted her head slightly against his hand, her neck arching backward, but still seemed totally unaware. Behind her lids, her eyes shifted rapidly from side to side. Just when he thought he couldn't take it anymore, they opened, but the beautiful blue-gray depths seemed empty, as if he were looking into a void. It was Erin's shell, but the girl, teenager, woman he had loved for so many years wasn't there.

Fear gripped him. If she had gotten so thirsty she drank a large amount of the water at one time, it was possible she might have overdosed on whatever was in the water. Based on what they'd found in Delacroix's car, he had to think it was ketamine, but it could be almost anything.

The distinctive rumble of a diesel engine grew louder. The ambulance. He heard it easing its way down the road. Flashes of red light bounced around the interior of the truck and off the dead, brown kudzu vines surrounding them.

"Help's here, baby," he crooned. "Hang on for me. I won't let you go. I'll stay right with you."

Jake opened the door.

"They'll be here with the stretcher in just a minute. I had the patrol cars and Jim's SUV pull past the entrance so we could get her out of here first. Then they'll come in to rope off the scene and do what evidence gathering they can right now. Any movement from her?"

Sam sighed. "Movement, no awareness. I tasted the water. It's got a bitter flavor like it might be spiked with something."

"Hmm. Take that with you so they can analyze it. And remind them about the vial of ketamine." Jake looked over his shoulder. "Here they are."

Sam looked into the eyes of Castle County's senior EMT. Over the years, they had worked a lot of incidents together, but nothing as important as this. "Be careful with her, Tony. I'll get out so you can move her."

Tony grasped Sam's hand for an instant longer than necessary. "Don't worry, Sheriff. We'll take care of her."

Sam nodded.

"Can I ride with you?" He'd beg if he must, fight if he had to, but no way was he leaving her side.

Tony's gaze filled with understanding. "Of course, sir."

Sam climbed awkwardly from the truck, grabbed his cane and the canteen, and limped to the ambulance. If this was all the time Erin had left, then at least he could spend it at her side. Even thinking it made his throat close right up.

Tony and his crew wasted no time getting Erin onto the stretcher and into the ambulance. One of the younger guys helped Sam inside. Sam sat to one side near her feet, staying out of the way as they worked on her. An oxygen cannula was hooked onto her, and a saline drip started. The EMTs were careful of her left hand, using her right arm to hook up their drip before gently attaching a blood pressure and pulse monitor to her finger. Heated blankets were tucked around her, dirt and all. Sam had seen how filthy and scraped her feet were before they tucked the blankets around those too.

Erin would hate being helpless like this. He swallowed as he looked again at the tear tracks on her cheeks. He had made her shed a tear—once—but not weep as those stains indicated. What had happened to her?

They bounced along the farm road. The ride didn't smooth out until they hit the black top. Sam's eyes never left hers, so he was the first to notice that the rapid movements of her eyes beneath her lids had speeded up. Twitching began in her feet and hands.

"Tony," Sam said sharply, fear bubbling up inside him. "What's going on?"

The EMTs were strapping her down as quickly as possible.

"Seizure," Tony grunted as he tightened a strap across her lower legs.

Sam's heart pounded. He didn't want to distract either man working on Erin, but he recalled seeing a drug overdose in which the victim had gone into seizures before dying. While Tony and Drew talked back and forth about blood pressure and pulse, the siren blared as the ambulance raced along the narrow highway.

Jesus, Sam prayed, don't let her die. Please don't let her die.

He started to breathe a sigh of relief as the seizures suddenly stopped just as they turned into the hospital parking lot, then everything crashed. Her breathing had nearly ceased, her blood pressure plummeted, and her pulse beat erratically. Tony and Drew worked silently now, something that petrified Sam more than their earlier staccato conversations.

Sam slammed himself as far into the corner as he could, his heart thudding heavily and his breathing rasping. His mind screamed no. They couldn't get this far just to lose her when they'd finally found her and gotten her to safety.

As soon as the rear doors opened, Sam scrambled to get out of the way, half- running, half-hopping in pursuit as Erin was wheeled into the emergency room. The driver must have radioed ahead. Medical staff surged forward to take charge.

So did Stoner and Catherine, who'd obviously beaten them to the ER. Their shocked expressions were no doubt a mirror of what he was feeling.

"I thought Jake said she was okay?" Catherine cried in disbelief, as they watched everyone frantically working on Erin.

Sam paused in his hopping half-run after them. "This just happened as we turned in. I'm going with them."

He made it as far as the treatment room before an apologetic nurse blocked his way. "Sorry, Sheriff."

Sam peered over her shoulder. "Come on, Karen. I've known you since you started kindergarten."

She shook her head. "I can't give that okay. You get Doc to give you a nod and that's a different matter."

"Can I stand right here?"

Karen sighed. "Yes."

Sam refused to leave. Thank God it was a small emergency department. From his vantage point, he could see everything they were doing. Other than the bruising that discolored her cheek, her skin was deathly pale. Erin had always had beautiful skin, but now she looked nearly waxen, and that made Sam fear once again that he would lose her after all.

"Her breathing is stabilizing," the young man near her head said.

"Blood pressure's coming back again and her pulse is nearly back to normal," another nurse added.

Now he would be able to tell her family she was okay. At least he hoped so.

"Sam? What are you doing out here?" Jenny asked as she hurried toward the room. She was still clad in surgical scrubs. Her gaze found his before traveling to the young doctor bent over her sister-in-law.

"What's up?" she asked from the doorway.

"Looks like a drug overdose. The sheriff brought in a canteen containing water laced with something. We're testing it right now, but he and Chief Allred both suspect Ketamine based on other evidence they found. What we're seeing is consistent with that, so we're treating accordingly. Respiration, pulse, and blood pressure crashed as the paramedics brought her in, but we've stabilized her."

Jenny glanced at the monitors hooked to Erin before taking a moment to study Sam and nod. "Come on in. I need to ask you some questions while we're working on her."

Sam limped in ahead of her and moved to a place along the wall where he would be out of the way but still able to see what was going on.

"You're moving pretty well, Sheriff. Everything okay?"

"I thought you needed to ask me about Erin, not about me." Sam scowled. He didn't want to be in here chatting about himself, so he replied shortly, "I'm getting around fine, Doc. It's Erin I'm worried about." He glanced at her, lying so still, tubes coming from an IV and more tubes providing an oxygen feed. "Is... Is she going to be okay?"

"We should know soon. How long has it been since you found her?"

Sam glanced at his watch. "About an hour."

Jenny nodded. "Well if it's Ketamine she's taken..."

"Ketamine she's been *given*," Sam corrected softly but distinctly. "Jenny, she was cuffed in the crawlspace of a trailer, probably for almost three days, with nothing but a canteen full of spiked water. There was no choice here. She didn't *take* anything." Sam's jaw clenched. The distinction might be small but it mattered. Big time.

Jenny nodded. "Sorry. You're right. Thirst would have forced her to drink to stay alive." She pulled off her colorful cap and shoved it into her pocket. "Ketamine's effects are short-lived, Sam. It hits quick and resolves quickly. Depending on how much she's been given since her kidnapping, she could be disoriented, even slightly amnesiac about her experiences. If you'd like, I'll go with you to talk to everyone. You can come back here after that to stay with her. We'll want to keep her, so we'll admit her and move her to a room once we're satisfied she's stable enough."

She glanced over to where Karen carefully cleaned Erin's wrist, and her golden eyes narrowed. "If I haven't already said so, I'm really glad that son of a bitch is dead."

Sam rested his hand on her shoulder. "Then you understand exactly how I feel."

"Dr. Richardson," the nurse interrupted, "she's regaining consciousness."

* * * *

Erin didn't want to leave the party she'd dreamed of. All her relatives were there and so nice. But the great-grandmother, who had looked so much like Erin they could be twins, told her she had to. It was time to go back. Go back where?

Other noises now intruded, and the radiant light of her great-grandmother's world faded to be replaced with a harsher one. Even from behind closed lids she felt the pain of this reality. She cringed away from it, trying to go back to what was surely the best dream she had ever had, but the gentlest of pushes sent her away.

"Come on, open your eyes for me," a pleasant male voice urged.

She wanted to hang on to where she'd been, but she couldn't quite remember it. There had been friendly people there who made her feel competent and confident. People she knew. Her lids fluttered, and the harsh light invaded. She wanted to close them and keep it out.

"No, no. Open your eyes for me."

There was something important she should remember.

"Can you tell me your name?"

That was ridiculous. Who would forget…their name? She shook her head slightly.

"Let me try," a female voice spoke from the other side so she turned her head that way. What a beautiful woman with the most amazing golden eyes, like a lioness. "It's Jenny, honey. How are you doing?"

"I'm fine." Was that her voice? She didn't recognize it, and it hardly even seemed to come from her.

"She's not recognizing me," the golden woman said and gestured toward someone just out of sight. "Come over here. Maybe you'll trigger her."

A large shadow fell over her, and she looked up a long way until her eyes encountered his face. His skin was pale, his mouth tight as if he held it that way to keep it from trembling. Lines of weariness slashed his cheeks and purplish circles hovered below his eyes. His eyes. She stared into depths that appeared almost black, and in those velvety depths she saw pain, weariness, and an unshakeable love. She had dreamed of him ever since she was a little girl, ever since he had cradled her in his arms and told her she would be all right. She had believed him then and believed in him ever since.

"Sammy."

One word. It came back to her in a rush.

"Sammy," she whispered again in wonder.

As she looked at him, his dark eyes filled with tears that overflowed and ran unheeded down his beard-shadowed cheeks. The mouth he'd held so tightly broke and trembled.

"Oh, Sammy. Matty…killed you. I didn't think they would let me in heaven, but I must be… 'cause you're here."

"I'm not dead, baby," he whispered. "Neither are you. We found you in time."

His huge palm engulfed her hand, but the pressure he put on it as he squeezed was gentle and steady. Warmth radiated from his grasp, along her arm, and into her mind and heart.

"Can you tell them who you are?" he managed to ask.

She smiled, feeling a confidence she'd never had before flood through her.

"I'm Erin. Erin Richardson," she stated firmly and turned her gaze back to the man hovering at her side. Her voice was a whisper as she continued, "And I love you, Sam Barnes."

"I love you too, baby, for as long as I can remember and until my last breath on my dying day. I'll tell you every day, Erin. I should have said it sooner."

She had waited an eternity to hear those words on his lips. She wanted to leap up and throw her arms around him, but weakness held her immobile, so she put everything she could into the smile she gave him. "You can say it as much as you want, but I can see it, Sam, and that's even better."

He held her hand while the medical staff prepared to move her to a room. Erin stared at Sam's face and refused to release his hand. She never wanted to let go again. When he stepped reluctantly back so they could shift her onto the gurney to take her to a private room, Erin saw the cane he held in his left hand. Her gaze bounced to his questioningly.

Sam's lips twisted ruefully. "They nearly succeeded in killing me, baby. I took a bullet through the leg and one through the arm."

But he was alive. She swallowed thickly, blinking back tears of joy as she watched the fluorescent hospital lights flash by above her head while they wheeled her along the corridor. In deference to Sam, they moved slowly enough now so he could keep up. Erin watched him struggle, and tears stung her eyes yet again. She had brought Matty and Andre, and they had nearly killed the most precious thing in her life. Sam limped beside them, and she saw how he kept his right hand in his pocket, providing his arm with some support. Erin closed her eyes, willing away the tears that hovered, ready to fall at any moment.

The old Erin would have viewed this as yet another screw up, but the last few days had taught her a hard lesson. She wasn't to blame for Andre Delacroix or any of the events his actions had set in motion. Some things were simply out of her control, out of Sam's control. Some events just had to be gotten through in the best way possible.

And she had.

She was okay. Sam had found her and right now she didn't even care how, just that he had. More important than that, Sam was alive. He might be hurt, but he was still alive, still hers, and he'd told her he loved her.

"Okay, Erin," the nurse at her head said, "we're going to shift you from the gurney over to the bed."

She closed her eyes, fighting the faint dizziness when they lifted and shifted her. Tubes were readjusted and covers tucked. The control for the bed was set next to her and pillows plumped behind her head.

"Is there anything else you need right now?" an older nurse asked.

Erin blinked and looked at the nurse. "I'm hungry."

"Doc's ordered something brought up for you, but just a little bit. Your body's got to readjust to eating."

She nodded. The door shut behind them.

"Sam?" Her eyes searched for him.

"Right here, baby."

He moved back to her side, pulled a chair forward, and sat heavily. Erin eyed the cane. She bit her lip to stop its trembling.

"I'm so sorry, Sammy," she choked. "All of this is my fault."

He took her hand. "No. It's mine. I was supposed to protect you. I failed."

She turned her head to study him, seeing the immense pain in his face.

"No! If I had never agreed to meet Matty and Rick…"

"They would have found you anyway, and if I hadn't met Rick, he might be dead, and I might never have been able to get you back."

Rick was alive. What about the other two? Should she know? There was only one way to find out. "What about Matty and…and Andre?"

Sam stroked the back of her hand with his callused thumb. "Both dead, baby. From what we've been able to piece together, Andre shot Matty, not too long after they took you. Your friend Rick agreed to work with us so we could get Delacroix. Things turned critical, though, before we were able to take him alive. He pulled a gun and was getting ready to shoot, so one of the snipers took him out."

Laura Browning

Sam paused for so long she turned her head toward him and saw his head was bowed as he continued to rhythmically stroke the back of her hand. She had never seen him this…distraught. It was the only word that seemed to fit.

"Sam?" she questioned in a whisper.

"I thought I'd lost you." His voice was hoarse and tight. When he looked at her with his intense, dark eyes, she saw the tears again.

"Oh, Sam."

He swallowed, sitting quietly for a moment to compose himself. He was such a proud man. Big, masculine, and she was sure the last thing he wanted was someone to see him cry.

She needed to get him talking before his feelings overwhelmed him. "How did you find me?"

"I ran over to Delacroix and tried to get him to tell me where you were, but even with his dying breath, he wouldn't say. Sweet heaven, Erin. You can't imagine… You've got Jake and my chief detective to thank. A house key with Matty's name on it is what led us to you. Jake and Jim decided he had either rented or purchased a house or apartment to hide you. We worked the realty companies and also the private classifieds for places within a specific distance from the restaurant where Rick met with Delacroix for dinner."

Erin blinked. There were so many rentals in the area she knew it had been a monumental undertaking. She blinked again, thinking of all of the people involved in getting her home safely.

"Erin? What is it, baby?"

She shook her head. "I can never thank everyone enough."

Sam squeezed her hand. "Look at me." When she did, he continued. "Seeing you safe and whole is all the thanks they'll need. That's why we do what we do."

They were silent, just gazing at each other, drawing comfort from being able to touch, to feel. Sam ran his hand over her hair, then cupped her cheek in his palm. Erin reached up and covered his hand with her own. This was exactly what she had longed to feel during the entire time she was cuffed underneath that trailer.

"I don't think I'll ever get tired of feeling your hand on my skin," she whispered.

Sam smiled. "And I will never get tired of touching you. I just hope the feeling is mutual."

"Just wait until we're both back to full speed. I'll show you just how mutual it is."

The door opened a crack. Jenny poked her head in. "I have dinner and your family. Which do you want first?"

Erin laughed. "Both."

Chapter 14

Stoner and Catherine stood outside the room beside Tabby and Joseph. Stoner looked around him, wondering how the other three could look so serene. From the moment he'd heard Erin had been found, worry nagged him. He wanted to know what had happened to her. Jenny had mentioned drugs, and he feared more than anything else that he might walk into the room and see once again the brittle, strung-out Erin from the past.

"Come in," Jenny told them. "You can't stay long because she's not very strong, but she wants to see all of you... Where's Evan?"

"Here."

Stoner glanced over to see his son carrying a stuffed bear. "Dare I ask what that's for?"

"In case Jenny's cruel enough not to let Sam stay with Erin, I've brought her a substitute."

At the grin on Evan's face, Stoner smiled, some of the tension leaving him.

Jenny shook her head. "Come on. She's anxious to see all of you."

Stoner let the others precede him. It wasn't fear, he told himself, just good manners. But in the back of his mind, he knew the reality. They had always seemed to be at cross-purposes where Erin was concerned, as though everything about their lives was just a step out of synch. Before her kidnapping, he'd finally begun to feel things were going to be all right. But now?

He stepped into the room and pushed the door shut behind him before turning to face her.

"Daddy?" Her voice was hoarse, but alert and lucid. Such a surge of relief poured through him that Stoner was barely able to raise his gaze. When he did, though, he saw clear, blue-gray eyes that, though they were shadowed with pain, looked at him with love.

"Oh, baby," he whispered, barely even noticing as everyone moved back so he could reach the side of the bed opposite Sam. "We were so afraid, and I'm so sorry we didn't do a better job protecting you."

She shifted her hand on the bed, covering his. He turned his palm, cradling her delicate fingers. The last time she'd showed this kind of trust she'd been just a girl. "Don't, Daddy. If it hadn't happened at Sam's house, it would have happened somewhere. Andre was determined to kill Rick and Matty."

"And you?" he asked, his heart thumping at just how close they had come to that becoming reality.

She shifted her gaze to Sam. "Eventually. He made some comments about taking me back to the islands, but I don't think he would have in the end."

Stoner stroked her short hair. "Are you all right?" He didn't want to ask about the drugs, but she seemed to understand.

"I will be." She looked at their joined hands. "Great-grandmother Richardson sends her greetings."

Concern knitted Stoner's brow. He'd always thought Erin looked remarkably like his paternal grandmother. From the stories he'd heard as a boy, he suspected their personalities weren't too far apart either. "You saw her?"

Erin shrugged. "I guess. It must have been a dream, but it seemed so real at the time."

"I saw her too," Tabby offered quietly, "while I was in surgery after my accident. I didn't realize who she was until later when I saw her picture at the Homestead."

Stoner sucked in a breath, feeling his heart pound heavily. They had nearly lost Tabby then, so it seemed logical the same applied to Erin. He looked around at all of his children and felt immense gratitude. He'd come so close to losing them either to injury or alienation, but now he felt like he'd been given a gift, a second chance.

"I love you, Erin," he told her.

"I knew I was doing the right thing when I came back. I love you too, Daddy."

* * * *

Jenny kept her in the hospital a couple days. Sometimes Erin wasn't sure if it was solely for her. She glanced over to the recliner where Sam was now stretched out, still sleeping as the first rays of light filtered through the window. They would be going home today. Erin felt so much stronger. Her wrist was still bandaged, but her lip and her cheek were well on the way to mending, and a butterfly bandage had closed the cut near her hairline.

She wondered just how strong Sam was feeling. She was desperate to get him home where he could finally relax, and she could get a look at his injuries. Erin needed to reassure herself that he would be all right. The focus had been all on her, but she still couldn't get the picture out of her head of him lying so still and silent in the muddy farmyard.

"Erin? What's wrong, baby?" His eyes opened, concern coloring their dark depths.

She shook her head. "It's nothing. I just want to go home, Sammy."

"Home as in my farm?"

"Yes. Our home." Peace settled deep in her soul. Sam's farm was home.

He smiled, the concern vanishing. "God, Erin, you have no idea how wonderful that sounds." He shifted, gingerly lifting his injured leg and setting it on the floor. Grabbing his cane, he pushed to his feet. "I'll see if I can get the ball rolling."

A couple hours later, she was being wheeled downstairs while Sam limped next to her. Stoner and Catherine awaited them at the door. "If you don't mind," her dad said, "we'll be your chauffeurs until Jenny clears both of you to drive."

When they pulled off the highway and approached Sam's old farmhouse along the gravel drive, Erin's fingers tightened on his hand.

"Okay?"

She leaned against him. "I will be. I keep seeing you sprawled there so still. Oh, Sammy, I thought you were dead." She bit her lip and blinked back tears. This was supposed to be a happy event. She shouldn't be dragging up that nightmare.

"Don't remember that, squirt," he murmured. "Think of some of the other happier memories."

Stoner glanced in the rearview mirror. "You mean like the day I arrived and both of you were covered head to toe and wallowing in the mud?"

Sam flushed, laughing a bit nervously, and Erin's tension eased. "Thank you, Daddy. I'll picture that instead." To Sam, she whispered, "I also remember how much fun we had washing the mud off each other."

"I heard that," Stoner growled.

"Mind your own business, Senator," Sam growled back.

* * * *

Over the next week, they had plenty of visitors. Friends and family came by with food or to handle work around the farm. Sam limped around, hoping his strength would return, but he was also keeping a close eye on

Erin. On the surface, she seemed much better, but at night, nightmares haunted her, and by day she would only leave the house in his company. Finally, as they sat on the couch watching the news, Sam figured out what it was that had been bothering her. He'd been paying only half attention to the announcer while he read Amanda Brown's account of the investigation in the local paper. Suddenly, he felt Erin tense, and he looked up.

"What's wrong?"

"Look!"

He saw a white-haired man in what appeared to be a wrinkled linen suit being escorted away from a shimmering, pastel yellow mansion. "Who's that?"

"Andre's father!"

Sam snagged the remote and increased the volume.

"Authorities on St. Thomas today arrested the head of the powerful Delacroix family on charges of drug trafficking and conspiracy to commit murder. Sixty-year-old Philippe Delacroix has headed the family's business ventures for the past twenty years. Charges of drug trafficking surfaced after his son's death at the hands of police snipers in Virginia earlier this month. Former private cruise ship captain Rick Nelson also faces charges in the case, but prosecutors say it's possible he'll be granted immunity in return for his testimony against Delacroix."

Sam muted the sound and gathered Erin against him. "It's over, baby."

Erin sucked in a deep breath, let it out slowly, and smiled. "I was so afraid they'd come back."

"I know you were, but you wouldn't talk about it. Why?"

"I felt silly."

He slid two fingers beneath her chin and tilted it. "There was no reason to feel silly, but I don't want fear to rule our lives. There are always going to be some risks out there each and every day. You've faced probably the worst you'll ever have to face—and you made it. Do you know how proud I am of you? And how much I admire the way you've kept on going—working with Rachel, working with everybody's investments?"

She touched his cheek with her palm, then leaned in to kiss him slowly and thoroughly.

Sam groaned. "I love you, Erin. I'll never get tired of saying it. I wanted to do it all up with hearts and flowers, maybe a dinner someplace out of town, but that's not who I am. I'm just a county sheriff and a farmer. Will you marry me? I can't give you anything fancy like Richardson Homestead...."

"Oh, Sammy," she said and laughed. "I don't care about that. I never have. Wherever you are, that's where I want to be. If that means we never leave Castle County and Mountain Meadow again, then I'm happy to be here at your side. I think the real question is can your career stand my reputation? Can you stand a wife who'll always need some help reading any complicated correspondence?"

Sam tweaked her nose. "Tell you what, you can manage my finances on my next campaign, and I'll find someone else to make the election signs."

"You're on."

He kissed her again, his hand wandering down to cup her breast. "If we're careful, you think we could...?"

Her slender fingers began undoing his belt buckle. "Oh definitely."

* * * *

Two months later, Erin looked out the window of her mother's sitting room at Richardson Homestead. Late spring flowers bloomed in the beds lining the walk out front. All along the driveway, as far as she could see, cars were parked and people walked up the drive and around to the gardens behind the guest house.

"Erin?" Tabby spoke quietly from behind her. "You should probably go ahead and get your dress on now. Jenny's gone to get your garter, but she'll be back in a minute."

Erin looked over her shoulder at Tabby, beautiful in a sapphire satin sheath, her dark hair swept up off the slender column of her neck and a sapphire pendant hanging from a fine gold chain nestled against her chest. Erin's eyes shifted just beyond her to a photograph that hung among several other family pictures. It was black and white, softened with age, but the man and woman in it still leaped vividly from the paper. She was tiny and curved against his long, lean frame as he leaned back against a shiny luxury car. The woman's face was turned in profile, gazing adoringly at the man beside her.

Erin turned and looked at Tabby.

"You remember I said I saw our great-grandmother that day Jake and Sam found me? It was strange, like I was at a big party..."

"...and the guests were all our relatives," Tabby finished quietly.

Their eyes locked.

"She talked to me."

"Me too."

"She told me to use my gifts and talents and to stand on my own."

Tabby smiled. "I think we may have gotten similar pep talks."

"Was it real?" Erin asked her younger sister with a tilt to her head.

"I have no idea, but it does seem like an odd coincidence." Tabby brought her dress over. "What you need to believe right now is that you are less than an hour away from marrying one of the best men I know. Sam is a rock, Erin. He will never desert you, and he would move heaven and earth to make you happy."

Erin blinked. "I feel the same way about him. I spent so many years feeling like a misfit and trying to get away from here. I never suspected when I came back just how much I had really missed having a place I could call home…having this place to call home.

* * * *

Sam was so nervous, he was afraid he'd embarrass himself and start crying in front of the eighty million or so guests it seemed Stoner and Catherine Richardson had invited. Either that or he'd get sick. At this point, though, it scarcely mattered. He'd shed so many tears over Erin he knew his tough guy image had been blown all to hell. Now he'd blow it in front of the whole county. He looked out the window of Stoner's study. County hell. Half the doggone state must be here. He could already see Amanda Brown moving around, camera clicking away as she shot photos for what would no doubt grace the front page of the next issue of the *Castle County Messenger*.

He gulped the shot of bourbon Evan had poured for him and nearly choked. Sam had agreed to the big wedding to make Erin and her parents happy, but he would have been just as content if they'd gone to the courthouse and tied the knot in front of the magistrate.

"Ready?" Jake said from the doorway. "We're needed out on the terrace."

Sam swallowed, wanting desperately to loosen the tie and collar that now felt like they were strangling him. He'd tried to reach Luke, Jake's older brother, to see if he could serve as best man, but he'd already planned a family vacation. Jake was by no means a second best choice. He was about as close a friend as Sam had. As he stepped out onto the terrace, he nodded to a few acquaintances and moved to take his place next to the flowered archway where Joseph stood. When Joe winked at him, Sam managed a smile that was nearly painful. He glanced at the guests again and swallowed.

Yeah, the justice of the peace idea had real merit. Then they could have already been on their honeymoon and he could be peeling off… *oh God!* He felt his cock stir, his face flush, and he quickly turned back to Jake who stood next to him as his best man. He saw Jake's eyes flick downward and back up. A wicked grin curled his wide mouth.

"Try reciting multiplication tables. It helps me."

Sam looked at his friend's twinkling hazel eyes.

"Will it always be like this?"

Jake laughed. "You better hope so. Turn around, buddy, your bride's getting ready to walk down the aisle."

Sam was vaguely aware of Melodie, Jenny, and Tabby preceding her, but his eyes were only on Erin. He wished she didn't have that lacy veil thing over her face. It would help his nerves a lot if he could see her expression, see that she wanted this. But as they got closer, and he could make out her features beneath the veil, what he saw was the most radiant smile in the universe. His eyes shifted to Stoner, whose gaze held his. In addition to the seriousness, he thought he saw a twinkle there.

The next few minutes flew by, but Sam wasn't sure how. He spoke when Joe told him to, and he must have done all right. No one laughed. Then he was lifting Erin's veil. His hands shook, but he couldn't worry about that. When he gazed into her blue-gray eyes, what he saw shining back at him was a love so intense it blazed. Sam was amazed she didn't set the whole dang garden on fire.

"I love you."

He wasn't sure which one of them had spoken. Their lips met and everything else faded but that single moment and the feeling of coming home.

Also from Lyrical Press, Book #2 of Melissa Shirley's
Storybook Lake series, available now!

Falling Grace

Finding the fairytale in Storybook Lake . . .

Grace Wade left Storybook Lake hoping to escape her crazy family
and the demands of her job as a defense attorney. But not twenty-four
hours after landing in a small Texas town where she hopes to find new
beginnings, Grace instead finds herself in the middle of an investigation
that's turning the town inside out. Once she agrees to be the defense
attorney on the case, Grace suddenly finds herself torn between twin
brothers Blane Sheperd, the bad boy prosecutor on the case, and Jamie
Sheperd, the sweetheart town Sheriff . . .

Grace thought life in a small town would be simple, but simple has a way
of eluding her. To find her way to a happy ending, she'll have to master
the art of following her heart . . .

Learn more about Melissa at
http://www.ekensingtonbooks.com/author.aspx/31684

Visit us at www.kensingtonbooks.com

Chapter 1

"My wife killed our daughter."

Nathan Gabriel strolled into the office and threw out the line as though he said things like that every day. For such a serious statement, he'd said it with no stuttering sense of urgency, no affect whatsoever. The sheen of sweat on his face and his pinhead sized pupils spoke to something underlying his serenity as he spoke.

"Your wife killed your daughter?" As a criminal attorney, I dealt with some big baddies, but never with someone who confessed so readily for his wife.

"They *think* she did." He twitched and scratched the side of his face. "She wants Rory Allden to defend her."

"But you said…" I shook it off. "Rory isn't here. I'm her partner, Grace Wade. I might be able to help you." I never offered services without knowing the actual client's name and never without a few more details than a statement condemning the person meant to be my client, but something about him…

He looked around, glanced back as though waiting for the door to open. His wife was suspected of murder, and he needed a lawyer. I fit that description. What was the hold up?

After a few long minutes, a couple of frustrated huffs and puffs of his chest, and more waiting, he nodded. "Fine. Let's go."

I jogged with him across the street to the police station armed with only his name and what I could remember of his words. His first damning statement spun around my mind.

It wasn't my usual mode of attack on a case, but I brushed my confusion aside and peppered questions at his back. He hurried faster than I could keep up in my pencil skirt and four inch heels.

Conveniently located in viewing distance from the new offices of Allden and Wade, Attorneys at Law, the police station looked more like a refurbished coffee house, with a picture window in front under a black awning with its edges flapping in the wind and a park bench on its wide sidewalk. The whole town had been designed right out of a Rockwell and the sheriff's department was no different.

I stepped inside a heavy glass door and breathed in the pungent smell of sweat and chilidogs. Pinching the bridge of my nose, I approached a counter marked Information in crooked gold lettering.

An officer behind the waist-high counter that doubled as a desk barely looked up from his *Bikes and Babes* magazine. "Can I help you?"

I curled my fingers in my palm to resist the urge to smack his feet off the cluttered Formica. "I'm Grace Wade, and I want to speak to my client."

"What client would that be?"

"I'm sorry. I didn't realize your town was so rife with crime that you could possibly be confused." *Well, more confused.* "Mrs. Quinn." I didn't even know her first name, for goodness sake.

He rolled his eyes and flipped a page. "Have a seat over there." He nodded to a semi-stained seating arrangement that I wouldn't risk my clothes to sit on. "I'll let the detective know you're here."

The magazine crinkled as he brought it closer to his face, investigating something on the inside. He'd missed a button when he dressed and more of his lunch dotted his shirt than could possibly have landed in his mouth.

He ignored the long, huffy breath that billowed between my lips. I counted down the ten more seconds I waited by drilling my fingers against the counter for each one that ticked off. *Enough.* I snatched the magazine from his fingers and shoved it behind my back as he reached for it.

"I can charge you with assaulting a police officer."

"Not until I smack you with it." I slammed the flimsy paperback down in front of me. "Listen, *Einstein.* If your detective is in there questioning her and she's asked for counsel, anything she says is going to get thrown right out of court, and who do you think is gonna get the blame? Hot shot detective or desk jockey?" I gave my most endearing and practiced grin as I mimicked his twang. "So, if I were you, I would get my big, lazy, too-many-biscuits-dipped-in-gravy ass out of that chair and let your detective know I'm here."

His white cowboy hat tilted as he shoved a phone receiver to his ear and punched a single digit into the phone. "I know that, Detective. Her attorney is here." He looked up at me. "Name?"

"Grace Wade."

"*Miss* Grace Wade." He took a pointed look at my ring finger, and I slid my hand off the counter to my side.

The sassy *miss* he added to my name was in an accent that drew out the syllables.

"I'll let her know." He took his time, polishing the receiver with his soiled shirt, then replaced it in its cradle. "She's in the interview room." After extricating all seven feet of his body from the chair, he made his way around a wall to stand beside me.

At five-foot-seven with another four inches of heel, I barely made it to his shoulder. "Right this way, *Miss* Wade." I didn't have to ask how he felt about single women.

His white T-shirt hung beneath the tail of his button down as I followed him down the hall. He stopped in front of an unmarked door and turned to me. "She's right in here."

I hid my mental eye roll with a wink and walked past him, noting his name for future avoidance. "Thank you for your hospitality, Deputy Wesley."

He grunted a reply and shut the door behind me, keeping her husband, Nathan Quinn, locked outside.

A plain clothes detective leaned across the table on his fists in front of a woman so shriveled I disguised my muttered "Whoa" with a cough.

He straightened, then looked me up and down, his eyebrows creeping up his forehead as his eyes made their way lower. A slow smile spread across his lips and he extended a hand. "I'm Detective Paul Roan, Texas State Police."

After the initial handshake, he continued to hold on. His slimy palm sweat slithered onto my skin. I yanked my arm back to my side and wiped my fingers down the outer seam of my skirt. "Grace Wade."

"You must be new in town. I'd remember such a pretty face."

You'll remember it now. "Detective, I know you weren't in here questioning my client after she asked for her lawyer."

He cocked his head to one side and crossed his arms over his chest. "No, ma'am. We were having a little chat is all."

"Of course, you were." I nodded to the woman. "Looks like she was enjoying it."

"She never asked me to stop."

His eyebrows issued a dare and I smiled in return. The quiet recesses of my mind came to life, and I started mentally counting the piles of money I would earn suing this police department.

"Well, Miss Wade, if you'll excuse me, I'm gonna go get my paperwork in order and call the prosecutor in charge of this case to let him know that we're booking your client on first degree murder." Honey didn't drip with such sweetness as his tone. He smacked his big, black hat on his head and grinned as though he'd won a war with his words.

I flipped a glance at the clock ticking loudly on the wall. Four o'clock, Friday afternoon. "Impeccable timing. I would expect nothing less."

He twisted the knob and tossed a wink over his shoulder. "See you soon, *Miss* Wade."

As soon as the latch clicked into place, I looked at the woman in the chair. "I'm Grace. Your husband hired me to be your attorney." She frowned. "Rory wasn't there, so I came instead. Right now, I want you to tell me everything that happened with your daughter, and I need you to do it as quickly as you can." She didn't move, didn't seem to breathe. I wanted to shake her, show her the urgency of her situation. Instead, I pulled a chair around the table and sat close enough to smell her coffee breath. "Listen, detective tall-hat is gonna be back in a minute to book you into the jail. They're going to fingerprint you, change your clothes, and put you in a cell. Because it's Friday, and this is Backwater U.S.A., you won't see a judge until at least Monday."

She didn't look up from the table.

When she continued to ignore me, my guilt-o-meter got confused. In my experience, guilty clients either gave me *the stare* or shouted too many details of their innocence like chirping fools. Catatonia was new, though. I had no expertise to call on to deal with that kind of response.

"Mrs. Quinn, I know this is awful, but I need you to focus on what I'm saying." I snapped my fingers in front of her. "What happened to your daughter?"

"My husband can tell you." Her voice wavered on the words.

"No." The sharpness of my tone caused her to look up while simultaneously becoming smaller. I softened my voice. "I need you to tell me."

"We went out to a movie and for a couple drinks with some friends. When we came back from Dallas, I checked on the kids while he drove the sitter home. Emily was already asleep, all tucked in, so I went to bed. When Nathan got home, he came up, and we went to sleep. Emily was fine." She broke into a sob.

"Okay. She was sleeping. Did you touch her or cover her or anything that told you she was okay at that moment?" I checked the clock as minutes sped past during her silence. She needed to move this along. "We don't have much time."

"No. I looked in and she was covered up. She liked to sleep with the blankets over her head. I could see her hair and I didn't want to take the chance of waking her up."

"What happened in the morning?"

"When I woke up on Sunday, I got our boy dressed and went in to take a bath." She twisted the fingers of one hand in the fisted grasp of the other. "I liked having some time before Emily woke up. She was difficult in the mornings and I thought if I could just get myself ready without her wanting me to hold her and... And I heard Nathan screaming. I ran down the hall, and he was holding Emily. She was dead." She shook her head and a wave of tears brimmed over her lashes. "So much blood."

"Okay. What happened to her?"

"Someone killed my baby." Her voice cracked, then shattered on a sob.

I ran a hand over hers, gave it a squeeze. I needed five more minutes of coherency. "Who could have stabbed your daughter?"

The withering continued. Mrs. Quinn slunk farther into her chair and fat, sloppy tears streamed down her cheeks. "I don't know." She mumbled the phrase three more times.

I covered her hand with mine. I didn't usually coddle my clients, but she needed contact, a sympathetic touch. "Okay. We're going to figure this out, but you have to listen to me. They're going to put you in a cell. Whatever you do, don't speak to them, at all. If anyone asks you anything, or tries to start a conversation, you ask for me. Do not say anything to them." I couldn't stress that enough. "To anyone. Especially if they put you in a cell with someone else." She continued to sob. "Do you understand?" Her body shook as she ignored my question. "Do you understand?"

"Yes."

"What's your first name?"

"Gabrielle. My husband calls me Gabby."

"Okay, Gabby, listen. Because of what they're charging you with, I probably can't get you out on bail, but I will do everything I can to make your stay here as short as possible."

A bubble of something I hoped was only gas formed in my stomach. In law school, it was drilled into us that asking the wrong questions limited our ability to defend our clients, but in this case, I had to know. Even if the answer meant I could never put her on the stand, a fire burned in me to get the answer. "Did you kill your daughter?"

She looked around the room, at the floor, the paint peeling from a far wall, the doorknob, a mirror that doubled as a window. Everywhere but at me.

"Gabby, did you kill your daughter?"

"No. Nathan didn't do it either. He's a wonderful father."

Oh, for him she was willing to spearhead a defense? In the words of William Shakespeare, *the lady doth protest too much.* I made a mental note to launch a little investigation into wonder daddy. I had a tingling feeling her case would live or die by whatever I discovered about him. Her shoulders slumped forward as she lifted her gaze to slide over me and finally land on a spot in the center of the table. She wouldn't meet my eyes, wouldn't look up again. That bubble in the pit of my stomach expanded.

"Okay." For the moment, I couldn't care about her husband or whether the world believed he did it. He wasn't the one holding down a chair in the interrogation room. I cared about this broken woman, thin and aged beyond her years. "Then let's figure out how to make sure a jury knows you didn't do it."

Meet the Author

After a long career in journalism, **Laura Browning** changed gears and began teaching English. The change in pace allowed her to ramp up her love of writing fiction. After a push from her hubby, her hobby morphed into a book contract. When not teaching or writing, you can find her on her farm or in the woods with camera in hand. Visit her website at: www.laurabrowingbooks.com.